VITAMIN P—FOR POISON

"Just how do you think I can help you?" Antony asked.

Roddy opened his cigarette case absentmindedly and helped himself. "I expect the police think I did it."

"Why should they?"

"Because Aunt Janet accused me right out. She said I'd have done anything to stop my father from making it public . . . what grandfather had done, I mean. And that's almost true," he added reflectively.

"A motive," said Antony. "How about opportunity?"

"That makes it worse," Roddy admitted. "You see, I collected a new bottle of tablets from the chemist for him. I handed them over to him about nine o'clock that evening, and at eleven he took one, and died an hour later. How could anybody have tampered with them, once they were in his possession?"

"I don't know. But there must have been some way; unless you're telling me you did it, after all."

THIS LITTLE MEASURE

Sara Woods

AVON
PUBLISHERS OF BARD, CAMELOT, DISCUS AND FLARE BOOKS

Any work of fiction whose characters were of a uniform excellence would rightly be condemned—by that fact if by no other—as being incredibly dull. Therefore no excuse can be considered necessary for the villainy or folly of the people appearing in this book. It seems extremely unlikely that any one of them should resemble a real person, alive or dead. Any such resemblance is completely unintentional and without malice.

AVON BOOKS
A division of
The Hearst Corporation
1790 Broadway
New York, New York 10019

Copyright © 1964 by Sara Woods
Published by arrangement with the author
Library of Congress Catalog Card Number: 85-91518
ISBN: 0-380-69862-5

First Avon Printing, May 1986

AVON TRADEMARK REG. U. S. PAT. OFF. AND IN
OTHER COUNTRIES, MARCA REGISTRADA, HECHO EN
U. S. A.

Printed in the U. S. A.

K-R 10 9 8 7 6 5 4 3 2 1

O mighty Caesar! dost thou lie so low?
Are all thy conquests, glories, triumphs, spoils,
Shrunk to this little measure?

JULIUS CAESAR, III, i.

To avoid confusion it should be stated that the events narrated in this book occurred at an earlier date than those recorded in *Trusted Like the Fox*. The death of Roderick Gaskell, senior, and everything that happened as a result of the unexpected reappearance of the lost Velasquez, took place while Antony Maitland was still at the junior Bar.

RODERICK GASKELL, senior
m. PRISCILLA GASKELL
(his cousin)

ANDREW   JANET   GILBERT
m. Eleanor Danvers m. Edward
        (Ted) Blake

RODERICK DORCAS EDWARD
(Roddy) (Dorrie)

CHAPTER I

"IT ALL BEGAN," said Roderick Gaskell, a little more loudly than could have been considered necessary in the quiet room, "it all began with Grandfather's will." He paused and eyed the man he was addressing doubtfully, as though wondering whether he had, in fact, succeeded in obtaining any part of his attention.

Antony Maitland did not look up from the plan he was studying. He was, for the moment, absorbed by what he was doing; and he had reached this state hardly enough to wish at all costs to retain it. What on earth had possessed young Roddy to come . . . or Gibbs to let him in, for that matter? "I could recommend a good solicitor to you," he said, without raising his eyes, and heard a chair scrape as his visitor came to his feet.

"I thought at least you'd listen." Roddy spoke stiffly, but Antony heard also the hurt resentment in his voice, and looked up quickly and smiled.

"I'm sorry, Roddy. Of course I'll listen." He dropped his pencil on top of the plan, and it rolled out of reach across the thick blue paper. "I didn't realise it was important."

Roddy looked doubtful. "I don't want to bother you," he said, with obvious insincerity. And Antony laughed and came round the desk.

"Tell the truth, and shame the devil," he advised. "We might as well make ourselves comfortable . . . don't you think?" He was moving towards the fireplace as he spoke, and his mind, released from the discipline of considering a particularly uninteresting title, rushed helter skelter after this new—and far more intriguing—problem. It was surprising enough, of course, that Roddy Gaskell should be here at all . . . a young man he knew only in the most casual way, and almost half-a-generation away from himself in age; but Roddy looking troubled, with no sign for the moment of his usual rather aggressive self-confidence . . . there was a puzzle indeed. Old Mr. Gaskell—Roderick senior—had been dead for at least six months now. He threw a log on the fire, and turned to wave invitingly towards the chair on the right of the hearth. "Tell me," he said, "about this will of your grandfather's."

Roddy Gaskell seated himself obediently, but he still had a wary look. He was a good-looking young man, of medium height and rather stocky build, and in general all his movements were quick and decisive. He said now, "It's not an easy thing to explain," and shifted in his chair as though he were physically, as well as mentally uncomfortable.

"Were the dispositions so very complicated?" Antony bent as he spoke to open the cigarette box on the table at the visitor's elbow, but his eyes did not leave the younger man's face. Roddy helped himself absentmindedly, but relaxed a little once the cigarette was between his fingers.

"It isn't that," he said. "I mean, everything was straightforward enough, and much what we expected. Even Aunt Janet wasn't particularly dissatisfied. The trouble was . . . he'd added a codicil."

"Not, in itself, unusual," said Antony.

Roddy frowned at him. "No, but . . . just wait till you hear it," he said. The momentary diffidence had disappeared now, and his usual vitality was becoming very evident. " 'To my son Andrew,' it said, 'I leave the problem of the Velasquez.' " He leaned forward and added eagerly, "The thing is, you see, there wasn't any Velasquez . . . there never had been."

"And, therefore, no problem?"

"Well, that's what we thought, of course. But—"

"It might be helpful to get the dates straight. When did Mr. Gaskell make his will?"

"Fifteen years ago," said Roddy. He seemed to regard the question as a gratifying evidence of interest on his companion's part. "I'm afraid I can't remember the exact date, but the codicil was added three years later."

"I see. And you were going to explain the problem."

"Yes, well, I said we didn't understand the codicil, and we gave up trying after a while. My father made enquiries, of course; at the Bank, at our solicitors, but nothing came of them. So we more or less forgot about it until a week ago.'' He paused, obviously with dramatic intent; but Antony, whose patience was by no means inexhaustible, ruined the effect by saying unsympathetically:

''Where was it found?''

''Behind a panel in the study,'' said Roddy. ''And my climax is too good to spoil, so don't be so damned depressing.'' (Antony grinned, and shifted his position a little because the fire was beginning to burn up again). ''A genuine, hidden panel,'' Roddy went on, with relish. ''We none of us knew it was there, and Dad only learned of it accidentally when he was having some alterations done, and it was the same carpenter who'd done the work—''

''All right, so the picture turned up. You still haven't told me where the problem came in.''

''I'm just coming to that,'' Roddy protested. But obviously he had no intention of being hurried. ''Naturally, the first thing Dad did was phone Uncle Gil. I mean, *we* only thought it might be a Velasquez because of what the will said. But Uncle Gil got fearfully excited when he saw the picture, and said it was a very famous one. He raved about it a good deal, and actually, you know,'' added Roddy, with the air of one who tries to be perfectly fair, ''it is pretty stunning. But the real pay-off was that Uncle Gil says it belongs to some provincial gallery or other, and was stolen from them years ago. *That* caused a stir, I can tell you.''

''Yes, I should think it might.'' Antony's tone was startled, and the visitor sat back in his chair again, obviously satisfied with the effect he had created. ''Er—am I to infer that your revered grandfather—?''

Roddy grinned, and looked for the first time that afternoon completely like himself. ''I don't see what else we can think,'' he said. ''Do you?''

''There's no doubt, I suppose, that it really is the one that is missing?''

''I can't see Uncle Gil being mistaken about a thing like that, you know. But of course he checked up. I'm not sure what these experts do to satisfy themselves, but whatever it is, he did it.''

''But . . . why?''

"You mean, why did the old pirate pinch the thing? Well, he didn't *need* to, you know."

"That hardly puts the matter in a more favourable light," said Antony, suddenly tart.

"No, but . . . I can see the fascination, can't you? If a thing isn't for sale . . . and then there'd be the feeling he'd put something over—"

"What I don't see," Antony interrupted him, "is what you think I can do about it."

"As a matter of fact," said Roddy, "I hoped you'd persuade Sir Nicholas to talk to my father."

"But it's perfectly obvious what you must do. Send the thing back."

"Yes, but do you think there's any point in making a scandal?" Roddy was serious now. "There must be some way of doing it . . . well, privately. But you know my father; he's thoroughly shocked . . . well, so am I, of course," he added hastily, and without any great conviction. "But he's talking about justice, and retribution, and the lord knows what. And that's all very fine, but it can't be particularly nice for Gran."

"No, I can imagine not."

"She won't say a word, of course." Roddy sounded aggrieved. "I mean, he's practising what she preaches, so she can't very well complain. So it seems to be up to the rest of us . . . the ones who aren't . . . who aren't—"

"Respectable," Antony suggested. Roddy took the thrust smoothly.

"Conventional," he substituted. "Well, you see what I mean."

"And you really think your father might listen to Uncle Nick?" (Antony was trying—and failing—to visualise the meeting).

"Well, he might," said Roddy doubtfully. "It seems worth trying, and Liz said—"

"I see," said Antony, relieved that so much at least was explained. Liz Watson was his wife's cousin, and if she was a friend of Roddy's it was only too obvious why he had been cast for the rôle of intermediary. It was one he had little taste for, particularly as there seemed so small a chance of success. He was thinking how best to word his refusal when he looked down again at Roddy and saw that he was really troubled, and forgot in that moment the rather tiresome nature of the demands that were being made on him. After all, who'd have thought it of old Roderick? There should be some amusement, surely, in getting to know his descendants better. "What exactly do you want me to do?" he asked.

The Gaskell family were, of course, a legend. It wasn't only their wealth and long run of success in business, but a certain spectacular quality which caught the imagination, ever since the late eighteenth century when an enterprising member of the family had founded his fortune on a mixture of privateering and a sheer genius for the possibilities of trade in the more unlikely corners of the world. Since then, the Gaskell Line had grown over the years to its present magnificence: the great passenger liners which gave it its prestige . . . the more humble trading ships which were the real backbone of what could fairly be called an empire. And in all that time, no member of the family had ever been known to do things by halves. They were saints or they were sinners: cold, fanatical, puritan saints; or cheerful, swashbuckling sinners, careless alike of public opinion and the convenience and peace of mind of their nearest and dearest. And old Roderick Gaskell (whose will was now causing his grandson so much concern) had nobly upheld the family tradition. "The Pirate King" he had been called by his contemporaries, and still was by the less reverent members of his family; the name was apt enough to have stuck to him throughout a long career. All the same, the idea of him stealing—or causing to be stolen—a world-famous painting seemed utterly fantastic.

It was this point that was occupying Antony as he went back to the study after seeing Roddy out. The plan was still where he had left it, with the bundle of accompanying documents piled neatly on the edge of the desk. For a moment he gazed down at it absently, running his finger down the thick red line that marked the disputed boundary. He even took his mind from the Gaskells for long enough to wonder, vaguely, why this particular difficulty had been sent to him. But there was no getting back now to its intricacies; he folded the plan and began to look for the deed from which it had been separated.

It was Sunday afternoon, and he had come down to his uncle's study to work, to escape the possibility of visitors . . .

not very successfully, as it turned out. Sir Nicholas Harding (that eminent and irascible Queen's Counsel) was a busy man; and Antony—his nephew, and in his chambers—generally found himself even more fully employed. His own quarters (into which he and his wife had moved "temporarily" at the end of the war) were at the top of the house in Kempenfeldt Square; and glancing at the clock he realised that, by a sort of Box and Cox arrangement, Jenny was most likely giving Sir Nicholas tea at this very moment. As good a time as any to broach the matter, especially as Roddy had seemed to think it so urgent; though his status as a guest was unlikely to inhibit his uncle's comments in any way.

He stowed the deeds away safely where Sir Nicholas was unlikely to find and disarrange them, and went out into the hall. The house was quiet, and he wondered as he went up the stairs how long this state of affairs would continue, once he had propounded "the problem of the Velasquez".

He found Sir Nicholas and Jenny gossiping peacefully over their tea. Sir Nicholas had his favourite chair, and—rather unfairly—seemed to have disposed of the greater portion of the hot-buttered toast. Jenny was curled up in a corner of the sofa, with her cup balanced precariously on the arm. She moved it to the tray when she heard him come into the room, and stretched out a hand for the teapot. Sir Nicholas, still apparently languid, directed a piercing look at his nephew, and enquired: "Have you reached an opinion yet?"

"Not yet, sir." He accepted the cup Jenny was holding out to him, and bent down to forage on the bottom shelf of the trolley, whose contents he hoped might so far have escaped attention. Surfacing a moment later with three sandwiches and a slice of fruit cake, he put down his provisions on the mantelpiece and turned to survey his family. "I had a visitor," he told them. And paused for the inevitable questions.

"Who?" said Jenny, obligingly. But something in his tone had alerted her, and she was watching Sir Nicholas as her husband answered.

"Roddy Gaskell . . . of all people."

"What on earth did he want?" asked Jenny: and

"I hope you made it clear to him that you were busy," said Sir Nicholas, with a maddening lack of interest.

"It wasn't a social call," said Antony. He retrieved his

plate from the mantelpiece, and demolished the first of the sandwiches. "It was . . . well . . . a sort of SOS," he added. Sir Nicholas gave him a cold look.

"As I see you are determined to unburden yourself," he remarked, with an air of resignation which was very far from encouraging, "it will save your time and my patience if you do so without further preamble." His nephew had no hesitation in discounting the optimism of the second part of this statement; and rightly, as it turned out. For a few minutes later Sir Nicholas, in possession of most of the story, was angry enough to have stopped protesting and become very quiet . . . . a dangerous state of affairs that couldn't possibly be allowed to continue.

"As for Andrew Gaskell," said Antony, "I can't see him listening to you, but of course, he might. Roddy says his father thinks you're the only honest lawyer in town." He had moved across to the window and was looking out as he spoke, and his uncle was unable to catch his eye. "And the only one with any sense," he added, for good measure.

"If he had made a slightly less sweeping statement," said Sir Nicholas, icily, "I might have inclined to agree with him, at least on the latter point. How you could be idiot enough to let young Gaskell talk you into this . . . this lunatic interference—"

"I'm not going to interfere, sir; it's your help he wants, not mine." He turned from the window at last—the prospect, that February day, was bleak and uninviting—and came across the room again into the circle of firelight. Jenny looked up and smiled at him. It was as well, perhaps, that her face was in the shadow; her expression of amused sympathy would not have pleased Sir Nicholas.

"It's fascinating though . . . isn't it?" she said with an air of innocence that didn't even begin to ring true.

"It is a serious matter," said Sir Nicholas crushingly; "not a farce being played for your amusement."

"Well, seriously then, sir . . . if you have any influence with Andrew Gaskell—" Antony spoke with a tentative air; but, like Jenny, he had no intention of being soothing. All the same, he was surprised by the vehemence of his uncle's reply.

"Nobody has any influence with Andrew Gaskell. I doubt if anybody ever had. He's thoroughly obstinate and pigheaded, and sanctimonious into the bargain,'' said Sir Nicholas, obviously pronouncing the final condemnation.

"Yes, I know. But there are the other members of the family to consider."

"They're no better. And I haven't your passion for meddling." Sir Nicholas remained aloof, but for all that Antony had a feeling that the topic of the Gaskells was one on which he might be induced to enlarge. It seemed that the same thought had occurred to Jenny, for she said now, casually:

"You've known them for ever, Uncle Nick?"

"They have lived in Kempenfeldt Square—on the wrong side of the square—as long as I remember. When old Roderick was a young man he was thought to be very wild." He paused, and smiled at Jenny with one of his unpredictable changes of mood. "I am telling you what my mother used to say, my dear. She told me that when Roderick married his cousin everyone thought she would be a good influence on him. Priscilla Gaskell was as hide-bound and puritanical as her son has turned out to be . . . and that's saying something," he added malevolently. "But as for influencing her husband, it didn't work out that way at all. They just seemed to react on each other, so that each one became more extreme."

"How . . . how depressing," said Jenny.

"And as for the children," said Sir Nicholas, now happily launched on this flood of reminiscence, "well . . . just look at them! There's Andrew, a damned, sourfaced, killjoy of a fellow; and Janet, who's no better . . . and who goes about looking like a scarecrow into the bargain," he added bitterly.

"I've met the other brother, Gilbert," said Jenny. "He seems nice, and quite ordinary."

"Well, so he may. But mark my words, he'll have a queer streak somewhere," said Sir Nicholas.

"The . . . the next generation are absolutely normal," she protested.

"Do you think so? I don't know about the girl . . . what's her name?"

"Dorcas." Jenny sounded apologetic. "They call her Dorrie. Someone told me she takes after her mother."

"Then perhaps there is some hope for her." He paused, and then added emphatically: "It was utter madness. She should never have married him." And somehow Antony had the impression that he had forgotten for the moment that he was not alone.

"Who?" asked Jenny; she was as curious as her husband, and even less inhibited about displaying the fact.

"Eleanor Gaskell."

"Did you know her, Uncle Nick? I thought she died ages ago."

"I knew her well when she was a schoolgirl. She was a friend of your mother, Antony. They were at the Convent together,"—he smiled suddenly—"and at that time I remember I thought them not a particularly good advertisement for the sisters' care. I lost touch with her after Ann married your father, and didn't see her again until she was engaged to Andrew." He paused, and reflected on this, and added: "She'd changed a good deal by then." But obviously the remark was to be taken as a understatement.

"Then perhaps," said Jenny, cheerfully, "it's a good thing Dorrie's like her." Thus prompted, Sir Nicholas returned abruptly to the point he had been making.

"Yes, but she isn't the only one of that generation. As I was saying, she seems a quiet little thing. But there's Janet's son, Edward . . . he's got some odd ideas, if Andrew's telling the truth. And then, take Roddy—"

"At least, you can't call him a puritan," Antony put in.

"Better perhaps if I could," said Sir Nicholas darkly. "But at least, he's alive," he conceded.

"I think Liz is falling in love with him," said Jenny, incautiously. Sir Nicholas sat suddenly bolt upright, as though the back of his chair had become red hot. For a moment he seemed to be struggling to find words, then he looked up and succeeded at last in catching his nephew's eye. The look he gave him could hardly have been termed affectionate, but his voice when he spoke was quiet, almost gentle.

"So that's it," he said. "I might have known there was something behind this . . . this vicarious altruism."

Antony gave him a sympathetic grin, and prepared to do what he could to retrieve the situation. "The monstrous regiment of women," he agreed. "You might as well give in gracefully, Uncle Nick . . . we'll neither of us get any peace until you do."

"You traitor!" said Jenny, indignantly; but Sir Nicholas,

with another of his abrupt changes of mood, was returning his nephew's smile with comparative amiability.

"It is some time," he remarked, "since I saw old Mrs. Gaskell. Besides, the Velasquez—though perhaps not worth a journey into the provinces—might certainly be felt to merit a quiet stroll across the square." He got up purposefully as he spoke, and smiled down at Jenny. "I cannot believe that this is anything but a fool's errand," he added, unfairly; "but if it will give you pleasure, my dear, who am I to argue?"

CHAPTER II

THE GASKELLS' HOUSE might be on the wrong side of the square, but it presented to the passerby the same air of elegance as its neighbours. There was nothing to prepare the eye for the scene of out-moded splendour revealed by the opening of the front door, and Antony—crossing the threshold in the wake of Sir Nicholas—blinked a little at what he saw. Pure Victorian, but nothing was worn or shabby; the colours of the Turkey carpet leaped to the eye as fiercely as the day it was laid. And that, of course, he realised, wasn't so very long ago. He glanced at his uncle, who appeared unmoved and was asking in a placid voice for Andrew Gaskell. But the parlourmaid obviously had her instructions. She said: "I'll tell Mr. Andrew, sir. If you'll come this way, Mrs. Gaskell is expecting you," and set off firmly towards the staircase.

Mrs. Priscilla Gaskell was in her drawing-room; a well-proportioned room on the first floor which might possibly have acquired some beauty if the covers and curtains had been allowed to fade into a decent obscurity. But here again, the Victorian furnishings had been renewed at no very distant date, in all their original hideousness. Antony's eyes, seeking relief, fell upon the one incongruous item . . . a portrait of Roderick Gaskell that hung over the fireplace. No mistaking the Pirate King . . . the vigour of the painting matched the subject's own vitality. It might or might not be a masterpiece, it was certainly an extraordinarily good likeness. And it emphasised what hadn't occurred to him before: the almost uncanny resemblance between Roddy and his grandfather. The same dark, tightly-curling hair; the same rather square face, at once good-humoured and masterful.

But the old lady could hold her own with her surroundings,

and even dominate them. She was enthroned (there could be no lesser word for it) on the right hand side of the fireplace, her white head erect against the crimson velvet of the high chair back. Her expression did not soften as she watched the two visitors cross the room towards her, but it seemed that the maid had been right in saying they were expected.

"Well, Nicholas?" said old Mrs. Gaskell.

If explaining himself to Roderick's widow had been no part of Sir Nicholas's plan, he gave no sign that it perturbed him. "I trust, madam," he said, feeling his way, "that you will not regard this as an intrusion."

The old lady bowed her head, and her tone ironically matched his own. "You are very welcome," she told him. "Both of you." Antony, encouraged, came up to his uncle's side.

"Did Roddy tell you he'd been to see me?" he asked.

"Certainly he told me. Do you imagine I allow myself to be uninformed where my family is concerned? I was expecting you . . . both of you," she said again. Her eyes went from one to the other of them. "I never could stand being hovered over," she remarked. Sir Nicholas subsided into a chair, and Antony—in whom a certain unholy joy in the situation warred with his own embarrassment—chose a smaller, spindle backed affair, violently upholstered in Prussian blue, a little removed from the others. He was thinking, as he seated himself, that a little of old Roderick's irrepressible self-sufficiency—as portrayed so well by the unknown artist —would have been helpful in dealing with the unexpectedly difficult state of affairs. But as the talk went on he noticed that Priscilla Gaskell, in spite of her unbending attitude, was extremely aware of the portrait above the fireplace, and several times he saw her eyes turn in its direction.

"I should explain," Sir Nicholas was saying, "that our business—"

"Is with my son, Andrew." The old lady nodded her head. "I know all about that. But it is a long time since I saw you, Nicholas, and I have my share of curiosity. Just what do you propose to say to him?"

"My dear Mrs. Gaskell!" Sir Nicholas gestured despairingly. "If this seems to you an unwarranted interference, please understand it was not my idea."

"That I believe," said the old lady. "I have heard of Mr. Maitland," she added, and turned a cold eye on Antony for a moment.

"It is not a matter," said Sir Nicholas, warming to his explanation, "upon which I feel myself fitted to advise. If I may make a suggestion, your family solicitor—"

"That old woman!" Her displeasure was emphatic. "Don't be a fool, Nicholas," she added, sharply.

It was difficult to see what answer Sir Nicholas could possibly make to this downright comment, so perhaps it was as well that there was an interruption. Two people came into the room, both of them known to the visitors. Andrew Gaskell seemed to be in a hurry, and obviously did not know that his sister was only a pace or two behind him. He allowed the door to swing almost in her face, and crossed the room with quick, angry strides. Janet Blake disentangled herself from the door, and followed him at a pace only a little less urgent.

Antony's first thought was that they were very much alike, and obviously very near together in age. Both were sturdily built, with straight, greying hair, and fresh complexions. There were similarities of expression, too . . . a sternness about the eyes; mouths tight-lipped, ungenerous. But whereas Andrew Gaskell was almost excessively neat in his person, and in his dress, Mrs. Blake had carried carelessness to the other extreme, so that she had a dingy, down-at-heels air.

Coming to his feet, Antony was glad that he had chosen a chair a little withdrawn from the centre of things, and backed away, unobtrusively, a little farther still. An awkward enough situation, it would be instructive to see how Uncle Nick handled it. And he wondered, briefly, if Andrew was angry that they had come at all, or just that his mother had worked herself in on the deal.

However that might be, Andrew had obviously no time to waste on preliminaries. He came to a stop not much more than a foot away from Sir Nicholas, and said belligerently: "I don't know what nonsense Roddy's been giving you. My mind's made up, and there's no more to be said."

Sir Nicholas stood looking down at him, faintly surprised at so much vehemence. "I'm relieved to hear it," he remarked. "It is always refreshing to meet someone who knows his own mind. But I came to see the Velasquez . . . surely you won't deny me that pleasure?''

"Why . . . no.'' He was clearly at a loss, but added disagreeably, and with more assurance, ''I didn't know you had any interest in art.''

''A considerable interest,'' Sir Nicholas corrected him. ''Though not, I admit, much knowledge. This picture now—''

''Don't . . . don't mention it!'' Janet Blake had clasped her hands against her chest, and her interruption was made in a dramatic tone. (Now, even supposing Roddy had no choice but to confide in his grandmother, why, why, why had he stirred up the family to this extent?)

''Don't be silly, Janet, of course we must mention it.'' Andrew spoke over his shoulder, and his tone was definitely testy. ''Besides, what does it matter? Everyone will know in a day or two—''

''A wrong has been done, and must be put right,'' his sister agreed. Antony couldn't decide whether there was irony in her tone, or whether it was merely submissive. Andrew, too, seemed in some doubt as to her intention.

''Mother agrees with me . . . don't you, Mother?'' he appealed to old Mrs. Gaskell.

''Certainly I do. I've told you that before.'' She sounded firm enough, but for the first time Antony thought he detected a faint note of uncertainty. He looked at the old lady, and saw that her eyes had turned again to the picture that hung above the fireplace. He said, impulsively and unwisely:

''You could do what you say must be done, and still not make a song about it.''

That brought the eyes of all four of his companions on him, so that (as he confided to Jenny afterwards) he felt like nothing so much as the man in the Bateman cartoons. Sir Nicholas was smiling faintly; old Mrs. Gaskell's lips were tight, her expression inscrutable . . . much thanks he'd get in that quarter for letting his sympathies run away with him; Andrew looked shocked and outraged; only Janet Blake hastened to answer him with quick angry words.

''I agree with my brother. I agree with him absolutely. There is nothing else to be done.''

''There are ways and ways of doing things,'' said Antony,

stubbornly, but he only spoke because the silence was becoming uncomfortable. Janet's voice went up a note or two, and she repeated excitedly:

"There's the difference between right and wrong; and when wrong has been done, it must be put right again."

Sir Nicholas turned to look at his nephew, and shook his head at him. "Justice must not only be done, it must be seen to be done," he murmured.

"Exactly!" said Andrew. "But I didn't need you to tell me that," he added, ungraciously.

"I'm sure you didn't." Sir Nicholas's tone was cordial. "But . . . forgive me for reminding you . . . I should very much like to see the picture while it is still in your custody."

"Yes, well . . . yes, of course." He seemed to hesitate, and then made up his mind. "So long as you understand the position," he remarked, and turned towards the door.

"You have made yourself reasonably plain," said Sir Nicholas; and this time there was an edge to his voice. Antony, making in turn his farewells to the ladies, followed the other men out of the room with an air of meekness that was, perhaps, one-tenth the genuine article.

Andrew Gaskell's study, which until six months ago had been his father's, was a sharp contrast to the other parts of the house they had seen. Each piece of furniture seemed to have been carefully chosen for its individual beauty, and had the appearance, at least, of being an antique. But it was all a little overdone . . . flamboyant. And perhaps that was because, in this room, old Roderick's personality had had free play. His son looked out of place here . . . one of Cromwell's soldiers in possession of a Cavalier stronghold. But the paintings were another matter; Antony reserved for future consideration the fact that they fitted nowhere into his preconceived notion of the Pirate King's character.

Sir Nicholas, meanwhile, having unnecessarily quelled his nephew with a glance, was proceeding to speak his mind. "I did not wish to pursue the subject in Mrs. Gaskell's presence, but since I am here, and since Roddy has asked for my advice, I think I must make my opinion clear: the picture must be returned to its owners, so much is obvious. But you are under no obligation to court publicity in making restitution. If you do not wish to entrust the negotiations to your own solicitor, I can certainly put you in touch with someone who will handle the matter discreetly.''

''You lawyers!'' said Andrew Gaskell. He almost spat out the words. Obviously, Antony thought, it was at that moment the ultimate insult he could offer.

''I do not wish you to be in any doubt about my position. I did not speak more openly before, for fear of distressing Mrs. Gaskell further—''

''Distressing her?'' said Andrew. ''She agrees with me. And so does Janet.''

''In that case, there is no more to be said.'' The overtone was one of relief, but Antony could hear the bitterness in his uncle's voice, and wondered again at the obvious dislike between the two. Meanwhile, it seemed that they might be manoeuvred out of the house without even a sight of the controversial picture. He began to look around him, misleadingly casual.

''The panel Roddy mentioned must be very well concealed,'' he said.

''In the circumstances,'' said Sir Nicholas, ''that is understandable.''

Andrew made no direct reply, but took three quick paces across the room and put up a hand to the panelling. A moment later, quite silently, a wide section slid back . . .

Andrew was staring stupidly. Antony, coming up eagerly to his uncle's side, heard his quiet comment before he took in the meaning of the words. ''That would seem, my dear Gaskell, to settle the problem very effectively,'' said Sir Nicholas.

The space behind the panel was quite empty. Of the picture that had been causing so much excitement there was no sign at all.

''So that was that,'' said Antony to Jenny, much later that evening, when they were on their way to bed. ''We got away as quickly as possible. But it's a pretty problem, isn't it?''

''I just don't understand,'' said Jenny. She spoke slowly, thinking it out. ''Who would have taken it?''

''*I* don't know,'' said Antony. ''Nothing seems to make sense.'' He yawned elaborately, and sat down on the edge of the bed.

"I've been longing to know what happened, all the evening," said Jenny. She picked up her hairbrush and sat down in front of the mirror. "But I could see you didn't want me to ask questions."

"I didn't." Her husband spoke with feeling. "It would only have started Uncle Nick off again."

"Was he very cross?" asked Jenny sympathetically.

"He was deeply moved, and expressed himself rather freely. I don't blame him altogether," he added reflectively.

"Well, what happened to the picture?" asked Jenny, brushing vigorously. "Do you think . . . do you think perhaps Andrew moved it himself. I mean, he *said* he was going to send it back publicly, but perhaps he never meant to."

"A face-saving operation? It's a good idea, but I don't think it was that way. He was absolutely furious, and it sounded genuine."

"He might have been putting it on," said Jenny, reluctant to abandon her idea.

"Well, he sounded furious," Antony repeated, declining to be drawn into an argument. "And he said he'd find out who had taken it . . . if it was the last thing he ever did."

"It might have been Uncle Gil," said Jenny, disregarding this attempt to introduce a note of melodrama. Her hair was brushed up into a wild disorder, and she paused to admire the effect. "He'd be bound to covet it, and perhaps it didn't seem like stealing, when it had already been stolen once, you know."

"You may be right," said Antony, peaceably.

"Or it might have been Roddy." She exchanged brush for comb, and began the less amusing task of reducing order out of tangle. "To prevent his father making a scandal," she explained, unnecessarily.

"In that case, why come to me?"

"As a blind, of course. That's obvious."

"Well, if it was . . . whoever it was, I'm sorry for them if Andrew finds out. He wasn't pleased, I told you that, didn't I? He looked . . . positively malevolent," said Antony, laying it on thick, but rather spoiling the effect by yawning again as he spoke. "But I expect we've heard the last of it, anyway."

"Do you think so?" It was hard to tell whether her tone

was sceptical or disappointed. "We'll be seeing the Gaskells—the young ones, that is—at Aunt Carry's dance, you know."

"So we shall," he agreed, a little too dutifully.

"If you're thinking how to get out of it, Antony, I'll never forgive you."

"Don't worry, I'm counting the days."

"I know . . . counting the days until it's over. But I have to go, darling, and it's no fun alone." Antony grinned at her reassuringly, but made no direct reply. "You ought to be grateful to Aunt Carry, anyway," she went on. "You'd never have got Uncle Nick to go with you to the Gaskells' if it hadn't been for her."

"Now, why on earth—?"

"Well, it was what you said . . . and it was very clever of you, even if it was horrid."

"You've lost me, love. What are you talking about?"

"The monstrous regiment of women," said Jenny, with a great air of clarity. "You said we'd give you no peace, and—don't you see, Antony?—Uncle Nick wouldn't care if I nagged him for a month, and he wouldn't care what Liz said either. But Aunt Carry is Liz's mother, and he's terrified of her." Antony began to laugh. "Well, you know he is," she insisted, putting down the comb and giving the result of her labours a critical look.

"I'll take your word for it," said Antony. "But I have a feeling he meant to go all the time. Will you be long, or can I open the window now?" Jenny pulled a face at her reflection, and got up purposefully. "And as it happens," he added, crossing to pull back the curtains, "Uncle Nick would be in a much better mood now if we'd never succeeded in persuading him."

"Oh, no, he wouldn't," said Jenny. "His conscience would be plaguing him for not doing all he could to help; and that would be Much Worse."

CHAPTER III

THE NEW PROBLEM posed by the disappearance of the Velasquez was one that Antony Maitland would dearly have liked to solve. There didn't seem to be much he could do to satisfy his curiosity, however, unless Roddy chose to take the matter up again; and he was perfectly well aware that the sensible course was to lie very low and say nothing at all. Sir Nicholas, having spoken his mind on the subject, had not mentioned it again. They were busy that week—not an unusual state of affairs—and Antony perforce put the whole thing out of his mind.

Old Mrs. Gaskell would never have admitted, even to herself, that she was glad the picture was gone. She was by habit a busy old lady, persistently interfering in the housekeeping duties which could quite well have been left to her daughter. But when Andrew ventured to remonstrate with her, as he did from time to time, she told him roundly: "You wouldn't be nearly so comfortable if I stopped worrying, my dear."

This was probably true, but Andrew had not quite finished propounding his ideas. "You've earned a little relaxation, Mother, at your age. And Janet could quite well—" But that was an unwise remark. Priscilla drew herself up to her full height, and looked up at him with eyes that sparkled with indignation.

"We'll leave my age out of the argument, Andrew, if you please. Janet has no control over the servants, as well you know. And she's quite happily occupied with all those charities of hers." She paused, and then added shrewdly: "If your conscience is troubling you because you think I shall be hurt when you return the picture to the gallery, you may set your mind at rest. I never gave in to your father's ideas when he was alive. And I don't propose to start now.''

Andrew made haste to disclaim any intention of attributing to his mother principles less rigid than his own. ''Though the point doesn't arise, as a matter of fact,'' he added disconsolately. ''We've searched the house from top to bottom, and the picture just isn't here.''

''Then it must have been taken away,'' said Priscilla briskly.

''Yes, but how? It's too big to be carried out openly, even rolled up, without being noticed. It's too big for a brief case, and nobody has taken any luggage out of the house.''

''It was managed somehow,'' his mother pointed out.

''Yes. I wonder now—'' He paused, to think out whatever point had struck him, and the old lady took the opportunity to stoop and run her finger along the ledge under the hall table. It seemed to be free of dust, but she had her suspicions of that girl. Too cheerful to be really respectable . . . flighty. Andrew's voice interrupted her reflections.

''Is Roddy coming in to lunch to-day?'' he asked. His tone had an urgency that seemed to convey to her more than was actually said.

''He said he'd be out. But Andrew—'' For once in her life her voice faltered. ''Are you telling me Roddy stole the picture?''

''I don't know yet, that needs some thought.'' He was more nearly excited than she had ever seen him, less punctilious in his speech. ''But I think I know how it was taken out of the house. *That* was his doing, or I'm very much mistaken.''

''Oh, no, Andrew.''

''Don't say a word about it,'' he warned her. ''I want to be sure.''

Having given her word on this point, the old lady had no intention of breaking it; but it was not her way to allow anything to go on under her roof that she did not know about, and she determined therefore that the picture must be found, whatever her own misgivings. ''You're an old reprobate,'' she said, shaking her head reprovingly at her husband's picture, ''and must take the consequences, as Andrew says.'' Roderick Gaskell was the only man whose sins she had ever, to any degree, condoned, and she had fought him and loved him all her life; it was to the extent that he resembled his grandfather that she was sometimes tempted to forgive Roddy even the more outrageous of his exploits.

With her other grandchildren, the case was different. Janet was inclined to become shrill when her son was criticised (one day it would be ''he spends too much time here . . . can't have enough to occupy him''; and another ''better things to do than visit us, my dear''). ''I can't see why you should always pick on Edward,'' said Mrs. Blake. ''I'm sure if he'd had Roddy's advantages—'' But if Edward was present, she had learned to let him fight his own battles. For all his polished ways, he had a tongue and could use it.

It was different again where Dorrie was concerned . . . her aunt and grandmother were at one over her short-comings. ''Sit up straight, child . . . don't sit there idle . . have you done your practising? . . . where's your needlework?'' Dorrie, who hated arguments, raised voices, and—even more—being ''talked at'' about her imperfections, did her best to comply; but she had been becoming increasingly restless, and in the weeks that followed the disappearance of the Velasquez—with the atmosphere at home coming obviously up to boiling point—she finally resolved to take the first step towards independence and try to find a job.

''It's wrong that I should be idle,'' she told her father, with more cunning than Roddy (her chief confidant) would have given her credit for. But it did her no good. Her grandmother was held up as an example—''a woman still busy about her household cares.'' (''She doesn't really *do* anything,'' said Dorrie mutinously. But she said it to herself). And until she was married, with a home of her own, there were always Good Works. (To do Andrew justice, this was Dorrie's translation of what he said to her). ''Your Aunt Janet's activities fill her life.''

''But it would be better if they left her some time to shop, and to visit the hairdresser,'' said Dorrie to her brother that night.

Roddy grinned at her. ''Spiteful little cat, aren't you? Well, if Dad won't help, you'll just have to take matters into your own hands. Defy him!''

Dorrie looked horrified. ''You know I couldn't.''

"How do I know? You've never tried." But he realised as he spoke it was hopeless, she could never stand being bullied or shouted at. In fact, she was a complete misfit in that stormy household, and the only reason he had himself remained so long under his grandparents' roof.

"Besides," said Dorrie miserably, "I've not been trained for anything."

"Oh, come now!" said Roddy. "The pianoforte . . . water-colour painting . . . what I'm always expecting Gran to call 'your stitchery'. No expense spared, my girl!" In spite of her depression, Dorrie giggled.

"Too, too Jane Eyre," she agreed; and went on to explain, unnecessarily: "I meant things people do in offices."

"Well, nobody trained me," said Roddy.

"But, you're a man. And they let you go and . . . and practice until you learned something. I shall ask Edward to give me a job," she added, with sudden inspiration.

"Good idea," said Roddy. "Let's see what he says." Which was reprehensible, because he knew well enough what the answer would be.

"Anything up to half my kingdom," said Edward, shaking his head at Dorrie regretfully. "But not a job."

"Well, why not? You needn't pay me anything while I'm learning," she encouraged him. Roddy grinned at the pair of them.

"Cold feet, Edward?" he enquired.

"Ice cold," said Edward, firmly. He looked at Dorrie, and added gently, "We'd never hear the end of it, either of us."

"But you're a man," she protested, as she had protested to her brother. "You don't mind rows."

"No," said Edward. He did not elaborate; and Roddy, with unaccustomed forbearance, steered the talk to less uncomfortable matters. His cousin might not mind rows, though Roddy doubted he had any particular zest for them; but no one could stand hysterics, and there was no doubt Aunt Janet's nerves gave her son plenty to worry about.

"But I could offer you a different sort of job," said Edward later, when the other two were about to leave his flat.

"What sort of a job. You said—"

"Housekeeping," said Edward. Roddy gave a hoot of laughter.

"He's asking you to marry him," he told his sister. "At least . . . I hope so."

Dorrie looked up at her cousin doubtfully. "But Edward, you don't want to marry me," she protested. "If you're trying to be kind—" She saw his smile, and laughed back at him. "We know each other much too well."

Lunching with his cousin next day Roddy said glumly: "What on earth did you want to bungle it like that for? You meant it, didn't you?"

Edward was studying the menu, but looked up with a gleam in his eye that might have been amusement. "Asking me my intentions, Roddy?" he said.

"Yes . . . well . . . not exactly." For once in his life Roddy seemed taken aback. "But I'll tell you what it is, Edward," he went on seriously. "We'll be having her marrying Michael if we don't watch out, and I'm damned if I want him for a brother-in-law."

"Pratten?" said Edward; and frowned over the information. "Do you really think—?"

"That's what I said, isn't it? While you're fooling around—"

"What else can I do? She said herself we know each other too well."

"If she thinks of you as a brother, whose fault is that?" But he allowed himself to be distracted to a study of the wine list, and for some reason found himself unable to re-open the subject when they were alone again. The thought occurred to him that if you felt deeply enough about something—or somebody—you might have an over-sensitive fear of a rebuff; but he put this revolutionary idea aside for later consideration, and devoted himself to his lunch.

But because he was fond of Dorrie, the matter stuck in his mind. He would have been the first to admit that he was perhaps not the best judge of her preferences, but Edward (with all his faults, thought Roddy, with his sarcastic ways and the odd ideas Dad talks about) seemed to him a much better proposition that Michael Pratten; in the business world, Michael would undoubtedly go further than Edward; his position in the firm was now far more managerial than his original rôle of secretary to "the Pirate King," and there was no denying . . . he knew the business backwards. As far as character went, he was more stable than anyone connected with the Gaskells could ever hope to be. Roddy respected his ability, thought his principles a nuisance, and his conversation a dead bore. But Dorrie saw a lot of him, and perhaps she didn't realise that he wasn't exactly scintillating company. (It never occurred to Roddy that she might not care). He was so much preoccupied with the problem that he answered his father's questions at random when he saw him before dinner, and never wondered until very much later what was behind them. Nor did he notice that his grandmother's eyes were on him even more frequently than usual as the meal progressed.

Michael Pratten thought the old lady looked anxious, and wondered what sort of a scrape Roddy was in this time. He didn't consider that it might have to do with the loss of the picture . . . it was as well for everyone that it was out of the way, and the sooner the whole thing was forgotten the better. He was quite well aware that Andrew would like to get his hands on it again, and was even more eager, perhaps, to get his hands on the person who had moved it. But it wasn't very likely he'd ever find out who it was.

Meanwhile, Dorrie was even quieter than usual. Pale, too. He wondered what had happened to upset her. Perhaps it was Roddy again, she was fond of him . . . too fond. The bond between them was of a kind that usually existed only between members of a much larger family, where two kindred spirits might find themselves united in sympathy against the rest. The sooner he got away from here, the better; but he had to be sure of her feelings. She was so quiet, so self-contained, it was difficult to tell what she thought on any subject . . . especially difficult to tell if her emotions were engaged. Since old Roderick died, Michael's position as a member of the household had chafed him; he had loved and respected the old man, but no such feeling united him to Andrew. The job was another matter; his knowledge of the firm's affairs gave him power, which was satisfying, and which he hoped he could retain. He wasn't sure enough of his standing to know what the outcome of marrying Dorrie would be; but he thought as he watched her that if he could be sure she loved him he wouldn't care for anything else.

Gilbert Gaskell heard of the new problem from Edward, who took the trouble to go round to his flat one evening with the news and got only abuse for his pains, on the grounds that he didn't take the disappearance of the picture seriously enough.

What Edward didn't understand, of course, was that to Gilbert the personal problems which were solved by this disappearance were as nothing; only the picture itself was of any real concern. But for all that, Edward was shrewd enough to come to another conclusion. "You know where it is, don't you, Uncle Gil?"

"As a matter of fact, no."

Edward looked around him. The room was warm and fire-lit, but to his eyes not precisely comfortable. Too many antiques . . . too many curios. And the pictures: nothing startling, perhaps—Uncle Gil's finances wouldn't run to that, he supposed—but, "it would make a pleasant addition to your collection, wouldn't it?" he suggested.

Gilbert eyed him with some amusement. "Do you really think I'm such easy game?" he demanded. "Even if I had it—" Edward had the grace to look a little abashed, but thinking it over afterwards he decided that his opinion was unchanged. He still thought Uncle Gil knew . . .

But all these things happened in the week before "Aunt Carry's dance," to which Antony and Jenny Maitland were looking forward with such different feelings. And though all the people concerned were troubled to some extent with a feeling of foreboding, only one had any idea of the precise climax towards which their affairs were moving.

CHAPTER IV

JENNY'S "AUNT CARRY" was Mrs. Thomas Watson, though to be fair all round it must be admitted that she was by far the more forceful member of the partnership. Uncle Tom, however, though easy going in his personal relationships, was a stock-broker with a flair. This was fortunate, as his wife had a passion for large-scale entertaining. They had brought up, and launched, a numerous family; and now Liz, the youngest daughter, was the only one at home.

Antony was late, of course, having been all the afternoon in court, and then delayed by a frantic telephone call just as he was leaving chambers. He got home at last, to be irritated—though not surprised—by the news that Jenny, summoned imperiously by her aunt, had gone on ahead of him. Mrs. Watson had a way of getting what she wanted . . . in this case, Jenny's help in dealing with any last-minute emergencies. Antony, sharing a cold meal with his uncle (for Tuesday evening had been Mrs. Stokes's night out as long as he could remember) was moved to dissert bitterly on the unreasonableness of Aunt Carry's demands; but Sir Nicholas, secure in the knowledge that nothing was going to disturb his evening, remained blandly unsympathetic.

Going upstairs a little sulkily when the meal was over, Antony decided there was no point at this stage in hurrying, he might as well take his time; an unnecessary decision, as it turned out. His tie proved completely unmanageable, and he was reduced at last to the dreadful expedient of going downstairs and begging Gibbs's help.

Gibbs was Sir Nicholas's butler, a saintly-looking old man of disagreeable temper. He dealt with the tie with depressing efficiency, but not before he had taken occasion to deliver an improving homily upon the virtue of punctuality. Antony left the house with his morale at very low ebb, and even later than he had intended.

Jenny always maintained that Uncle Tom had chosen his house solely with an eye to having somewhere big enough to lose himself in when his wife's instinct of hospitality got the better of her. It was not a comfortable house, nor one you could feel at home in, but on occasions like this it came into its own: a fitting background for the colour and glitter of a fashionable crowd, the rooms large enough to absorb the disharmony of high-pitched chatter without quite allowing the listener to be deafened.

The hall was empty of guests when Anthony arrived. He took off his coat, realised suddenly that the scarf he had picked up in a hurry was an old, frayed one, which Jenny had condemned months ago, stuffed it into the overcoat pocket, and started upstairs a few minutes later with a quite irrational feeling of guilt. The sound of voices and music came down to him, mercifully muted by distance. There must be a pretty good crowd, and how he was going to find Jenny . . .

His hostess met him at the top of the stairs. Caroline Watson was a handsome woman, who made the most of an imposing figure. She gave him a small, tight smile by way of greeting, and eyed him critically; wondering—not for the first time—what Jenny, a sensible child in many ways, saw in him. Presentable enough, she conceded; good-looking, even . . . if you cared for that dark, thin type, and could tolerate the amusement that showed only too often in his grey eyes. But his manner was far too casual for her liking; she had never seen him in court, and would only have murmured "playacting" if she had done so . . . a comment Antony would have been the first to acknowledge as fair. Besides, there was something odd about his background; not the family, of course, she knew all about that, but there was a certain reserve, a lack of openness. She was old-fashioned enough, she would have told you, to consider frankness a manly virtue. His army service, for instance . . . intelligence work, she had heard, whatever that might mean. And there had been some not-altogether-sympathetic publicity about one or two of his cases. It added up to a lack of conformity she could not but deplore.

"Poor boy," she said, in a tone that fairly dripped with honey. "So late!"

Antony, recognising this for the rebuke it was meant to be, grinned at her amiably. He was not particularly fond of Aunt Carry, and had arrived early in their acquaintance at a pretty accurate estimate of her opinion of him, but there was no denying she had a stimulating effect. "What is one," he asked, waving a hand towards an archway on the left of the wide landing, through which poured a multitude of sound, "what is one among so many?"

"We missed you," Mrs. Watson told him, insincerely. She was eyeing him up and down as she spoke, and Antony said defensively:

"I know you enticed Jenny away from me, but my tie was tied by an expert." He caught her eye, and added with the amused look she disliked so much: "Really, Aunt Carry, you ought to have been a sergeant-major. Do I pass inspection?"

"I suppose," said Caroline Watson, abandoning her cooing tone for one with a certain amount of ice in it, "I suppose we should be grateful you've found time to come here at all."

This being quite unanswerable, Antony attempted no comment. "Is Uncle Tom well?" he asked, diplomatically.

"Quite well, thank you."

"I suppose I'll find Liz—" He was about to move on when he caught a fleeting expression on Mrs. Watson's face, a troubled look . . . if that didn't seem so unlikely. "What's wrong, Aunt Carry? Has Liz been up to something?"

"I don't know why you should think so. I don't know why you should suggest such a thing." Antony gestured vaguely, and she added no less stiffly: "What exactly are you suggesting, anyway?"

"I don't know," said Antony. "I just thought you looked bothered. She might be in love with the dustman, I suppose; or planning to elope with a heathen Chinee."

Aunt Carry relaxed suddenly, and gave one of her rare laughs. "Not quite as bad as that," she admitted, with unexpected candour. "She's seeing a lot of Roddy Gaskell." (And what obscure impulse possessed her, he wondered, to choose him as a confidant . . . when she was bound to regret it almost before the words were uttered?) "I shouldn't like to see her make a mistake, Antony. Girls can be so head-strong.''

"Like Jenny," he agreed.

"Yes, perhaps." It was no use, he reflected ruefully, trying to get a rise out of Aunt Carry. The briefest of pauses acknowledged that the point had not gone unmarked, and then she was continuing smoothly. "Elizabeth is so young, and there have been rumours."

"About the Gaskells?" His interest was caught now, but his tone remained casual.

"Oh, nothing definite. I'd know what to do if there was anything definite. Just vague hints of something wrong . . . Tom says it isn't the business, but—"

"I shouldn't worry if I were you, Aunt Carry. I'd back Liz to cope, even with the Gaskells."

She looked at him stonily for a moment, obviously regretting her unpremeditated frankness. "The girl's name is Elizabeth," she remarked. "She was called after your mother-in-law."

"Good lord," said Antony, blankly. His hostess did not actually say: "Jenny's mother, you fool," but her thought was obvious. He grinned at her apologetically.

"She never actually was, you know," he said, not very lucidly. "She died too soon."

A wave of her hand at once dismissed him and made him free of the rooms beyond the archway. "Dear boy," she said. "Have a wonderful time."

The first of the big rooms was the one given over to dancing, and as he knew from experience that it was here he was most likely to find his wife, Antony did not endeavour to penetrate any further. It took a moment to adjust to the noise, which he mentally condemned as an infernal clatter; a few more minutes passed before he saw Jenny, dancing with a red-haired man who looked vaguely familiar. He found a strategic position near a pillar, and settled himself to watch their gyrations. Jenny seemed to be enjoying herself, despite her preliminary forebodings. She was also looking particularly well, he thought, and took a little time to consider the point; all experience to the contrary, he had expected to find her worn out by coping with Aunt Carry's demands. The dress was a new one . . . a birthday present, Uncle Nick had called it, and just as well because the exchequer was pretty low just now. He was interrupted by a voice at his elbow.

"It isn't decent," it complained, "to come to a party and have eyes only for your wife." He turned to find Derek Stringer at his elbow, a tall man of about his own age, whose receding hair-line gave him an older look.

"She's worth looking at, don't you think?" said Antony, complacently.

Derek turned to follow his glance. "You'd better find yourself a partner," he declared pessimistically. "She looks set for the evening."

Anthony, who—for reasons he considered to be good ones—hated to dance with strangers, gave him a look of stern dislike. "How long have you been here?" he demanded.

"Half an hour . . . a little longer, perhaps."

"And still at large?" Stringer's determined bachelorhood was the despair of all his friends' wives, but there could be no denying he knew how to enjoy himself.

"She's dancing," he said now. "I'm just biding my time. You see that fair girl over there—"

Antony identified and approved the fair girl, though rather too guardedly to satisfy the other man completely. The music stopped for a moment, but started again almost without a pause. Derek disappeared unceremoniously, and Antony began to work his way slowly round the edge of the dance floor.

He had not gone very far when he was pounced on by his cousin, Liz Watson. Liz was a tall girl, who would one day be as heavy as her mother; though her lighthearted manner gave little promise that she would ever achieve an equal majesty of bearing. She had thick, dark hair, cut in a short "bob," which she kept through every change of fashion. And now she had obviously been waiting for Antony, because her first question was almost in the nature of an attack.

"What was mother talking to you about?"

She must have overheard something, he thought, for it ever to have occurred to her to ask the question.

"She told me, among other things," he replied, "that your name is Elizabeth."

"I see." Liz spoke ominously. "So you *were* talking about me. I can guess the rest, I suppose." She gave him a fierce look. "I know what I'm doing," she said. "I'm not a poor, deluded girl . . . do I look like one?"

"Never, to my knowledge, having deluded anybody in my life, I am not familiar—"

"Don't play the innocent," his cousin advised him. "And if you don't look out," she went on, "you'll end up sounding exactly like Uncle Nick."

"Well . . . thanks for the warning." But she was quite right . . . if she knew what was worrying her mother it was no use sparring. "Look here, Liz, what have you been up to?"

"If you mean Roddy, I'm going to marry him," she said.

"Are you indeed? Er . . . does he know?"

That brought the first lightening of her expression, and she gave him quite a friendly smile. "Of course he does." Then she was suddenly anxious. "Antony, darling," she said, "you don't hate Roddy, do you? I mean . . . some one must like him, mustn't they?"

"I think," said Antony, deliberately, "that you'll make an ideal couple."

"Do you really?" She saw his smile and added suspiciously, "What exactly do you mean by that?"

"You'll lead each other the hell of a life . . . just what you both deserve." But she was not to be cajoled into treating the subject lightly.

"I can't think," she said, spitefully, "what on earth Jenny sees in you."

"That's another thing Aunt Carry said to me," Antony told her. "Only she didn't put it quite so crudely." But Liz had already forgiven him, and her frown was for her thoughts, not for his flippancy.

"What do you think," she asked, "about this picture?"

"It hasn't turned up again?" He took a quick glance round as he spoke, but their nearest neighbours were obviously taken up with their own affairs.

"No, it hasn't."

"In that case," said Antony, carefully ignoring the ethical problem involved, "I wonder how Aunt Carry got wind of a possible scandal."

"Well, I didn't tell her," said Liz, "and I don't know who

would. But there has been some vague sort of talk, and the funny thing is, Roddy's worried."

"Why?"

"That's what worries me . . . he hasn't told me."

"Is he here this evening?" Antony was looking about him as he spoke.

"He's dancing with Marjorie Lawson; I made him," said Liz. "I didn't know it would go on for ever," she added, disconsolately.

"Well, don't worry. If the thing has disappeared for good there can't be anything much to worry about," he told her. And had no means of knowing, at the moment, how very wrong he was.

The music stopped soon after that. A few moments later, Roddy was crossing the floor towards them, alone. He held out a hand to Liz, and greeted Antony politely enough, but seemed disinclined to meet his eyes. A moment later the two young people were moving away together. Antony turned to look for Jenny, and found her only a few paces behind him, with the red-haired man still in tow.

"Have you met Edward Blake, darling? He's a neighbour of ours, so perhaps you know him."

So this was Janet's son: a man in his early thirties, whose colouring and general appearance could not have formed a greater contrast to the dark flamboyance of the Gaskell family. A man, thought Antony sourly, who obviously had no trouble in dealing with his tie, and achieving perfection at the first shot; in fact, as different as possible from Janet Blake, who seemed to equate slovenliness with virtue.

"Not exactly a neighbour," Edward was saying, "but I do visit frequently in the square. My uncle and cousins live there, and my mother with them."

"I was wondering where I'd seen you," said Antony. He spoke a little absently, because his mind was occupied with a problem. Had Edward sought out Jenny, wishing—with whatever motive—a closer acquaintance with himself? Or was this one of Jenny's tricks, to keep his interest in "the problem" alive by interesting him in the family? There was an air of smugness about her that lent colour to the latter possibility . . . or perhaps the fellow had been making her pretty speeches? "I met Mrs. Blake a week or so ago," Antony remarked.

"So Dorrie told me." But if he knew there had been anything unusual about the meeting he gave no sign. "I wish I'd been there," he added (and obviously, thought Antony, *that* couldn't be sincere). "I've often thought I'd like to meet Sir Nicholas Harding. He must be an interesting man."

"For those who can stand the strain." He still sounded vague, and Jenny glanced at him, and frowned a little.

Blake said, perhaps deliberately misunderstanding, "I suppose your profession can be very trying. But I've always felt the law had a . . . a sort of glamour."

"Not so much as a shipping line . . . far flung corners of the world, and all that." He felt Jenny's eyes on him, silently reproachful. "Or aren't you in the family business?"

"Not exactly, though you might say there's a connection." Edward's tone was dry. "I work for a travel agency; well, I manage their West End Branch. 'Sunshine Unlimited'; the name, I might add, was not my invention."

"Sounds jolly," said Antony.

"It's a damnable sort of existence," said Blake; his vehemence was startling in contrast to his previous manner. "Well, it just happens it isn't exactly my cup of tea," he added, with an apologetic look at Jenny. The subject had evidently been previously discussed, because she looked at her husband and said with an air of geat clarity:

"Mr. Blake would like to be a beachcomber."

Antony, knowing Jenny's explanations of old, took this rather startling pronouncement calmly, with no more than an enquiring look in the other man's direction. Blake seemed to have regained his composure, and said with an amused look, "Nothing quite so dramatic. But I'm sick of civilisation . . . or what passes for civilisation these days."

"At least, you're in a position to know the best places to go to get away from it all."

"Yes," said Edward. He seemed to have lost interest in the subject, and turned to take his leave of Jenny. As he left them a moment later, she looked reproachfully at her husband.

"I thought you'd be interested in meeting him."

"Well, so I was."

"It didn't sound like it."

"Damn it all, love, I couldn't cross-examine the fellow."

"You didn't have to sound half-witted, or trot out one cliché after another," said Jenny severely. She seemed to have taken his shortcomings unduly to heart, and Antony grinned at her.

"Blame your relations," he said. "I'm never at my best after a session with Aunt Carry; she's got the wind up about Liz and Roddy, by the way. Someone seems to have been talking out of turn."

"I ought to have waited for you," said Jenny, characteristically going to the heart of his complaint.

"Never mind. I can quite see it was more amusing to start a flirtation with Blake. Are you booked up for the rest of the evening, or may I have the pleasure?"

"Don't be so silly." She tucked a hand under his arm, and smiled up at him. "You want a drink, and I know exactly where everything is. And after that we can dance, if Derek doesn't find us first. I sort of promised—"

"Derek," said her husband firmly, "has other fish to fry. The last I saw of him, he had his eye on a blonde, and I imagine he'll have succeeded in picking her up by now."

"Aunt Carry is quite right," said Jenny, with her nose in the air. "The practice of law has an extremely vulgarising effect—"

"You can't say that," said Anthony, shocked. "Think of Uncle Nick."

"You didn't let me finish," Jenny protested. "She said, 'except on the most elevated minds' . . . I expect that would cover Uncle Nick, don't you?"

They found friends in the smaller room where the buffet was established, and Jenny remembered that she had had no time for dinner. Antony was rather silent; he was wondering about the Gaskells, and what had been happening to them during the past week. There wasn't much they could do by way of reparation so long as the picture was missing, but the mystery surrounding its disappearance could not possibly be encouraging a happy atmosphere in the family circle.

After a while he became aware that Jenny was tugging his sleeve. "That's Uncle Gil over there," she told him, taking the trend of his thoughts for granted.

"The Gaskells are here in force, aren't they?"

"Well, he's a friend of Uncle Tom, you know."

"I didn't. But that doesn't explain the others. I saw Dorrie while I was waiting for you, dancing with a chap who looked like an intelligent egg. And there's your friend Blake as well, and Roddy. Aunt Carry must be losing her grip."

"You can't just *not* ask people when you know them as well as she does the Gaskells. It isn't done," said Jenny, with an air of finality.

"I'll take your word for it. You know, love, Liz has got me worried. She told me something was bothering Roddy . . . and I'm pretty sure she was serious."

"It needn't be anything to do with . . . with old Mr. Gaskell's will," said Jenny, cautiously.

"No, but . . . I think we'll just have a word with Uncle Gil as we go out."

Gilbert Gaskell was some years younger than his brother and sister, and his hair was still dark with no sign of greying. He had the same square build as the other members of his family, but there the resemblance ended. His manner was relaxed, almost lazy, and he greeted Jenny—and Antony, when the introduction was effected—with quiet friendliness. In fact, Antony could not place him at all: too quiet for one of the wilder Gaskells . . . too amiable for one of the puritans.

"I've been hearing about you," he told Antony, "from my niece Dorrie. I'm afraid you had a somewhat uncomfortable visit to my family a week or so ago."

"A wild goose chase," Antony admitted, not quite sure where this was leading. (One thing was certain, if all the Gaskells felt the same urge to bring up the subject of the Velasquez at every possible moment, it wasn't surprising Aunt Carry had heard rumours of something wrong).

"It wouldn't have mattered," said Jenny, "if Uncle Nick hadn't wanted to see the picture."

"That I can understand," said Gilbert. "It is . . . very lovely." The words had no effect of triteness, perhaps because of the tone in which they were spoken; almost, thought Antony, as though he were talking about a person . . . someone he loved.

"From the description Roddy gave me," he said, bringing out the suggestion with a diffidence which was completely misleading, ''I have wondered whether it was not a companion picture to the 'Lady with the Fan'.'' Gilbert turned to him eagerly.

''You're quite right, of course. An informal portrait—there were not many, as you know—and we do not know the identity of the lady. It is believed to have been painted in 1648, just before the second Italian visit.'' He paused, apparently to contemplate the picture they were discussing. Antony said solemnly:

''A subtle and delicate work, remarkable for the sensitive portrayal of personal charm.'' He found Gilbert's eye on him, suddenly bright with suspicion, and grinned apologetically. ''Don't tell me I'm wrong,'' he begged. ''I've been reading the encyclopædia.''

''So it would seem.'' He spoke gruffly, and just for a moment Antony wondered if he had misjudged his man, and had offended him beyond forgiveness. But, ''you had me fooled for a minute,'' said Gilbert, and began to laugh. ''Do I really sound like that?''

''Of course not. It was merely a desire to keep my end up. But—if you will forgive me for returning to the subject—I should have thought your advice would have been of more value to your family than anything my uncle could say.''

''My advice? Oh, dear, no. Didn't Roddy explain to you?''

''Explain what?''

''The family don't mention me. I'm not considered quite respectable,'' said Gilbert, earnestly.

''Yet they asked your opinion.''

''On a matter they admit I am an expert in; a matter of complete indifference to them. But my advice on any more mundane matter . . . they wouldn't consider it for a moment. You see,'' he added gently, ''I'm the only one who never had the money-making urge. Never earned a penny in my life, as a matter of fact; and I'm certainly the only Gaskell you could say that about.''

''I see.'' Antony was a little bewildered, but Gilbert seemed quite unaware that his confidences were anything out of the way. ''Is your brother also an expert?'' he asked. (His companion, after all, had himself introduced the subject; surely there could be no harm in probing a little further).

''Andrew? Not a bit of it. My father was the only one . . .

well, he started my interest, I suppose, and I learned a lot from him.''

"His taste,'' said Antony, slowly, ''was not exactly what I would have expected. I've seen his study,'' he explained, as Gilbert looked at him enquiringly.

"I know,'' said Gilbert, cheerfully. ''More refined. You expect . . . a Reubens, perhaps? . . . and find instead—''

"Something gentle and imaginative by Turner.''

"The one in the corner behind the desk? I'm surprised you recognised it, it isn't one of his well known periods.''

"I didn't, I'm afraid. It was my uncle . . . and I think he was guessing,'' he added honestly.

"Well, after the rest of the house, I'm not surprised you wondered.'' He turned to smile at Jenny. ''Have you been there?'' he asked her.

"No, but Antony told me—'' At this point she realised for the first time where the sentence was going, and broke off abruptly. Gilbert took up the topic smoothly.

"The Victorian period is the only one my mother considers respectable,'' he said. ''And the only way my father could assert himself was by seeing that everything was renewed, only too frequently. To go back to the pictures, he was an enthusiast, you know; but he never had time to enjoy himself.'' He shook his head sadly. ''It's a great mistake, this preoccupation with money,'' he said. And added, surprisingly, with a direct look Antony could not avoid: ''Who do you think took the Velasquez . . . this time?''

"I . . . well, you know, I haven't any ideas on the subject.'' He wondered uneasily if Gilbert could have sensed his suspicion that *he* might have had something to do with the second disappearance. ''I wish I did know,'' he added, with truth.

"You may find out, sooner than you expect.'' Gilbert's tone was suddenly grim. ''Andrew's been throwing out hints . . . he said he'd find out, and I must admit he's a man of his word.''

"But surely . . . oh, I see you mean he'd make that public, along with the rest?''

"What would you expect?''

"I'd been thinking of the matter as closed,'' said Antony.

"Until to-night. But in any case," he added, firmly, "it's nothing whatever to do with me."

"No." Gilbert sounded doubtful. "I wouldn't count on that, if I were you. The children seem to have got it into their heads that you're reliable."

"Good lord," said Antony, blankly.

"So if anything else happens—" said Gilbert, and was interrupted by Roddy, who appeared suddenly in the doorway leading from the ballroom, and came across in a hurry as soon as he caught sight of them.

"I've just had a message, Uncle Gil. Dad's been taken ill. Could you get hold of Dorrie? Michael will see her home, but I ought to go right away."

"Yes, of course." Gilbert retained his quiet manner, but it was obvious that either the news or Roddy's manner of imparting it had shaken him. "Something serious, Roddy? Or one of Janet's panics?"

"Serious, I should think," said Roddy. "At least, it was Gran who phoned; she said he'd had a sort of convulsion." He looked from Jenny to Antony, and added unnecessarily, "I'm sorry. But I don't like the sound of that, do you?" He turned on his heel, and left them as abruptly as he had come.

CHAPTER V

ANTHONY VIEWED the world with a jaundiced eye next morning, and his temper was not improved by a series of setbacks which almost resulted in his being late in court. His opponent was long-winded, the judge caustic, the witnesses all—obviously—in bad faith. They sat late, without achieving anything in the way of progress, and though he went straight home after the adjournment it was almost a quarter to seven when he let himself into the house in Kempenfeldt Square.

Gibbs was hovering disagreeably in the hall, with information to impart. "A person called to see you," he said. "I would have let him wait downstairs, but he would have me tell Mrs. Maitland. And she told me to send him upstairs."

"Well, that's good," said Anthony, suppressing his irritation. "Who was it?"

"A police officer," said Gibbs, disdainfully, as though that were enough for anybody to know. But he relented sufficiently to add, as Antony turned towards the stairs, "I believe the name is Sykes. He has been here before."

"Yes . . . I see. Thank you." Antony had come to know Detective-Inspector Sykes well, and to hold him in some esteem. But an unheralded visit like this meant a matter of some urgency, and he couldn't think . . . He went up the stairs two at a time.

Jenny met him on the landing. "Gibbs told me—" he said as he kissed her.

"If you mean Inspector Sykes, I asked him to stay to supper," said Jenny, without waiting for him to complete the sentence. "Was that right?"

"Of course." He put up a hand absently to touch her hair.

39

His eyes were fixed on her face, but she knew he did not see her. "What does he want?" he asked abruptly.

"I don't know. He didn't tell me. But . . . Antony—"

"What is it, love?"

"I phoned the Gaskells this morning, to ask how Andrew was, you know. They said . . . he died in the night." She paused, and looked towards the closed door of the living-room. "Do you think—?"

"I don't think anything," said Antony, firmly. "And neither do you." He didn't look vague any longer, but sharply interested. "Business as usual," he ordered, "until we know."

When he went into the living-room a few moments later, Antony found the visitor comfortably established in the high-backed chair at the left of the fireplace, with a glass in his hand. Sykes was a square-built man with a rugged, pleasant face; he looked more like a prosperous farmer than a police-man, and too placid for either occupation.

"As you're going to eat my salt," said Antony, coming across the room, "I take it you aren't gunning for *me.*"

"I am also," said Sykes, "drinking your sherry." He raised the glass in his hand with the effect of a rather solemn toast.

"So I see. I take it that signifies a reprieve," said Antony. Sykes gave him a sedate smile.

"There's a matter I think you might help me with, Mr. Maitland, but I expect your good lady would prefer us to leave business until later."

"Well at least," said Antony, moving purposefully towards the tray with the decanter, "you can tell me what it's about."

Sykes waited until the drink was poured and Antony had turned again to face him. "A sad business, of which you may not yet have heard, Mr. Maitland. The death of Mr. Andrew Gaskell."

"I heard he was ill," said Antony, slowly. (The truth, if not the whole truth). "But, I don't understand . . . what's it to do with you?"

"We are making an investigation—"

"You're trying to tell me it wasn't a natural death? Oh, no!"

"I mean only that the cause of death is not yet known," said Sykes. "I can't say any more than that at the moment. But in the circumstances—"

"That's a beautiful phrase," said Antony, with a sudden show of anger. "In the circumstances . . . but you don't tell me what they are."

"I don't know . . . yet." Sykes's tone had a slight exaggeration of patience. "You know as well as I do, Mr. Maitland—"

"Yes, I'm sorry. You took me by surprise, Inspector." Sykes looked at him; a long look, which he could not but recognise as disbelieving. "We'll leave it till after supper," he said, pacifically. "But I don't see how I can help you."

As soon as the meal was over, Jenny announced her intention of going down to see Mrs. Stokes. As the point of the visit was still to reach, this did not require any explanation; but in any case, she went away quickly, before either of them could expostulate.

When they heard the outer door close, Sykes got up with an air of decision. "We'll just wash up while we're talking," he said. "Tell me, where does Mrs. Maitland keep her apron?"

"Behind the kitchen door." Antony followed him willingly enough, but not without speculating on the motive behind this display of energy. Perhaps the Inspector had some hopes of trapping him into incautious speech while his attention was distracted by this harmless task. And he felt the need for caution. What was worrying him was the possibility that the police had got wind of the stolen Velasquez, and that Roddy had lied to them about it. He had no real responsibility in the matter, but a strong, instinctive dislike for the rôle of informer.

Sykes had found the apron, and was tying it firmly round him. He shook soap flakes into the sink in a professional way, and turned on the hot tap full. Antony possessed himself of a tea towel, and abandoned himself to his companion's whim.

"Well, now, Mr. Maitland, you'll understand at this stage, with the doctor's report still to come, this is all fairly unofficial—"

"Yes, indeed," said Antony. Sykes turned to look at him, his face red with the steam, and grinned understandingly.

"It would be a great help to know something about the Gaskell family," he said. "You living so near, and all—"

"I see," Antony polished a glass with concentration, and put it down carefully on the table near the window. "I know the younger members of the family . . . fairly well," he conceded. "The older ones, hardly at all."

"I'm not asking for anything personal . . . well, it wouldn't be right at this stage," said the detective, with a maddening assumption of virtue. "Just things that are common knowledge."

"Then I expect I can fill you in pretty well." Antony picked up a handful of knives and crossed to put them on the tray. "What's more, I can tell you what my grandparents had to say about the family . . . unless you'd rather refer to Uncle Nick, as being one generation nearer the horse's mouth, so to speak." He was rubbing the knives dry as he spoke, and placing them on the tray quietly, without clattering.

"I don't think that will be necessary." Sykes, though not in the least deceived by this air of careful industry, was pretty sure the offer would not have been made had his host not been prepared, on this point at least, to be frank with him.

"Well, you know the Gaskell Line," said Antony. "That's who they are."

"Yes, I'd gathered that."

"There you are then. Plenty of money and not much taste," he added, recollecting the horrors of Mrs. Gaskell's drawing-room. "But I'm catching up with you, Inspector, you're not getting on with the job. And this fork isn't clean."

Sykes dropped the offending fork back in the bowl, and ran water into the pudding dish, before picking up the mop again. "I've heard tell of a man called Gilbert Gaskell. Would he be one of them?"

"Yes, and I wasn't thinking of him when I said 'no taste',"said Antony. "He's well known in artistic circles, and his opinion is highly regarded . . . on a purely amateur basis, of course."

"Well, tell me about the other members of the family."

"Andrew is—was—a widower. Come to think of it, I'm not very clear about dates. I think it was when his wife died that he returned to his parents' house with his family. The same thing happened when Mrs. Blake lost her husband; but that was later. I'm almost sure Blake was killed during the war, and after it was over she came back here.''

''Also with her family?''

''There's just a son. I think he was old enough by that time to live on his own.''

This had not taken long, but they had finished the pudding plates and started on the first course. Sykes unearthed the panscrub, and eyed the potato pan severely. Then he turned and smiled. ''So the present inmates of the house across the square—''

''Number 34,'' supplied Antony, helpfully. ''There's old Mrs. Gaskell; her daughter, Mrs. Blake; and Andrew's children, Roddy and Dorrie.''

''And, until recently, Mr. Roderick Gaskell senior,'' said Sykes reflectively. ''The one they called the Pirate King, that'd be, I daresay.'' Antony looked at him sharply, but he seemed intent on the contents of the sink. ''Would you say, now,'' the detective went on, ''that there'd be any business worries?''

''I don't think it's likely . . . but after all, how would I know?''

''Not 'of your own knowledge','' Sykes admitted. This was by way of being a joke between them, and Antony laughed but did not offer to amplify his statement. His companion scraped industriously at the pan, and up-ended it on the draining board with an air of achievement. Antony watched, fascinated, while he rinsed the sink, squeezed out the dish-mop, and hung the towels near the stove to dry. He then removed the apron, returning it to the peg behind the door, looked searchingly round the kitchen, and—apparently satisfied—picked up his jacket and put it on.

''Jenny will be pleased. She couldn't have left it neater herself.'' Sykes took the compliment complacently.

''My mother always taught me to siden up after a meal,'' he remarked.

They went back into the living-room, and Antony got out the cigars they kept for Sir Nicholas's delectation. Sykes subsided into a chair with an air of duty well done, while his host turned his attention to the fire. He was thinking as he did so, with a mixture of amusement and exasperation, that the unofficial nature of the visit must be regarded as established now, even to the detective's satisfaction. He put down the poker, and turned to take his favourite position, with one shoulder leaning against a corner of the high mantel.

"Well, now," he said, his smile acknowledging that the phrase was a borrowed one.

"There's just one small matter," Sykes admitted. He paused, and puffed luxuriously at his cigar. "A circumstance has come to my attention, and I'm given to understand that you can confirm it for me."

"Tell me more," said Antony. His tone was light, but the remark was dictated purely by an instinct of caution.

"Well, Mr. Maitland . . . put it that I'd like to know what you know."

"We'd get on quicker," said Antony, impatient—as well he might be—of this disingenuous approach, "if you told me, at least, what you want me to confirm. I *could* tell you everything I know, starting with the Kings of England, but the process would be a little tedious . . . don't you think?"

"It concerns the visit you paid—you and Sir Nicholas—to the Gaskells' house. A week ago last Sunday, unless I've been misinformed." Sykes's tone remained equable, but Antony continued to bristle.

"Well?" he enquired.

"I am told," said Sykes, "that your visit had to do with a painting."

Now who had told him that? Not Roddy, unless he had exhibited more wisdom than ever before in his life. Not Gil, because the detective had seemed in doubt as to whether he was a member of the family. Janet Blake . . . old Priscilla . . . Edward? "I wish I knew," he complained, "what really happened to Andrew Gaskell. I mean . . . it would make a difference."

"No doubt it would. But all I can tell you, Mr. Maitland—"

"I know. The doctor refused a certificate. That doesn't help me."

"What I was told," said Sykes, suddenly reaching a decision, "is that the old man—Roderick senior—had a stolen picture in his possession."

"A startling piece of information, Inspector." For the first time he saw a flicker of annoyance pass across Sykes's impassive countenance. Time to have done, anyway . . . it seemed he knew the whole story. "I was startled too when I heard it," he added. And went on to recount what had happened with an engaging air of candour which didn't deceive his companion for a moment. "Does that help you, Inspector?" he concluded.

"It confirms what I heard," said Sykes, slowly. "Up to a point, that is. But what I'm wondering, Mr. Maitland, is how you've justified to yourself your reticence on the subject. As a law-abiding citizen—"

"My dear Inspector! Hearsay evidence! My duty as a citizen would never allow me to mislead the authorities with what might well be a cock and bull story." Sykes was looking at him stonily, and he gave him an apologetic grin. "No, I mean it," he protested. "We never saw the thing, you know."

"No, I see." Sykes was not to be placated so easily. "But if I'd told you, for instance, that Andrew Gaskell had been poisoned—?"

"In that case, Inspector, even a cock and bull story might have its interest. As it is, I don't see what earthly good it's going to do you."

"If the doctor's report is what I think it's going to be, I shall be that much ahead of the game," said Sykes, bluntly. Antony pounced on the admission.

"That's more like it. What are you expecting?" But the detective was not to be drawn further.

"I mustn't guess, Mr. Maitland," he said. Antony, recognising the finality in his companion's tone, moved away from the fire to take the chair which was usually reserved for Sir Nicholas, and stretched out lazily.

"I call that unkind, Inspector; after I've been so frank with you. I don't think my uncle's in this evening. Do you want to question him too?"

"Not really. I imagine," said Sykes, honestly, "that he'd take it somewhat amiss."

"I think he might. It's probably a tribute to my saintly disposition . . . but what made you think you could rely on my forbearance?" Antony wondered.

Sykes took his leave a few minutes later, meeting Jenny on the stairs, so that his carefully worded messages for her were wasted. He seemed tolerably satisfied with the results of his probing. "I don't understand," said Jenny. "What did he really want?"

"To see what I was up to . . . if anything," Antony replied. "You know, love, it's quite reasonable; he doesn't trust me."

"I don't call that reasonable." Jenny was inclined to be indignant.

"Reasonable from his point of view," said her husband. "Just as what he thinks of as my lack of cooperation has always been—in my opinion—justified by circumstances."

"But who told him?" asked Jenny, abandoning her grievance. "About the picture, I mean. And do you think Mr. Gaskell was really poisoned?"

"Well, I bet Sykes is pretty sure, or he'd never have come here to-night. He did his best to keep things informal, but all the same—"

But Jenny was pursuing her own train of thought. "You said Andrew was cross, not unhappy," she said. "But I don't know whether it's worse to think he might have poisoned himself, or that someone else did it."

"That's bringing us back to 'who?' " Antony leaned back and closed his eyes. "Lord, I'm tired," he said. "Look at it how you like it's a messy business; and—have you thought, love?—Uncle Nick isn't going to be one bit amused." But before Jenny had time to give this more than momentary consideration, the house phone rang.

She went across the room to answer it. Antony said: "Tell them we've gone to the Riviera." The telephone growled volubly, and he saw Jenny's hand tighten on the receiver. When she spoke her voice was reluctant.

"Tell them to come up," she said. And turning back to face the room, she added without moving, "It's Dorrie Gaskell, Antony. We couldn't very well turn her away, could we? And a Mr. Pratten, Gibbs said. Do you know him?"

Antony shook his head. "Another relation?" he hazarded. His tone disguised, well enough, the distaste he felt for the coming meeting. He got up, and started across the room towards the door. "Go and sit down, Jenny. I'll let them in."

Dorrie Gaskell was a small, fair girl, with no resemblance to any member of her family whom Antony had so far met.

Her voice was quiet, her manner gentle, but she was obviously used to meeting her problems as they came. "You'll think it terrible of me, coming here to-day," she said, as soon as they were all in the living-room again. "But if you'll let me tell you—" She broke off there, and looked at Jenny appealingly. "I shouldn't have come out at all, to-day," she added.

"If you think we can help you," said Jenny, firmly, "you did quite right to come."

"Thank you," said Dorrie. She had been crying, Antony thought; and as it was not yet twenty-four hours since her father died, this didn't seem unreasonable. But better take a hand in the conversation, before Jenny's sympathies ran away with her altogether.

"Come and sit down," he invited. "And you know, Dorrie, you haven't told us—" His eyes went past her enquiringly to her companion.

"Oh, I'm sorry. This is Michael . . . Michael Pratten. He's . . . he was . . . my father's secretary." She sat down at one end of the sofa as she spoke; a sudden movement, rather as if her legs would no longer support her. "I made him bring me; he didn't want me to come," she added defiantly.

Antony looked at the other man with sympathy, and recognised—with one of those distressing impulses towards merriment which overtake us at the most solemn moments— the "intelligent egg" he had seen Dorrie dancing with the evening before. Even at a closer look, the description was not altogether an inapt one: a self-effacing little man, intelligent certainly, and younger than he had supposed. Pratten said now, apologetically, "Couldn't let her come alone," and his voice was surprisingly deep and pleasant.

"Of course not." Antony's response was hearty and—he felt as soon as it was uttered—inane. "Sit down," he repeated, and only just pulled himself up from the further inanity, "and let me know in what way I may serve you."

But Dorrie was ready to do this without prompting. "Roddy said you tried to help us," she said, "when we were in trouble about the picture. So I thought, perhaps you wouldn't mind my coming. You know Daddy died last night, and the doctor doesn't know why he died."

"You're upsetting yourself," said Michael, gruffly. "Let me tell them."

"No, I think . . . it's something I must do." Her voice was not quite steady, but she looked directly at Antony and went on firmly enough. "He was always very well, and we couldn't understand when he was taken ill like that. He died very quickly, you know, before Roddy or I got home. And then this morning Doctor Warbow came; I mean, he was there last night, of course, but it was this morning he told us there'd have to be a . . . a *post mortem,* and he said he'd got the tablets Daddy used to take, and asked if there was any other medicine in the house, or any . . . any poison." She stopped, and looked at Michael Pratten, and said as though asking him to help her, "It didn't seem real, did it?"

"I suppose the doctor thought," said Pratten, "that it might have been an accident. If he'd been poisoned, you know," he added, apologetically. The word seemed to worry him, but Dorrie went on resolutely.

"Well, there wasn't anything; and if there had been, how could he have taken it, by mistake? And he wouldn't have done it on purpose. Even if he'd been unhappy; he always said we should face up to things, not look about for the easy way out. But it's even more unlikely . . . I can't believe any-one else—"

"Look here," said Antony. "Aren't you worrying before you know—?"

"Not really. You see, later there was a policeman. He was very cautious, but he wouldn't have come—would he?—if the doctor hadn't been sure."

"Perhaps not."

"Well, that was when Aunt Janet had hysterics. She screamed that Daddy had been murdered . . . and that Roddy had done it." She sat back then, and gestured helplessly, as though having got so far she had reached the end of her strength. "Roddy wouldn't," she said. "I know he wouldn't. So I thought you'd help us."

Later, when he was alone with Jenny, Antony said explosively, "And what the devil does she think I can do?" His immediate reaction was more restrained. "The police won't believe that, just because Mrs. Blake says so," he protested.

"Won't they?" she said. She sounded exhausted, and

Pratten got to his feet and then stood irresolute, as though wondering at the impulse that had moved him. "You see," Dorrie went on, "if they start asking questions they'll find out . . . they were always quarrelling, you know. I don't see how anyone could understand. Roddy didn't mind at all; it . . . it stimulated him."

"They'd need a good deal more than that," Antony told her. She looked at him blankly, and he added, "Is there more?" but quietly, as though he thought the tone of his voice might alarm her rather than what he said.

"I don't know. Really, I don't know." (And for the first time he felt she was deliberately holding something back). "But I'd feel better if you said you'd help us," she added, insistently.

"You mean Uncle Nick, don't you?" he asked gently.

Dorrie looked at him without expression for a moment, and then—realising perhaps that he was answering her own, unexpressed fears—"Both of you," she said. "Both of you." And began to cry. So that Antony never had the opportunity of asking her the questions that were clamouring in his mind for an answer.

That was on Wednesday evening.

CHAPTER VI

THURSDAY WAS hectic, giving very little opportunity for drawing breath, and none at all for anything like connected thought. The case he was occupied with was a melancholy tangle, he was thoroughly out of sympathy with his client; and the final, favourable verdict—which might justifiably have been regarded as a triumph—was reached, he felt, for all the wrong reasons. Sir Nicholas was busy himself and preoccupied, and Antony had no intention of provoking a discussion of the Gaskells' affairs unless it became necessary. All the same, Dorrie's visit had disturbed him, and the remembrance of it was an uneasy undercurrent to all his thoughts.

He got back to chambers at four o'clock, found an urgent appeal awaiting him from his friend, Geoffrey Horton, and telephoned Jenny to say he was likely to be late. Her answer was almost a wail. "It's Meg's first night, darling. Had you forgotten?"

He had, of course. "It just can't be helped," he said avoiding the question. "I thought, perhaps, Derek might be able to take you. Or you could ask Joan."

"Yes, I could do that." She had recovered from her disappointment now, sufficiently at least to hide it. "I'll leave something in the oven, if you're sure you won't be too late."

"I just don't know. Don't worry, love. I'll get something on my way home."

He got back to Kempenfeldt Square just before nine o'clock; and Roddy Gaskell arrived five minutes later with his hair standing on end and a general air of harassment. Antony's conventional expressions of condolence were not allowed to proceed very far. "I know," said Roddy, obviously

50

not listening. "But he was *poisoned*, Antony. I just don't understand—"

"The doctor's report has come in, then?" A foolish question, but he had to say something. Roddy nodded.

"Some foul stuff called aconitine . . . something like that." He paused, and rubbed the back of his hand across his forehead. "You know," he added, earnestly, "he wouldn't have done it himself. And a thing like that . . . how could it have been an accident?

"Do they know how it was taken?"

"They think so." He was fumbling for a cigarette now, and took his time about lighting it. After a while he looked up and smiled rather half-heartedly. "I'm not being quite honest with you," he said. "It couldn't have been accident, or suicide, because of the way it was given to him. Only . . . murder . . . it's a difficult thing to bring yourself to admit, you know."

"How was it taken?" Antony repeated. And he sounded more patient than he felt.

"Those tablets of his . . . vitamins, or something, no harm in them," said Roddy. "Not tablets at all, really; they're sort of capsule things, and they melt when they get inside you—"

"How do they know?"

"Because he took one, about ten minutes before he began to feel ill." The cigarette was drawing well now, and he seemed glad to have something to do with his hands. "And he didn't have anything else around the right time, except a glass of water to swallow it. They said the poison couldn't have been in that, because of the taste."

"I see." He drew out the words thoughtfully, and Roddy interrupted impatiently.

"Yes, but do you see what it means? Someone we know well . . . perhaps even one of the family." He ground out the cigarette in the ashtray beside him with quick nervous jabs; and immediately was feeling for his case again. When it was in his hands he stopped, and looked directly across at Antony for almost the first time since he arrived. "I want your help," he said. "It's only fair I should be frank with you. But I don't like this at all; I just can't think who . . . or why?"

"I can understand that. But, before we go any further, just how do you think I can help you."

"Well, for one thing, I want to know. It isn't a thing you could live with . . . wondering." He looked down at the cigarette case in his hands, and opened it absent-mindedly, and helped himself. "That's one thing," he repeated. "The other thing is . . . rather difficult to tell you about. I expect the police think it was me."

"Why should they?"

"Because Aunt Janet . . . that was before we knew . . . she would have it it was murder. And she accused me right out."

"Yes, but why?" asked Antony again. "She must have had some reason; and if the police show signs of believing her, presumably they have some reason too."

"Well," said Roddy. He paused for a moment, and then began to speak faster than before. "She told them about the picture, and she said I'd have done anything to stop him making it public . . . what grandfather had done, I mean. And that's almost true," he added reflectively.

"A motive," said Antony, "if rather a weak one."

"Not really so weak. You know he was furious when the picture disappeared. Really angry, not just saying so. And on Tuesday evening he as good as told us he knew who it was."

"Did he say—"

"No. But the inference was, you see, he'd already had it out with the person concerned. And I had a row with him on Tuesday afternoon. Well, not about that, of course; but someone at the office is bound to have heard our voices."

Antony stopped to think that one out. There didn't seem to be any comment he could usefully make, so he asked instead: "How about opportunity?"

"That makes it worse," Roddy admitted. "You see, on Monday morning I collected a new bottle of tablets from the chemist for him; and I forgot about them, and had them in my pocket until I was dressing on Tuesday night . . . to go to the Watsons, you know. And Aunt Janet says he was right out of them, so it must have been one of the new ones he took."

"Not water-tight, Roddy."

"No, but . . . I handed them over to him about nine

o'clock that evening, and at eleven he took one, and died an hour later. How could anyone have tampered with them, once they were in his possession?''

"I don't know. But there must have been some way; unless you're telling me you did it, after all.''

"Well, I didn't.'' Roddy's explosive tone was all that he could have hoped, and Antony smiled at him.

"Oh, I say, you're having me on. But it isn't funny, you know.''

"I just wanted to see your reaction,'' said Antony, meekly.

"Well, I'm sorry, but . . . well, never mind.''

"Having set my mind at rest,'' said Antony, "tell me exactly what it is you want me to do. If it's a matter of defending you—''

"Do you think Sir Nicholas would? But it's not just that. I'm a little shaken,'' said Roddy carefully, "that anyone could think a thing like that. Even Aunt Janet. Still, he was my father; I want to know.''

"The police—''

"They're all right, I suppose. But I was hoping . . . well, people talk, you know.''

"About me?'' Antony's tone was gentle.

"I . . . yes, I did mean that. There have been cases when you've been able to find out—''

"Those have been cases where Uncle Nick was briefed, and was able to prevail upon the instructing solicitors to let me help prepare the case. There's a chance of getting somewhere then.''

"Well, I can't get myself arrested, just for your convenience,'' said Roddy, a little resentfully. But Antony's mind had gone off on another tack.

"Have the police searched the house?'' he asked.

"They asked if they could but Gran told them . . . well, she said no,'' Roddy replied. "I expect they'll be back. But if you mean the picture, we looked ourselves, pretty thoroughly, last week.''

"Yes, I suppose so. Have you any idea who took it, Roddy?''

"I only know I didn't.'' Strangely, his tone was defensive. "And if it was Uncle Gil, it isn't really like him, and I don't see how he'd have got it out of the house, do you?''

"If it isn't in the house," Antony pointed out, obviously, "someone must have taken it out."

"Yes, but . . . well, Uncle Gil's a visitor, even if he is family. I mean, he never roams around the house by himself."

"How about Blake? Would that apply to him?"

"Edward? He's in and out a good deal; but I don't really think—"

"Oh, for heaven's sake, Roddy, neither do I," said Antony, irritably. "Not at this stage. I don't even know whether you're telling me the truth," he added, roughly.

"I suppose not," said Roddy. Strangely enough, the suggestion did not seem to provoke any resentment in him. "It's no good my setting up as a plaster saint," he added gloomily, "but I do think I'd draw the line at poison." He sounded doubtful, but Antony laughed suddenly, and began to fumble in his pocket for pencil and paper.

"All right then," he said, "I'll do what I can, and Uncle Nick will probably expire of an apoplexy. But where do you suppose I ought to start?"

It was not actually raining when Roddy left half an hour later, but the air was still damp and raw. Antony, on an impulse, took a raincoat of his uncle's from the downstairs cloakroom, and went out with his visitor into the square. It would be some time before Jenny got home; his talk with Roddy had left him restless, and he thought a walk might clear his mind. They parted on the corner, and Roddy started to cut across the square by the shortest route towards number 34; but he stopped when he had only taken a few paces, and then turned back.

"There's a car outside the house," he said. There was something in his voice that Antony could not quite place . . . a half-suppressed excitement that did not seem to make sense.

"If you don't feel like visitors, why don't you come with me?"

"I think," said Roddy—and again he was speaking so rapidly as almost to slur his words—"I think it's a police car. Look here, Antony, if they decide to arrest me will you tell Liz?"

"Yes, of course, if you like." He thought back to the talk

they had just had, and closed his lips on the easy words of reassurance.

"I'm afraid," said Roddy, "that her mother will cut up rough. She's been looking at me crosseyed for quite a time now."

"I'll see Liz," Antony promised. "Meanwhile, perhaps we'd better find out—" Roddy muttered something, and turned again and made a good pace across the square. Antony kept close at his heels.

As they reached the house the door opened, and the over-bright light from the hall spilled on to the stone steps and across the pavement. There was no mistaking Sykes's figure, silhouetted in the doorway; Antony stopped at the foot of the steps, but Roddy went up quickly.

"Well, Inspector?" he demanded.

"Not very well, I'm afraid, Mr. Gaskell." The detective's tone was as placid as ever. "I had just left one of my colleagues to await your return; I'm sorry to tell you he has a warrant for your arrest."

Roddy was standing on the top step, just beyond the shaft of light; but Antony could see that he was holding himself stiffly, with his head back, and could have almost sworn that he was smiling. He spoke quickly out of the darkness:

"And the charge, Inspector?"

Sykes took the interruption calmly. "Good evening, Mr. Maitland. I didn't see you there. The charge—as I think Mr. Gaskell has guessed—is one of murder, but I'm sure the formalities would best be completed in a less public place." He looked again at Roddy. "Shall we go indoors, Mr. Gaskell. You'll be wanting to pack a bag."

"Thank you, Inspector. Yes, I . . . is my sister in?" he added, abruptly.

"Yes, Mr. Gaskell, she is." Roddy swore, and then turned to look down apologetically at Antony.

"Do you think they'll use that in evidence?" he enquired.

"In the circumstances," said Antony, "no. I'm here, and you haven't been cautioned. But—"

"All right," said Roddy. "I'll be seeing you, I expect." He went past the detective through the still-open door, and a moment later it closed behind the pair of them. Antony meditated for a brief period, and then went away to find a taxi.

* * *

Liz received the news mutinously, but—to his relief—without tears. "It's absolutely wicked," she declared, "to accuse him of a thing like that." Antony, who was occupied with his own thoughts, might have won an undeserved reputation had she not been too taken up with her grievance to notice his assumed air of sympathetic attention. But after a while came the inevitable question: "What will happen now?"

"They'll bring him up before the magistrate tomorrow. The arrangements are up to his solicitor; I don't know if Uncle Nick will be able to be there."

"But that's just . . . just a formality, isn't it?"

"He'll be committed for trial," said Antony. "Not a doubt of it. And we'll get busy about the defence."

"But . . . can you—?" This inarticulate air of appeal was so foreign to his cousin that Antony was touched, for a moment, with a sympathy that was no longer practical but something near panic.

"I don't know, Liz . . . I don't know." He thought again of his talk with Roddy. "I'll do my best," he promised; and the phrase, which was one he hated, fell ominously on his ears, to depress his spirits still further with a premonition of failure.

He left her a few moments later with his thoughts in a turmoil, and walked too fast all the way back to Kempenfeldt Square in a vain attempt to keep pace with them.

So much seemed to have happened that he could hardly believe, when he let himself into the hall, that it was still not quite eleven o'clock. There was a light in the study, and he fought a brief battle with himself before he crossed to tap on the door. He had had no talk with his uncle since the night of the dance, had not told him even of Sykes's visit, though Gibbs had probably done that; and as things had turned out it was high time he brought him up-to-date.

There were more ducks than usual. They marched singly across the top of Sir Nicholas Harding's pad, and in serried ranks back across the bottom of the page. One of them wore a judge's wig. . . .

"So that's how it stands," said Antony. "I was pretty sure

after Sykes's visit that there was something fishy about Andrew's death—" (Sir Nicholas closed his eyes for a moment, as if he were in pain) "—and so must the police have been to have got their case so far prepared." He broke off, and looked down suspiciously at the pad, where the older man had begun to sketch in one corner a severe-looking cod. "I say, Uncle Nick ... have you been listening?" he asked, in an aggrieved tone.

Sir Nicholas did not look up from his task. "I seem to have been doing nothing else for hours," he said, sweetly. "For my sins," he added, and at last threw down the pencil.

"Well, sir what do you think then?"

"I think it a pity," said Sir Nicholas, deliberately reverting to a point which he knew his nephew would have preferred to ignore, "that the mere mention of your name should be enough to bring the police to your doorstep."

"Only Sykes," Antony protested. "And I suppose, to be fair, it isn't really to be wondered at."

"No," said Sir Nicholas; and succeeded in investing the word with sufficient meaning to put Antony immediately on the defensive.

"They hate anything in the nature of unfinished business," he said. "And I must admit, each time he's been involved in one of our cases, there've been quite a few points that—from the police point of view—didn't really get cleared up."

"The fact had not escaped my notice. But I am obliged to you for explaining it so clearly." Sir Nicholas's tone was courtesy itself. Antony gave an impatient exclamation, and took a quick turn across to the window and back. "As to what I think," his uncle went on, in the same gentle tone, "you have given me very little on which to base an opinion. Young Gaskell has been arrested, and you—I gather—wish to embroil yourself in the affair. You have not informed me whether you believe what he told you."

"I believe it ... I think." Something was going wrong with the interview. Antony began to feel uncomfortable. This had happened often enough before, hadn't it? After all, it had been a foregone conclusion that his uncle would be angry, once he heard of Sykes's visit. But this time something was different; there was an undercurrent of feeling that he couldn't recognise, and that made him uneasy. He made one last attempt to get beyond the ice-barrier. ''Don't be so stuffy, Uncle Nick. You must admit—''

''If you are about to tell me that the affair is interesting, you may save your pains,'' said Sir Nicholas, outraged.

''I dare say.'' Antony left his pacing and went to take up his stand with his back to the fire with a deliberate assumption of ease. ''There's Liz,'' he said, but did not look at his uncle.

There was a silence. ''Hmm,'' said Sir Nicholas, presently. ''I suppose that confounded woman will be talking about keeping up appearances,'' he remarked, thoughtfully.

''I suppose so.'' Antony was doing his best to sound noncommittal. His uncle looked up, and gave him a surprisingly friendly grin.

''We can't have that,'' he said. ''And I cannot imagine why you should suppose me unwilling to accept the brief if it comes my way. I am in Mallory's hands, after all.''

This was a bland untruth, and Antony ignored it. ''Do you mean *you* believe what Roddy says?'' he asked; and did not bother to keep the incredulity out of his voice.

''You owned to some doubts yourself,'' his uncle pointed out. ''And I don't pretend to omniscience. Our clients aren't always innocent,'' he added.

''No,'' said Antony, and smiled reluctantly. ''The trouble is,'' he confided, ''I want to believe him.''

''Your instinct is probably right. But I think you should remember there may be occasions when the victim cannot be held guiltless of his own death.''

''I know that, but—''

''But it's easier to remember when you don't know the people concerned. You've no right to take this matter up, Antony, if you can't treat it objectively.''

''I might find it easier to agree with you, sir, if Andrew Gaskell hadn't been poisoned.''

''Then we must hope you find your faith in Roddy justified,'' Sir Nicholas went on, with surprising patience. ''But I know more of the family than you do. Would you say that a man who rears his children without affection or guidance is blameless if they hate him?''

''That's one thing, Uncle Nick . . . murder's another.''

He paused, and frowned, and then said less hesitantly, "You spoke of my instinct sir; I'm willing to back it."

"Who are the solicitors, do you know?"

"Hargreaves and Blunt. Specifically, the elder Hargreaves."

"Well, if Hargreaves wants us you'll have to take the preliminary hearing. I've got my hands full with Collier to-morrow, and I hear you finished with Bellerby's client to-day."

"Yes, I did." Antony was suddenly aware of weariness. He had gained his point, and the matter was best left for the moment; besides, he found Sir Nicholas's attitude disconcerting, and wanted time to think about it. So he cast about in his mind for a diversion, and achieved very fairly a casual air as he produced it. "There was an interesting point came up in court to-day—"

Sir Nicholas, amused and not in the least deceived, prepared to give this new subject his attention. But the faint frown between his eyes as he looked down again at his parade of ducks had nothing whatever to do with the impersonal problem his nephew was propounding.

CHAPTER VII

"I CANNOT conceal from you," said Mr. Hargreaves, sadly, "that the prosecution's case is a strong one . . . very strong indeed." The statement seemed only to increase his depression, and the look he directed at Sir Nicholas appeared hopeful of finding that he had succeeded in arousing in him a like emotion.

The solicitor was a tall, very thin man, who took a gloomy view of the human race in general and of his client in particular. For this Antony felt he couldn't very well be blamed; Roddy Gaskell had been that day in one of his more exuberant moods. But Antony had been in Mr. Hargreaves's company since ten o'clock that morning, and though it was likely the boredom was mutual he was now, at three thirty in the afternoon, relieved to find that his uncle had already concluded the affairs of Mr. Collier and returned to chambers. He had had, he felt, just about all he could stand of the solicitor's undiluted company. Besides, he wanted to tell Sir Nicholas . . .

Counsel appeared unmoved by his visitor's tragic air. He took off his glasses and pushed his chair back a little from the desk, leaning back with a relaxed look and an air of courtesy unusual in him when work on a new brief was in its early stages. "As Maitland may have told you," he said, "I already know something of the matter."

"There's more to come," said Antony. "They've—"

"There are a number of points which I believe will be new to you, Sir Nicholas," said Mr. Hargreaves firmly. "But nothing will be gained by taking them out of order."

"No, but this will interest you, sir—"

"In their proper order," said the solicitor again. Antony

muttered something which fortunately proved inaudible, and retreated towards the window. He propped himself up against the end of the bookcase, and looked back at the other two men. Hargreaves, who had chosen a straight-backed chair near the desk in preference to an easy chair by the fire, was leaning forward and talking again, earnestly and volubly. Sir Nicholas, who still seemed to be in that unusually mellow mood, caught his nephew's eye and smiled faintly. Antony listened to the solicitor's voice, and simmered with impatience.

"There is first," said Mr. Hargreaves, "the medical evidence. The immediate cause of death was respiratory paralysis, and having regard to the symptoms which preceded it—vomiting followed by a measure of paralysis—tests were made to determine whether one of the aconite poisons might be present."

"Monkshood," said Antony, brought back into the conversation by a questioning look from his uncle. "It can be mistaken for horse-radish, but they hadn't had beef for dinner, and anyway—"

"I do not think we can usefully discuss the nature of the poison at this stage." The visitor's tone was reproving. He paused to look across at Antony, as though daring him to re-enter the conversation; but Antony was looking out of the window and had apparently withdrawn his attention. Satisfied, the solicitor went on: "There is apparently a very strong suspicion that the poison was administered in a capsule, a soluble container which originally held some harmless medicament. Mr. Gaskell . . . Mr. Andrew Gaskell . . . is known to have taken one of these capsules a short time before he was taken ill—"

"Ten minutes," said Antony; but he did not look round from the window.

"He swallowed the capsule with a glass of water. It seems that aconitine—in whichever of its forms—would have a strong, unpleasant taste, which could not have been concealed in the liquid. We can assume, therefore, that it was contained in the capsule."

"For the moment," said Sir Nicholas, "I am willing to take that point as read. It will require closer study, I imagine, to find out whether or not the police are right in their contention.'' And again he glanced enquiringly at his nephew, who could at least be trusted to know the aspects of the problem he considered immediately important.

''I was endeavouring to convey to you that the theory seems reasonable,'' said Mr. Hargreaves. He spoke a little huffily, but went on without giving either of his audience the opportunity for comment. ''If we grant that the police are right in this—and as you point out we cannot at this stage disprove it—if we grant that they are right we must also concede that things are very, very difficult for Roderick Gaskell.''

''He had them in his pocket,'' said Antony, ''for well over twenty-four hours. But there's another thing—''

''Mrs. Blake has testified that Mr. Andrew took the last of his previous bottle of capsules on Sunday evening. She ordered a fresh supply by telephone on Monday morning, and asked Roderick to collect them, as the chemist's shop was situated quite near his place of business in the city.'' Sir Nicholas was still leaning back in his chair, though he had stretched out one hand to fiddle with a pencil that lay on the blotting-pad; he was smiling faintly and Antony, resentful of the solicitor's steam-roller tactics, wondered sourly what he found to amuse him. He allowed his mind to wander for a moment to this irrelevant enigma; but he wished old Hargreaves would give him a chance to relate the one new and interesting item that had emerged from the day's proceedings.

''Roderick Gaskell has admitted to me that he collected the package from the chemist.'' The solicitor was apparently impervious to Antony's fidgets or Sir Nicholas's gentle amusement. ''It remained in his possession until Tuesday evening, when Mrs. Blake reminded him about it, and he handed it over to his father. Andrew, in turn, pocketed it; and, as I have said, was seen to take the first capsule at about eleven o'clock. No detailed evidence of the events of that evening was given at the hearing.''·

''For which we may be thankful,'' Antony muttered. He forsook the bookcase as a source of support, and came across the room again to take the easy chair the visitor had spurned. The fire was bright, but it was chilly by the window. ''We'll get that later," he added. "It's not very important. What *is* important is whether someone else had the opportunity—"

"It is difficult to see how anyone else could have tampered with the capsules," said Mr. Hargreaves gloomily; and again Antony was moved to protest.

"It isn't difficult at all. It isn't water-tight." He remembered as he spoke that he had used the same words to Roddy . . . and wondered whether they were true.

Sir Nicholas looked up. "Well, for the moment, we must grant that the prosecution have a serious point against young Gaskell, one which it may be difficult to refute."

"Yes, sir, but the really interesting thing—"

"Really, Mr. Maitland, we must take these matters in due order. If you are content for the moment with the very meagre details I have given you concerning opportunity, Sir Nicholas, we may pass to the question of motive."

"That's what I was trying to do," said Antony. "At least—"

"A clerk from the firm gave evidence that he had heard loud, angry voices from Andrew Gaskell's office on Tuesday afternoon at a time when Mr. Roderick was with him. It is, perhaps, revealing that he mentioned he did not consider this unusual. These details are the more brief, Sir Nicholas," he put in, apologetically, "because Mr. Maitland seemed disinclined to challenge the witnesses—"

"And very properly," said Sir Nicholas, cordially.

"Well, I am sure . . . but it cannot profit us to argue the matter now. The main point about the motive is certainly the matter of the discovery of the Velasquez . . . of Mr. Andrew's intentions concerning it and my client's objections to the course of action he proposed . . . the subsequent disappearance of the painting . . ."

"My dear sir, I am quite familiar—"

". . . Mr Andrew's determination to find the thief, and the very strong presumption that he had done so. Mrs. Blake informed the court that from something her brother said at dinner on Tuesday evening she reached the definite conclusion that he had satisfied himself on this point, and had already spoken to the culprit about the steps he was going to take. I confess," he added, reproachfully, "I should have liked a little more detail."

"All in good time," said Sir Nicholas. "I gather," he went on, and now he was looking at Antony, "that Mrs. Blake is likely to be an important witness."

"I imagine so; and as she's already accused Roddy once, there will probably be no difficulty in getting her to go into some detail about his relationship with his father."

"I see. There were considerable problems, I imagine. The difference in temperament—" He broke off, looked once more at the solicitor, said vaguely, "Precisely," and was again silent.

"But the really interesting thing about the picture," said Antony, determined this time to have his say, "the really interesting thing is . . . it's turned up again." Sir Nicholas sat suddenly bolt upright, and put on his glasses again as though they helped him to hear better. "Yes, I thought that would surprise you," added his nephew, with satisfaction.

"Where?" asked Sir Nicholas, less precise than usual. The solicitor had a dissatisfied air, but for once he did not try to interrupt.

Antony got up. Having reached the point he had been trying to make ever since he came in, he seemed strangely disinclined to elaborate. As there was nowhere he could go, short of weaving an intricate course between the chairs to attain the wide open space between the door and the window, he contented himself with turning his back on the fire and looking down at his uncle in a troubled way. "It was found at the back of the safe in Roddy's office," he said. "The chief clerk's story is circumstantial: he and Roddy had the only keys, and to his knowledge no one else had been to the safe. Apart from that, I do think, sir, that anyone going in with the canvas under his arm would have been fairly noticeable."

"Yes, yes, I think so too." Sir Nicholas was thoughtful, but after a moment he added briskly: "Well, we shall see what our client has to say for himself."

"He says he never lent his key to anyone," said Antony.

"I might have expected that," said Sir Nicholas, bitterly. "I should like to see him as soon as possible. What about tomorrow morning, Hargreaves?"

"In the circumstances . . . in the unhappy circumstances," said the solicitor, a little stiffly, "I shall arrange to be free to accompany you."

"Well, no need for that. If you'll be good enough—"

"My duty to my client—" said Hargreaves, apparently determined to immolate himself on this unlikely altar.

"Will probably be best served by your absence," said Sir Nicholas, abandoning finesse with a suddenness that left the solicitor bewildered, and—for once—almost without words.

"Oh, very well then," he said, crossly.

"He will be more likely to speak freely to—er—to a comparative stranger," Sir Nicholas explained, with a sidelong look at the solicitor to see how he was taking this belated diplomacy. "Now you may know that Maitland has a particular interest in this case—"

"I consider it most unwise," said the solicitor, sniffing his disapproval, "to become emotionally involved—"

"There's not much emotion about wanting to see justice done," Antony put in, annoyed. Sir Nicholas quelled him with a look and went on smoothly with his explanations. It was amusing, Antony thought, returning to his arm-chair, to hear this watered-down description of what his uncle generally condemned as meddling; though, after all, if his ways were unorthodox, what did it matter? Someone had to do the work, and Uncle Nick wouldn't be content with anything less than a thorough investigation.

". . . some experience in these matters . . . willing to concern himself particularly in the preparation of the defence . . . feel we should be well advised to take advantage . . ." Sir Nicholas might perhaps be considered to be labouring his point.

"I shall be pleased," said Mr. Hargreaves, "to have Mr. Maitland's co-operation." He turned a cold eye on Antony, for the truth was that neither of them regarded the prospect of continued association with any pleasure.

"Well, then!" said Sir Nicholas.

But it was not, of course, quite as simple as that. There followed a period of skirmishing, during which Antony prudently remained silent; but the moment came, inevitably, when the solicitor, driven metaphorically into a corner, threw up his hands and resigned himself to Counsel's whim. "What exactly do you want?" he demanded, weakly.

Antony found his uncle's eyes on him, and came abruptly to life. "First," he said, "there's the chemist's evidence."

"We have heard it to-day."

"Yes, I know . . . but there's bound to be more. I mean, it's unlikely that anyone but Roddy Gaskell had the opportunity to poison that particular bottle of capsules, but if a substitution was made . . . well, the other lot had to come from somewhere."

"Naturally," said Mr. Hargreaves; who had certainly never considered the point before.

"The next thing is, who could have effected a substitution? I can deal with that myself, I expect. Then, I want to know more about the original theft of the painting; a whole lot more."

The solicitor was frowning over this one. "I don't see the value of that," he said at last.

"Quite honestly, neither do I." Antony's smile was disarming. "But everyone's taken it for granted that old Roderick pinched the thing—and that's queer when you think about it; anyway, it's in the highest degree unlikely that he actually committed the theft himself."

"The Pirate King, they used to call him," said the solicitor, with the first sign of humanity Antony had so far observed in him. "I suppose his family felt it was in character."

"Yes, but . . . oh, well, I suppose you're right. But that reminds me, you've looked after the firm's affairs for a long time and I suppose you know the Gaskells as well as anybody—"

"I think I may say that I do." He shook his head regretfully. "But there is nothing there to help you; rather the contrary, I am afraid."

Antony frowned over that. "What exactly do you mean?" he demanded.

"If you wish me to say that my client was on good terms with his father, I am afraid I cannot do so. And I think it unlikely we shall find anybody who will."

"Well, we know that." Antony relaxed again, but his fingers were drumming on the arm of the big leather chair. "Andrew and old Roderick, now—?"

"I imagine," said the solicitor, carefully, "there was little real sympathy between them. But Andrew was a man of principle, and a dutiful son."

"I suspected as much," said Antony mournfully. He

caught his uncle's eye fixed upon him and added hastily, "What about Roddy and his grandfather?"

"There were frequent disagreements. I cannot credit Roderick with any great propriety of feeling. And as for to-day," he added, bitterly, as an irrelevant grievance momentarily came to the surface of his mind, "I should say he was positively enjoying himself."

"I never thought of it before," said Antony to his uncle, "but what do you think Liz's children will be like if she marries Roddy?"

"I really cannot imagine," said Sir Nicholas. "And the point does not seem to be particularly useful." He looked apologetically at the solicitor as he spoke, but Mr. Hargreaves, surprisingly, seemed to be giving the question serious thought.

"You must remember," he said, after a moment, "that old Roderick married his first cousin."

"So he did," said Antony, with an air of relief. He smiled at the visitor, but again without getting any response. Mr. Hargreaves gave a cough, and looked at his watch.

"We're keeping you," said Sir Nicholas.

"Oh, I assure you—" He broke off and looked again at the younger and less congenial of his companions. "As for the firm itself—the Gaskell Line—it is a vast, prosperous organisation; and so far as I know has been very efficiently run."

"Were there policy differences between the generations?"

"I imagine Andrew would be more cautious than his father."

"And now, I suppose, it will be Roddy's turn."

"Yes, indeed. He is very young for such a responsibility."

"And we must hope, in the circumstances, that the firm will run itself." He spoke idly, but the solicitor answered him with sudden energy.

"We have heard already that he was at variance with his father. I told you, Mr. Maitland, that you will find nothing there to help you."

"No, I see." He looked at his uncle. "Not so good, sir. To confirm Roddy's story we must drag in the quarrels; and *that* stiffens the motive."

"They'll be dragged in anyway," Sir Nicholas pointed out. "Unless Janet Blake thinks twice about her evidence."

"As for the firm," said Mr. Hargreaves, who seemed to have grown restless again, "Michael Pratten is very capable, and knows the business through and through."

"I thought he was Andrew's secretary."

"He came to old Roderick in that capacity many years ago, and I believe it is still nominally his position. But his standing in the firm . . . he is a very capable young man," the solicitor repeated.

"Is he now?" For some reason, he seemed disinclined to pursue the subject. "I think that about covers everything for the moment, sir. I mean . . . I can take care of the family. By the way, does Pratten live at number 34?" he added, turning back to the visitor.

"Yes, he does. A fortunate circumstance for the Gaskells I have always thought it; he seems to exercise a calming effect—"

"A sort of sedative," said Antony reflectively. "How excessively dreary; why do you think he puts up with it?"

"Bread and butter," hazarded Sir Nicholas, laconically.

"There must be easier ways of earning a living. Such as the law, for example," he added, with an amused look.

"Precisely." Sir Nicholas's tone was dry.

"But I don't quite understand," said Mr. Hargreaves, having considered this exchange and decided it was irrelevant and better ignored. "You say, Mr. Maitland, that you will 'look after the family'."

"Yes, of course."

"If you mean, as I suppose, that you will obtain their evidence, it seems—if you will forgive me for saying so—a little unusual."

"I don't see that," said Antony. "I shall be acting as your agent, after all." He grinned at his uncle, and they both of them avoided the solicitor's scandalised look. They saw him leave a few moments later with expressions of polite appreciation, and no regret at all.

CHAPTER VIII

THAT EVENING Antony, having firmly declined to let Jenny accompany him, walked round to the Watsons' house. He put in a good deal of thought on the way about the best means of tackling the situation; but when he finally went up the steps and took hold of the old-fashioned bell-pull he was still no nearer a decision.

He found Aunt Carry with her husband in the smaller drawing-room. Uncle Tom was an inch or two shorter than his wife; a kind-hearted man with an incongruously hard head for business. He had mild blue eyes and sandy hair, and a habit of disappearing into some private fastness when his wife's social instincts got the better of her and the house became uncomfortably crammed with people. "I want to see Liz," Antony announced, without preamble.

"I suppose," said Mrs. Watson disagreeably, "you've just come to encourage her." Her tone made it abundantly clear that this was not a course of action of which she would approve, but Antony—who felt he had borne patiently as much as could reasonably be expected in one day—merely gave her an amiable smile and asked innocently:

"Of course I will, if you think it would help. What do you want her to do?"

"I don't want her to do anything." Aunt Carry's protest took her voice several notes up the scale. She paused, and gave him a tragic look. "She wants to announce her engagement," she declared.

Antony was startled; so startled that he forgot his usually urgent desire to bring Aunt Carry down to earth again when she started doing her Mrs. Siddons act. "She mustn't do that," he said, firmly. "I'll talk to her."

"Well, you can, of course." She sounded doubtful, and was obviously suspicious of the offered alliance. Tom Watson, who had silently been mixing a drink he knew would appeal to the younger man, now placed a glass at his elbow and returned to his own chair.

"What concerns me," he said, "is whether or not Roddy is guilty." He glanced at his wife. "Your aunt dislikes the connection in any case," he added. "But for my part I should be glad to be reassured on that point."

"I can only tell you what I think," said Antony. "I think he's innocent. Whether we can prove it is another matter; but I don't want Liz complicating matters."

"I don't quite see—" began Uncle Tom, temporarily diverted from his major worry.

"Friend's evidence," said Antony, elliptically, "open to suspicion. Engaged couple,"—he waved a hand expressively—"they'd expect her to be lying."

That brought Aunt Carry energetically back into the conversation. "I told you, Tom, we've got to get her away."

"No, look here, Aunt Carry, you can't do that. I don't know yet, but I may need her."

"Why?"

"Her evidence, of course."

"In court?"

"Perhaps. I told you, I don't know yet."

"She knows nothing of this . . . of this atrocious affair."

"She was with Roddy on Monday evening," said Antony bluntly. "If the police aren't interested in what happened then . . . I am."

"But . . . it's so sordid." The protest was weak this time, almost automatic. Tom Watson interrupted before she had time to say any more.

"She's very unhappy, Antony."

"The world won't come to an end because of that," said Antony, brutally. "But her world might, if you make her let Roddy down."

"Well, I only hope you can convince her." It was a measure of Mrs. Watson's perturbed state of mind that she accepted as an alliance what a moment ago she had opposed so bitterly. "She was talking about telephoning Fleet Street." Antony grinned at her.

"She won't do that," he promised. "But you'll have to leave her alone, Aunt Carry. She can be as stubborn as a mule, you know."

"Well, really!" She was obviously preparing something formidable in the way of protests, but her husband interrupted before she was fairly launched.

"He's right, my dear. At least," he added with belated caution, "in his estimate of the effect our opposition would have on Liz."

"And I can't see, Aunt Carry, what you've got against Roddy."

"I should have thought that obvious."

"Yes, *now* . . . you don't want to be mixed up in a scandal. That's reasonable enough. But you told me on Tuesday—"

"His reputation is not of the best," Mrs. Watson replied flatly. "And the Gaskells are an odd family, you must admit that."

"I should have thought they were wealthy enough for neither of those things to matter," said Antony. "Yes, I know that's vulgar, Aunt Carry, but—"

"Extremely vulgar," she agreed. But before the silence which followed this rather oppressive remark could lengthen unduly the door opened and Gilbert Gaskell came in.

Antony wondered later whether his own presence had in some way been guessed at by the newcomer, and provided, in fact, the reason for his opportune arrival. Gilbert merged into the group composedly, with the ease of long familiarity; and did not seem to notice either the nervous over-cordiality of Tom Watson's greeting, or the slight but unmistakable frigidity that crept into his hostess's manner. The most sensitive person could not have found fault with her greeting . . . the most insensitive must have felt it lacking in warmth. Antony picked up the tall glass which had been standing unregarded at his elbow, and leaned back to watch developments.

It was Uncle Tom who made the conventional enquiries. "My mother?" said Gilbert, as though the question surprised him. "Bearing up, you know, bearing up splendidly. Very tough old lady," he added as though that settled the matter. "Poor little Dorrie, now; that's another thing."

"Not to be wondered at," said Tom Watson, regretfully.

His meaning was clear enough, if the words were vague. "And Janet?" he asked.

The other man did not reply immediately. He tightened his lips as though the question displeased him, and spoke at last reluctantly. "Janet is . . . doing her duty," he said. "And talking about justice," he added, bitterly. "I couldn't stop her. And it's too late now." For the first time since he had greeted him he looked across at Antony. "Isn't it?" he asked. His tone was mild still, but conveyed, obscurely, a sense of challenge.

"If you mean it's all up with Roddy," said Antony, wilfully obtuse, "I don't agree at all. I'm not saying it's easy," he added.

"There," said Gilbert, grimly, "I agree with you. If only she'd kept her mouth shut." He broke off to take the glass Tom Watson was holding out to him, and Antony seized the opportunity to interrupt.

"I think, you know, the police would have reached the same conclusion, though perhaps not so quickly, even without Mrs. Blake's intervention."

The glass went down with a click that sounded sharply in a room grown suddenly quiet. When Gilbert spoke he might, from his tone, have been uttering the most commonplace remark; but his eyes met Antony's directly, and were full of awareness. "You're saying," he told him, "that Roddy killed his father."

"Does the idea shock you?" His voice was deliberately casual; so casual as, in the circumstances, almost to constitute an insult. Gilbert brought his fist down with a thump on the arm of his chair and said with suppressed violence:

"I don't believe it!"

Tom Watson's eyes went from one to the other of his guests. He was obviously distressed by the fear of a misunderstanding. "Antony was just saying—" he began; but was not allowed to finish.

"The children trust you, Maitland," said Gilbert Gaskell. He had reverted to his mild manner, but the words were a reproach.

Antony suppressed an inclination to protest, and said only, "Well, who do you think should have been arrested?"

There was a long pause. Antony was vaguely aware that

Uncle Tom looked unhappy, and that Aunt Carry's sense of outrage had congealed her expression and stiffened her back to an almost comical extent. But most of his attention was concentrated on Gilbert, who was considering the question as though it had never occurred to him before (and quite probably, thought Antony, with more irritation than sympathy, he was facing it for the first time). After a while Gilbert said slowly: "I suppose that is the next question, isn't it? It's rather a facer, you know."

"Then perhaps you can appreciate my dilemma."

"Yes . . . yes, of course. I'm sorry."

"Forget it." He got up as he spoke, and commandeered the hearthrug, and stood looking down intently at Gilbert Gaskell. For the moment he had forgotten where he was, or that Mrs. Watson was likely to object to the use of her drawing-room for the uncivil pursuit of asking questions. "You can tell me," he suggested, "about the Velasquez."

"But surely you know—"

"Go back a little. It's a famous painting; a man with your interests, your knowledge, must surely remember when it was stolen, some details of the theft."

"It was in the Stonehill Gallery, just outside Liverpool. There wasn't any great difficulty about the theft, from what the papers said; it was in 1946, so far as I remember, just after it had been brought out of its wartime storage. Afterwards, of course, they took precautions."

"And when Andrew called on you to see the picture, you weren't surprised to think that your father—?"

"Surprised?" exclaimed Gilbert, suddenly testy. "Of course I was surprised. But then I began to think."

"And you decided—?"

"He wanted it, you know. He had an eye for such things. I told you that when we met the other night; and he'd been in love with those two pictures for long enough. 'The Lady with the Fan'. Well, he knew there was no hope of that one; but a provincial gallery was different . . . he made them a whacking great offer for the picture as soon as the war was over."

"And found there wasn't so much difference after all, I suppose."

"They weren't having any," Gilbert agreed. "And he didn't like being refused."

"I see. So there's the motive. What about opportunity? Do you think he actually removed the picture himself?"

"I . . . just don't know."

"Was he in Liverpool at the time, for instance?"

"I don't remember. But he might well have been. Janet was living there, and he went north once or twice while she was clearing things up after Ted died. That was just before she came to live at number 34."

"And her son was with her, no doubt?"

"Yes. He was just about due for call-up, but as far as I remember he did his National Service after she came to London." For a while Gilbert had been speaking freely, but now he paused and looked doubtfully at Antony. "What are you getting at, Maitland. Do you think—?"

"Strange as it may seem," said Antony, with an unconvincing pretence of patience, "I ask questions because I want to know the answers, not because I've any preconceived notions on the subject of the query."

Surprisingly perhaps, Gilbert smiled at him. "I'm sorry," he said again. "But all the same—"

"I have been wondering about the original theft of the picture," Antony admitted. "I mean, if someone undertook the job of pinching it for your father . . . well, it's an interesting thought." But Gilbert seemed, rather, to find it amusing.

"You haven't asked if I was in Liverpool," he said, provocatively.

"Well, no. I can't see you taking the picture on someone else's behalf," said Antony. "If we are to talk about the more recent disappearance, now—"

"Oh, I say!" He was definitely startled, but after thinking the suggestion over for a few moments added briskly: "You may not believe me, but if I had taken it . . . I'd have it now."

"Very likely. But I've no means of knowing—"

"No . . . I see."

"Anyway, that's beside the point. Let's assume for the moment that the police theory is correct . . . that your brother found out who had stolen the picture, and was killed to ensure his silence."

"Well?" The word was sharply questioning. So that, for a moment, Antony wondered whether Gilbert's usual quiet manner was merely an affectation.

"The thief might well have intended to keep the Velasquez, and yet have found it too dangerous after circumstances had forced him to the added crime of murder."

Gilbert had no reply to that. A rather stunned look replaced the animation he had shown a moment before. Tom Watson uttered a shocked exclamation, reminding Antony for the first time in several minutes of his presence. He ventured a sidelong glance at Aunt Carry, who was sitting stiffly erect and looking more like Jove about to launch a thunderbolt than any woman had a right to. Antony looked back at Gilbert Gaskell and smiled at him. "I was only following through on your own suggestion," he said, and gestured with his left hand as though to disclaim responsibility.

Gilbert relaxed slowly. Aunt Carry said, "Really," with a decided effect of anti-climax, and Uncle Tom got up abruptly and poured himself another drink; perhaps for the first time in his hospitable life forgetting to ascertain his guests' desires.

"You don't pull your punches, do you, Maitland?" said Gilbert, heavily, and put up a hand to tug at his collar. "Just what are you trying to demonstrate?"

"That my present field of interest is very wide," said Antony promptly. "You needn't worry, you know. That kind of speculation may sound impressive, but it's quite harmless so long as it's unsupported. I could tear it to pieces myself in three seconds flat. To put it bluntly, I haven't an idea in my head; so I want to know everything. And I was asking you about the original theft."

"Yes . . . well." He returned to the subject without any great evidence of pleasure. "You're thinking the old pirate hired someone to do the job," he said reflectively. "It doesn't sound likely, somehow. He was nobody's fool, you know."

"I wasn't thinking of an outsider, exactly; not a professional. But . . . how old was Edward Blake?"

"Seventeen . . . eighteen." Gilbert made no further protest, but the glazed look was back in his eyes again. After a moment's thought he volunteered a little further information. "It wouldn't have been difficult, I grant you that. Things were pretty much in an upset at that time; and even in the normal way, gallery attendants are mostly alert just after there's been a theft, you know."

"That's very natural. But you haven't told me whether you think it likely—"

"Was that meant to be a question?" He sounded more energetic now, even a little angry. "I don't think it's likely Edward had anything to do with it, any more than any other member of the family. But obviously it isn't impossible."

"Why do you suppose Mrs. Blake accused Roddy? She brought him up, didn't she . . . surely she has some affection for him."

"I wouldn't say she had much hand in bringing him up," Gilbert said, doubtfully. "As for affection—" He shook his head over the thought, but before he could continue Caroline Watson had swept to her feet.

"I think you must both be mad," she said. "I'm ashamed of you, Gilbert, talking about your family in that cold-blooded way." She started towards the door, but turned before she reached it and fixed Antony with an icy look. "Don't hesitate to use my house *exactly* as you wish," she invited. "I ask nothing better than to provide a convenient place for you to . . . to torture my guests."

As the door closed behind her, Uncle Tom made again for the side table, but this time he bore with him all three glasses. "A bad business," he muttered, with his back to the room. "Made her nervous, poor girl . . . not to be wondered at."

"And she's right, of course," said Antony. "But it doesn't pay to be squeamish in a case like this." He looked at Gilbert, who at that moment received a replenished glass from his host and drank half the contents at a gulp. "So I won't apologise," he added; and almost made the words a question.

"No need," said Gilbert. He put the glass down and looked round with an air of bewilderment, almost as though he was surprised at where he found himself. "I shouldn't have come, really," he went on, vaguely. "A difficult time . . . I know that."

"Always welcome," said Tom Watson, firmly. He looked at Antony, who had put his full glass on the mantelpiece and was now kicking moodily at the fire. "You'll see Liz, won't you?" he asked. "Before you go."

"Yes, of course. Is that a hint you've had enough of me, Uncle Tom? Where is she?"

"In her sitting-room, I expect. I didn't mean—" He broke off as Antony smiled at him.

"It's time I went, anyway. Will you mind talking to me again, Mr. Gaskell? More formally."

"I don't expect I shall enjoy it, but I'm quite prepared to do so."

"Thank you." He turned and picked up his glass. "I'd better fortify myself," he remarked. "If I meet Aunt Carry on the landing she'll probably bite me. And I can't say I blame her," he added; and raised the glass to his lips.

Jenny was sitting on the hearth-rug when he got home, feeding the fire with the smallest pieces of stick she could find to keep it cheerful, and occasionally giving an anxious stir to the contents of a small, disreputable-looking saucepan which was perched on the hob. Antony sniffed appreciatively. "How did you know my life needed saving?" he enquired.

"I just knew," said Jenny, "that however hospitable Uncle Tom was feeling, Aunt Carry would be cross enough to have a . . . a neutralising effect."

"And how right you were." He pushed the sofa forward until Jenny could lean against it, and then went round the end and collapsed thankfully into its embrace. "Cassandra in person," he complained, "with all the stops out. However, I talked to Liz."

"Was she reasonable?"

"Not really. But I got her account of Monday evening, which may or may not be helpful."

"Then I don't see what more you want." Jenny was transferring the punch she had made from the pan to two heavy tumblers. "You can't expect her to like Roddy being in prison," she added.

"If ever I did," said Antony, with a sort of rueful amusement, "she disabused my mind of the idea very effectively." He received a glass with gratitude. "That should have a thawing effect," he remarked.

"That's the general idea," said Jenny. She twisted round to look up at him, one elbow on the sofa, the glass held between her hands as though she were trying to warm them.

"Antony . . . what's wrong with Uncle Nick?" she demanded.

He was still absorbed by his visit to the Watsons', and took a moment to adjust to the change of subject. "Uncle Nick . . . there's nothing wrong with him. Is there?" he asked. But as he spoke he remembered the uneasy feeling he had had when talking with his uncle the evening before; and how again, to-day, he had thought him too mellow, too easily satisfied. Jenny heard the uncertainty in his tone, and said accusingly:

"You've noticed it too. Haven't you?"

"He has been a little odd," Antony admitted. "He'll get over it."

"Well, that's what I thought," said Jenny. Her voice dropped impressively, so that her husband was reminded that she had been, only a few days ago, to Meg Hamilton's new play. "But to-night," she declared, "he was doing last week's Ximines."

"Are you sure? He never does crossword puzzles."

"He hasn't for years," said Jenny. "He used to when you were . . . he used to during the war," she corrected herself; and now she turned to look down into the fire, and started to sip her punch.

"I see," said Antony, startled.

"If they were easy,'' said Jenny, suddenly loquacious, "it used to make him fearfully angry. But the weeks when he hadn't made any headway by Tuesday or Wednesday were even worse. He used to say dreadful things about the man who makes them up. It was Torquemada then, but it comes to the same thing."

"That doesn't surprise me," said Antony. But he made the comment idly, and his voice was serious as he went on. "You've got some idea in your head, love. What is it?"

She did not reply immediately; what she had to say seemed to require some thought, perhaps even some degree of resolution. At last, "I think it's something personal," she told him. "It might be us, but it isn't . . . I mean, we're all right. So I wish you'd find out what's wrong."

"Who, me?" Antony was appalled by the picture this conjured up. He took an incautious sip, and coughed as the warm, spiced liquid stung his throat. "If it really is something personal,'' he added, when he had recovered, ''I can't possibly ask him about it. You must see that.''

''He may be ill.''

''Well . . . he may.'' Antony sounded doubtful. ''But I'll tell you one thing, love: he made all the routine protests when I told him about Roddy Gaskell's arrest, but I'm pretty sure he meant to take the brief right from the beginning.''

''He didn't like Andrew Gaskell,'' said Jenny, frowning over this piece of information.

''No. And I can't make out whether he thinks Roddy's innocent, or whether he feels someone ought to have murdered Andrew anyway.''

''That doesn't sound like Uncle Nick.''

''I know. I've been wondering about that. He seemed very interested in Eleanor Gaskell, didn't he? The day we first talked about the family.''

''Roddy's mother? Do you think he was in love with her?'' asked Jenny in an awed tone.

''Why not? It happens,'' Antony pointed out reasonably. ''So if you think I'm going to ask him any questions out of turn . . . I'd as soon face a man-eating tiger. He'd think it an intolerable impertinence . . . and what's more, my love, he'd say so.''

With that, Jenny had to be content. They finished what remained of the punch in an uneasy silence.

CHAPTER IX

AGAINST THE sombre background of the interview room at the prison, Roddy Gaskell's personality was as vivid and overwhelming as ever. He did not seem embarrassed by his position, or even particularly worried; and he answered Sir Nicholas's preliminary questions with a cheerful appearance of candour. Antony was sorting through some ragged envelopes which he had produced from his pocket, in an effort to find one with some space left for notes; the prisoner and his leading counsel took each other's measure with unabashed curiosity.

There came a point, however, when the routine of question and answer seemed to pall upon Roddy. He moved restlessly in his chair, leaned forward and interrupted Sir Nicholas without ceremony.

"I suppose we really have to go through all this, sir, even though you know all about me already. But there's one thing I want to know: will they drag all that out in court . . . about my grandfather?"

Sir Nicholas looked at him in silence for a long moment before replying. He seemed to be selecting his words with unusual care. "I think you must accept the fact that the theft of the Velasquez—the original theft, as well as the more recent one—is bound to play a major part in the case for the Crown," he said at last. "But that isn't all you have to worry about."

"Of course not." Roddy sounded impatient. "But I hoped . . . oh, well!"

"There are matters of fact which must be answered; for instance, concerning opportunity both for the second theft and for the murder. There are things which will be suggested in support of these facts . . . your relations with your father, for instance."

Roddy set his lips, but when he replied his tone was belligerent again, almost cheerful. "These matters of fact you speak of . . . it's quite simple so far as the police brought them out in court yesterday. I have no answer."

Sir Nicholas smiled at him. "If you're trying to make my flesh creep, Roddy, you may spare your pains," he said. "I think you'll find that quite a lot can be done."

"He means," said Antony, looking at the ceiling and speaking with an air of detachment, "that when you've been through the de-gutting process known as cross-examination you'll find we're all quite a bit wiser."

"I should not myself have put the matter quite so crudely," said Sir Nicholas, letting his eyes rest thoughtfully on his nephew's face as he spoke. "But I agree that these matters will be aired in court, and should be faced now, before you come up against counsel for the prosecution. And if my meaning is now clear to you, Roddy, I suppose I mustn't complain." Antony grinned to himself, and wrote 'without prejudice' across the corner of a foolscap envelope; but he still didn't look at his uncle.

"Yes, well . . . but if I don't *know*," said Roddy, stubbornly.

"I must still ask you to give me your attention," said Sir Nicholas. "I was asking you—"

"About the facts the police had gathered," said Roddy, a little too quickly. "What about them?"

Again there was a pause. Antony looked up from the notes he was making (or, more accurately, from the series of highly-complicated squiggles with which he was adorning the back of his envelope); he glanced at his uncle, whose face was expressionless, and then at Roddy, who still looked cheerful and aggressive, but whose hands were clenched on the table in front of him.

"The first—and perhaps most important—point we must answer," Sir Nicholas said at last, "concerns the capsules in which it is believed the poison was administered." Antony took up his pencil again, but before he began to write he saw Roddy's hands relax; the long breath he drew could only have expressed relief. "The prosecution," Sir Nicholas went on, "will bring evidence that your father's supply of these capsules was exhausted during the week-end prior to his death, and that Mrs. Blake placed an order for another bottle on the

Monday morning. You collected them from the chemist, I believe. How did that come about?''

"She asked me that morning to get them when I went out to lunch. The shop is only a couple of doors away from the office.''

"You kept them in your possession until the following evening.''

"I forgot I had them. I was out on Monday evening.''

"And on Tuesday—?''

"I found them in my pocket when I changed to go to the Watsons' dance. So on my way out I gave them to him.''

"What time was that?''

"About nine o'clock, I suppose.''

"Mrs. Blake says she reminded you . . . is that correct?''

"Near enough. She came knocking on the door when I was shaving, asking if I'd forgotten to get them. She might have known I wouldn't . . . she even had Edward phone me on Monday morning to remind me." He paused a moment, as though weighing up the advantages of frankness. "You know, sir, I can't help thinking the police theory must be wrong about those capsules. I mean, I swear they weren't out of my possession all that time.''

"And you handed them to your father yourself?''

"Yes.''

"When you were shaving, and your aunt came to the door of your room—''

"The bathroom door, actually. I share with Michael." He grinned, and then seemed to think his amusement called for some explanation. "Grandfather had extra bathrooms put in, of course; but Gran would consider it sinful luxury for us to have one each," he said. "She never let him have all his own way.''

"No, I see. And when Mrs. Blake knocked, and asked you her question . . . where were the capsules then?''

"Still in my jacket pocket; and my jacket was in the bedroom.''

"Then go back to Monday, after you had been to the chemist." For a moment Sir Nicholas looked questioningly in Antony's direction. "I want to know everybody you saw, that day and the next.''

"But nobody would have had time . . . really, sir, I've thought about this. It wouldn't be difficult to pull those capsules open, if you had some tweezers, or something of that kind; and you could put the poison in, and put the two ends together again. There might be some scratches, but nobody'd be likely to notice. It would be quite easy . . . but it wouldn't be quick. Nobody would have had time.''

''Nevertheless, I must ask you to take the question seriously.''

''Well, I had lunch with Michael.''

''Michael Pratten?''

''Yes. Afterwards, there was Miss Barton in and out of the office; she does my typing. And I was with my father for a while. And I suppose I saw some of the clerks, but I don't remember exactly. Yes, I do! there was Jenkinson—that's the chief clerk. And in the cloakroom I saw Coppins and Yates . . .'' He paused with an air of achievement.

''Go on,'' said Sir Nicholas.

''After work I went straight to meet Liz, and we went round to Edward's flat for a drink, because he had some stuff he wanted to show her. Travel literature, pretty dull I thought, but she's keen on reading about places she's never seen. After that we had a meal, and went to the theatre.''

''Could any of these people have taken the capsules from your pocket?''

Roddy frowned over that. ''I tell you, there wouldn't have been time; if someone took them, they put them back again.''

''Please answer my question.'' When there was no immediate reply he added sharply: ''I am thinking that some previously prepared capsules could have been substituted; that would have taken very little time.''

''Well . . . Michael, I suppose; or Edward; or even Liz, since you insist on precision. Not Miss Barton, I think; but perhaps Coppins or Yates.''

''Liz says you took your jacket off while you were visiting Blake; she says you threw it onto a chair in the corner of the room near the television set.'' Antony made his intervention in a tone that was deliberately expressionless, but Roddy whirled round on him with an abrupt and direct question.

''You're saying you think Edward—''

''I'm trying to find out what happened. And if you gather I don't think much of the amount of detail you're giving us,'' Antony retorted, ''you won't be far wrong.''

"No. I see."

"Blake turned on the television set for the news, but you were both looking at a map he'd given you, so you weren't looking that way," said Antony. "Is that correct?"

"It must be, mustn't it? If Liz says so."

"Don't be an idiot, Roddy, it's the kind of thing we have to know."

"Well, I suppose. But—"

"Did you see your uncle during the time we're talking about—while you had the capsules in your possession?" Sir Nicholas took up the questioning again smoothly, and Roddy turned back to him with a look that was almost bewildered.

"Uncle Gil? He came to tea on Sunday, and then I didn't see him until Tuesday evening, at the dance," he said.

"And during the night . . . could anyone have tampered with the capsules then?"

"Anyone in the house, in theory. I don't lock my door. But I'm not a particularly heavy sleeper, either."

"The next day?"

"The same people, at the office. I had lunch—a long, expensive one—with Sir Charles Conroy; and afterwards—" He broke off, and then added irritably, "I'm trying to remember. I think it would just be the people I've already mentioned."

"Then tell me instead, who knew you had the capsules in your possession?"

"Anyone at home, we all had breakfast together on Monday. Anyone any of us told. Anyone!"

"In addition to the people you have mentioned, you also saw your father at the office that Tuesday afternoon."

"Yes." He made no attempt to elaborate, and Sir Nicholas waited only a very short time before he suggested:

"Let us turn, then, to the poison itself. What do you know of aconite?"

"Nothing," said Roddy.

"Monkshood . . . *aconitum napellus.*" Antony turned over the envelope he was writing on, and read out the description from the notes he had previously made on it.

"Is that what it comes from? I've only heard of it." He looked at Sir Nicholas blankly for a moment, and then said, "Oh, my God!" and rubbed the back of his hand across his forehead.

Counsel made no pretense of misunderstanding him. "I'm

afraid this discussion of the means of death is distressing,'' he said. ''Unfortunately, it is also necessary.''

''We shall know more about aconite presently,'' said Antony, without looking up. He seemed to be offering a flat statement, but Sir Nicholas interrupted him testily.

''That's true enough, if you must state the obvious,'' he declared. ''But even now—''

''I'm not very clear about the stuff,'' said Roddy, in what was obviously meant to be a normal voice. ''But they couldn't prove I bought any, because I didn't.''

''It isn't quite as easy as that,'' Antony told him. ''If the root can be mistaken for horseradish I suppose anyone could go out into the country for some, if he knew where it grew.'' He raised his eyes as he spoke. Roddy had gone rather pale and said now, with difficulty:

''He was dead when I got home you know, but Aunt Janet told me . . . it wasn't nice, the way he died.''

''No.'' Again Antony's tone had no expression. He glanced at his uncle, who was scowling, and added: ''I've been in touch with Doctor Raven about some additional tests.''

''So I should hope.'' Sir Nicholas spoke repressively, but this time he left the subject. ''Let us turn our attention to the picture,'' he said.

Roddy greeted the suggestion without enthusiasm. ''It's just what I didn't want to happen,'' he said gloomily. ''I expect the newspapers will love it.''

''You were fond of your grandfather, I think.''

''Yes.'' He did not seem inclined to enlarge on the statement.

Sir Nicholas said: ''I can understand, then, that the idea of publicity is distasteful to you,'' and somehow made the words an invitation.

''It's damnable!'' Roddy became suddenly voluble. ''He was always so alive, you know; nothing ever worried him, nothing was too difficult, or too much trouble. He'd raise the roof if he was angry, but at least you knew where you were with him. He was never petty, and he never expected other people to be, either. There were always tales about him, of course; and I suppose the nickname . . . well, I suppose there was some reason for it. But I never heard that he did anybody any harm, and there must have been plenty of people who were grateful to him. Now they'll say they 'always knew' he was crooked; they'll say it couldn't have been the only thing. They'll forget all the worthwhile things he did, they'll forget he was a great man; and they won't care that some of us loved him.''

''And yet you think,'' said Antony, as though this outburst was nothing out of the ordinary, ''that he stole the Velasquez from the Stonehill Gallery.''

Roddy looked at him. He seemed to be considering the various possibilities this statement opened to him, but eventually he said, ''Well, it was there . . . he had it,'' in a tone which did not indicate any real doubts. After a while he added, but less positively, ''He wanted it, you know . . . he tried to buy it. Uncle Gil told me that. I suppose he thought—''

''Like swindling an insurance company,'' said Antony, helpfully. For some reason this simple remark appeared to infuriate his uncle, who came suddenly to life, banged his fist on the table, and snapped ''Be quiet!'' in a tone that invited no argument. Antony went back to his doodling; Sir Nicholas eyed him suspiciously until he was sure no retort was forthcoming, and then turned back to Roddy Gaskell again.

''Were you responsible for the second disappearance of the picture?'' he asked abruptly.

Again Roddy took his time about replying, and when he spoke it was in an injured tone. ''I thought you believed me,'' he complained.

''Perhaps I did not make myself clear. You might be guilty of that, and still innocent of the crime of which you are now accused.'' (He's being careful, thought Antony, not to commit himself).

''Well, I suppose . . . but I didn't, anyway.''

''Have you any idea who did?'' Sir Nicholas pressed his question.

''None whatever.''

''But the picture was found in your safe. How do you explain its presence there?''

''I told you,'' said Roddy, ''I can't explain it.''

''Do you agree with what the clerk—Jenkinson, I believe—had to say: that only two keys existed, one in his possession, one in yours?''

''Yes, that's quite right.''

''Do you think that Jenkinson might have put the canvas in the safe, either on his own account, or because some other person asked him to?''

Roddy took his time to think that one out. "On his own account . . . that's ridiculous," he said. "And I'm pretty sure he wouldn't be open to a bribe."

"What's more to the point," said Antony, venturing to insinuate himself into the conversation again, "nobody'd be likely to saddle themselves with an accomplice, in a case like this."

Sir Nicholas ignored the interruption. "When did you last open the safe?" he asked.

"On Tuesday morning, the day my father died. I needed a copy of the contract we have with Conroys . . . before going to work on the old boy at lunch time, you know."

Sir Nicholas frowned. "You're trying to tell me the picture wasn't there; that it was introduced into the safe at some time between Tuesday and whenever-it-was the police made their search?"

"Well, that's what I don't know. It could have been there."

"Good heavens, Roddy," said Sir Nicholas, exasperated, "you couldn't have missed seeing it. Even rolled up—"

"But that's just it. There were some old charts, rolled up and stacked on end at the back of the safe. It could easily have been among them." He turned his head, and found Antony's eyes fixed on him, and added with sudden excitement: "That's how it got there, I expect . . . I can't imagine why I didn't realise . . . when I put the charts back."

Sir Nicholas closed his eyes and appeared to be praying. "I suppose it would be too much to ask you to explain," he said eventually. "You had the charts out, you say? Were they of a size comparable with the rolled canvas?"

Roddy measured with his hands. "Various sizes," he said. "Quite big enough."

"I suppose you are inferring that you took the charts away from the office?"

"I took them home," said Roddy patiently, as though the whole thing should now be obvious. "Dad wanted to show them to someone who was coming to dinner. There were eight of them, and they were tied together loosely with tape. They were like that when he gave them to me next morning to take back, but I took the tape off before I put them in the safe; they fitted better that way. And I never gave them another thought. Not till just now."

"Where were they overnight? I mean when you had them at home."

"In the study . . . at least, I suppose so."

"You think their presence might have suggested to someone a means of getting the canvas out of the house?"

"Yes, don't you?" His excitement left him suddenly. "But that means—"

"Who else was at dinner that evening?" Sir Nicholas had no intention of wasting more time than necessary on his client's sensibilities, and his tone was bracing.

"I don't know, I was out," said Roddy. "And now I remember, it was on the Wednesday I took them home; and on the Friday morning my father asked me if I'd forgotten about taking them back to the office. Well, I had, of course."

"And when was this?"

"The week before I came to see Antony. Just before we found the picture was missing," he added.

"I . . . see. And about that visit of yours, Roddy. Did you mean to inform your whole family what you were doing?"

"Of course not." He looked at Antony. "I meant to do just as we said: tell my father Sir Nicholas wanted to see the picture. He'd have cut up rough about my lack of discretion, but that couldn't be helped. Only Gran heard us talking; she was only guessing, but when she put it up to me it didn't seem worth while denying that I hoped—" He gestured slightly, an oddly indecisive movement of his hands, and turned back to Sir Nicholas again. "I'm sorry," he said.

"And not without reason," said Sir Nicholas; but he smiled as he spoke, and his mind seemed already to be taken up with the next of his points. "You have evaded the question once, Roddy, but now I'm afraid we must revert to this matter of your relations with your father. You will certainly be faced with cross-examination upon this subject when we get into court."

"Yes . . . well." Antony had expected a flare of anger, but Roddy's tone held no emotion of any kind. "We didn't get on very well," he volunteered at last.

This was too much for Sir Nicholas, who rose from his chair (as Antony later told Jenny) like a rocketing pheasant, and began to stride angrily backwards and forwards across the width of the narrow room. "I am obliged to you for the information," he said awfully.

Roddy was leaning back in his chair now, and strangely the look of strain had left him for the moment, and been replaced by genuine amusement. He said, reflectively: "I wouldn't have needed two motives, would I?"

Sir Nicholas ceased his pacing, and came back to stand at the head of the table, gripping the back of his chair as though only with difficulty did he restrain himself from hurling it at his client's head. "One would have contributed to the other," he explained. "In view of Mrs. Blake's attitude, you must realise that the Crown will have plenty of ammunition. They will say, I believe, that the immediate motive was this business about the picture; but, obviously, you would have been more likely to resort to drastic measures if a state of ill-will already existed between you and Andrew." As Roddy showed no immediate signs of answering, he added, deliberately: "Counsel for the Prosecution would be failing in his duty if he ignored such matters in a case of patricide."

"But it wasn't . . . I didn't kill him."

"That is the charge, however. We must answer it."

"I don't see," said Roddy sulkily, "how it would help you to know—"

"That you hated your father?" Sir Nicholas prompted gently. Roddy gave him a hurt look, but said after a moment, quite calmly:

"Funnily enough, I didn't. It might have made things more interesting. I didn't like him, though," he added, conscientiously.

"The prosecution will have details of every cause of disagreement between you," said Sir Nicholas. "I imagine you must have come up against Andrew's rather stern principles quite early in life. Will you tell me—?"

"All right." He was leaning forward now, and his hands were clenched on the table in front of him. When he spoke it was quickly, almost eagerly; but neither Antony nor his uncle was under any illusion . . . he found the necessity almost intolerable. "We only need go back to the end of the war," he said. "Mother took Dorrie and me down to the country; we have a cottage at Temple Guiting, but nobody goes there now. We didn't really see much of Dad in those days: an occasional week-end, but the trains were pretty bad; and sometimes a bit more in the summer. At the time, of course, I took that for granted, and I do realise now how busy he must have been. Anyway, I went away to school a year before the war ended, and it was during that year Mother died.''

"Yes,'' said Sir Nicholas. "I remember.''

"Do you, sir? It's funny to think you knew them all quite well. My mother was . . . well, that was a bad year,'' Roddy said; and sounded as though the admission surprised him.

Sir Nicholas did not comment on this assertion. He said only: "And so you went back to London.''

"Not straight away. Not till the following spring,'' said Roddy. His voice was carefully level. "There was a governess sort of person for Dorrie, and I expect it seemed the best thing. You see, our London house—which I don't really remember at all—had been bombed, and Dad moved in at number 34. I suppose it was after Mother died he decided to stay there, and by the time we got back Aunt Janet was already installed, and all set to take the burden of us off Gran's shoulders.''

"From what I know of Mrs. Gaskell, she would have been able to deal with the situation.'' Sir Nicholas was smiling, and after a moment Roddy relaxed and smiled back at him.

"Of course she would,'' he agreed. "But it sounded well, and Aunt Janet likes being a martyr.''

"Which brings us to the question: why doesn't she like you?''

Roddy frowned over that. "It sounds conceited if I say I don't know,'' he said. "I suppose it's just incompatibility. She's very like Dad in some ways, you know.''

"Yes,'' said Sir Nicholas. It was obvious that he contemplated without pleasure the picture that was being drawn for him. "Well now,'' he went on more briskly after a pause, "what will Mrs. Blake be able to tell the police about that period of your life?''

"She'll say, when I was home there was always trouble of one sort or another,'' said Roddy. He paused, and then added explosively: "Nothing was right . . . nothing I could ever do. And if Dad by any chance came to the end of his list of sins, Aunt Janet could always be relied on to think up one or two new ones.''

"Did this . . . this constant bickering trouble you?'' asked Sir Nicholas. Roddy grinned at him.

"Not particularly. How did you guess?''

"Then tell me about the first major disagreement.''

"It won't really need Aunt Janet to tell the police about that," said Roddy. He might not have been speaking in a boastful spirit, but certainly he was unabashed by the recollection. "Uncle Gil says all the Gaskells but him are money-grubbers, so I suppose that was why—"

"What in heaven's name are you talking about?" demanded Sir Nicholas.

"I started a book-making business at school," said Roddy, with a sidelong look to see how his companions were taking this revelation. "It seemed a good idea at the time. Well, I daresay it was illegal," he added, making a concession to what he obviously regarded as the eccentricity of his audience, "but there wasn't anything *wrong* about it."

Sir Nicholas was eyeing him coldly. "I can well imagine," he remarked, "that you found your grandfather the most congenial member of your family."

"I don't think," said Roddy, slowly, "that's intended for a compliment."

"It is not."

"Oh, well! To go back to the business venture, it wasn't exactly a popular move; there was a row at school, and the newspapers got hold of it. I don't suppose you'd remember, sir, it wasn't in all the papers. I mean . . . probably not in the ones you read."

"And how did your family feel about that?"

"Just as you'd expect. Righteous indignation. I never particularly minded Dad being angry, you know, but I couldn't stand him being shocked."

"Your grandfather, however, did not share his sentiments?"

Roddy grinned. "He wasn't exactly sympathetic," he said. "But at least he made a push to do something about it. He came roaring down to school; well, I don't know how he fixed it, but they were all set to throw me out . . . and then they didn't."

"You surprise me," said Sir Nicholas. He seemed to be thinking something over, and added after a moment, "Er . . . Roddy. If you have occasion to speak of this in court, try not to do so with quite so much enthusiasm."

"Should I shock them?"

"Not precisely. But I think it would be unwise to give the impression that you were in any way enjoying yourself."

"Oh!" said Roddy, blankly. And added quite meekly a moment later, "Is that how it sounds?"

"That's exactly how it sounds," Sir Nicholas told him.

"Well . . . I'll do my best." He sounded doubtful. "What do you want to know next?"

"The next major cause of disagreement with your father."

"Well—" said Roddy. "Business, I suppose." And now he was watching Antony as he spoke. "That's just since grandfather died, of course. Dad was so cautious."

"Before that," said Sir Nicholas. Roddy looked an enquiry, and Antony again took upon himself the task of explanation.

"He means his taste in newspapers is rather more catholic than you might suppose," he said. The statement seemed only to bewilder Roddy, but Sir Nicholas nodded his approval.

"The occasion you have mentioned was not the only time your affairs have been taken up by the press," he remarked.

"No," said Roddy. He seemed disinclined to add anything to this, and Antony broke in again, saying crossly:

"If you're thinking I'll run to Liz with the information, you're wrong. Anyway, she probably knows already."

"And if she doesn't," said Sir Nicholas, at his blandest, "she certainly will by the time the trial is over."

"Yes . . . I see," said Roddy.

"You needn't worry, I don't suppose she cares. Girls have no sense of decency these days. And don't delude yourself Liz is different," Antony added firmly, "because it's just as well for you she isn't."

"All right!" said Roddy. He sounded angry now. "My father was a puritan . . . I'm not. That isn't very original, or interesting. But I seem to have inherited the old pirate's knack of making the headlines."

"It was probably," said Antony, reflectively, "your rather indiscreet choice of—friends." (No members of the chorus for the Pirate King's grandson . . . when he went adventuring in the world of the theatre it was with a leading actress, some fifteen years his senior. And again there had been . . .)

"I am not concerned to embarrass you," said Sir Nicholas. If he really had any scruples on this score, they were obviously unnecessary. "What concerns me is that you couldn't deny these matters made bad feeling between your father and yourself."

"No," said Roddy. "I couldn't deny that."

"And you say there was a more recent disagreement, concerning the management of the business?"

"A sort of running battle," said Roddy, with renewed gusto. But when he went on there was a hint of awkwardness in his manner. "I told you, we were quarrelling that afternoon . . . the day he died. It wasn't about the picture, but after what he said at dinner it must sound as if it was."

"What did he say?"

"That he knew who had stolen it, and the person knew he knew. That he intended to deal with the matter 'as justice dictated'; it would be unpleasant for all of us, but couldn't be avoided. He was—" He broke off; obviously it was important to find the right words for what he wished to say. "He was bitterly angry, and quite determined to do what he thought was right."

"And who was there when he said this."

"All of us . . . all the family. Gran and Aunt Janet—oh, and Edward—and Dorrie and Michael. But not Uncle Gil."

"Were you sure he was referring to someone who was then present?"

"I thought he was 'talking at' somebody; but . . . I don't really know . . . I can't be certain." He paused, and Antony had the impression that he was deliberately taking stock of the situation, facing—perhaps for the first time in spite of his protestations—the full implication of what had happened. "It wouldn't be so bad," he said after a while, "if it were just getting me out of this mess."

"You said you wanted to know," Antony pointed out.

"So I do. So I do, really." He shrugged. "What next?" he asked.

"Back to the beginning again," said Sir Nicholas. "We'll have a little more detail this time," he added, and pushed a foolscap pad across the table to his nephew, whose envelope was showing signs of overcrowding. "For heaven's sake, boy, make some legible notes this time," he growled. Antony received the loan without comment, but as soon as his uncle was fairly launched again took out his penknife and slit his envelope down the sides. When he passed the pad back an hour later, it was still unsullied. Sir Nicholas glared at it; took off his spectacles and looked at it again; but put it away in his brief-case at last without more open comment.

CHAPTER X

By a complete reversal of mood on the part of the Clerk of the Weather, Sunday morning was pale gold and mellow, a delightful foretaste of pleasures—perhaps—to come. Antony, who had got his plan of campaign pretty well worked out the night before, put Roddy Gaskell's troubles firmly out of his mind and took Jenny out to Richmond to walk in the park. They lunched at a restaurant where the waiter was an old friend, and could be relied on not to look patronisingly at a slightly windswept, if not actually dishevelled appearance; and they lingered so long over the coffee cups that it was turned three o'clock when they got back home.

Gibbs appeared like a jack-in-the-box from the back of the hall almost before they were fairly indoors. He looked harassed, and for the first time in Antony's recollection seemed to have abandoned hostilities. "It's a Mrs. Gaskell on the telephone," he said in a distraught way. "Mr. Maitland . . . will *you* take the call?"

Antony grimaced at this sudden reminder of the problems he had temporarily shelved. "Well . . . all right," he said reluctantly, and started towards the study. Gibbs padded after him, still explaining.

"She was asking for Sir Nicholas . . . I told her, Mr. Maitland . . . it's the fourth time she's called." Antony smiled at him over his shoulder.

"All right," he said again. "I'll do my best to pacify her." But as soon as he took up the receiver and spoke he knew this wasn't going to be easy.

"Is that you, Nicholas?" Old Mrs. Gaskell's voice was sharply suspicious.

"I'm sorry, Mrs. Gaskell; my uncle is out of town for the week-end."

"Oh, it's you! That's what your man told me." She sounded discontented, and not especially as if she believed the statement, even now. "Well, Mr. Maitland?" she added; in a tone that seemed to expect some precise answer to this vague query.

"Can I . . . is there anything I can do?" asked Antony cautiously.

"I should have thought that was obvious. Roddy's still in prison, isn't he? I thought you were supposed to be doing something about that."

"These things take time, Mrs. Gaskell."

"Lawyers!" The old voice was scornful. "All alike, and not a ha'p'orth of gumption among the lot of you," she grumbled.

"We're a useless bunch," agreed Antony, more cheerfully. If all she wanted was to abuse him, he could cope with that all right. But it wasn't to be so easy.

"You'd better come over here. If that uncle of yours weren't gallivanting all over the country . . . but you'll have to do."

"Yes . . . of course. Has something happened, Mrs. Gaskell?" He realised as he spoke that the question was not particularly well phrased, and was not surprised at the scornful snort which nearly broke his eardrum.

"That seems rather obvious, doesn't it?"

"I'm sorry," said Antony meekly, but without any hope that his tone would deceive her for an instant.

"Well, if you mean anything else," she said flatly, "what do you think I'm making a fuss about. I'm not doing it for fun."

"I suppose not."

"If you must know . . . no, I can't tell you on the telephone. Gilbert is here and Janet is having hysterics. And Michael has some absurd story from the office." She paused for an instant, and then added briskly. "So you'd better come."

"Now?" said Antony, gloomily.

"Well, I don't mean next Christmas. And bring that girl with you . . . Jenny . . . whatever her name is," she ordered. "She looks as if she had a head on her shoulders."

"But you needn't come, of course," said Antony, relating the inaudible half of this conversation a few minutes later. Jenny looked at him consideringly, so that he thought for a moment she hadn't even heard what he said.

"I think I'd better," she replied at last. "She may not bully you if I'm there. Besides, Dorrie must be having a pretty grim time, don't you think?" She turned towards the stairs as she spoke, and caught sight of her reflection in the long mirror which hung in a rather bad light at the other side of the hall. "But not until I've tidied myself," she added, firmly.

This time it was Michael Pratten who opened the door to them when they arrived at number 34. He looked more nearly agitated than Antony would have thought possible, and said in a conspiratorial undertone as he led the way upstairs: "It's a pity the old lady found out. The trouble is, she *will* know."

"What's up?" said Antony. He sounded detached, as though he were only most casually concerned with the affairs of the Gaskell family.

"You'll hear," said Michael, making the prophesy without pleasure. "I daren't stop and explain," he added over his shoulder; and paused for a moment for them to join him on the landing. A moment later he was ushering them into the drawing-room.

Sorting out his impressions afterwards, Antony thought it was strange how little outward effect the events of the past week had had upon the family. The quietness with which the house had greeted them was misleading: the normal hush of Sunday afternoon, rather than the chill which follows bereavement. Unhappy the Gaskells might be, in their own highly individualistic ways, but still there was no impression that they were drifting with the tide; so far as circumstances allowed, they had retained some measure of control over their lives.

They were all there except Janet. Gilbert had seated himself at the far end of the room near the window; he looked chilled and aloof. Edward Blake had apparently been turning the pages of an album on a side-table, but came across immediately to greet them; Antony thought his welcome a little exaggerated. Dorrie was sitting on the edge of a small, overstuffed sofa to the left of the hearth; she looked flushed, and Antony thought they had probably interrupted an argument, which could only have been with her grandmother.

Priscilla Gaskell was enthroned as regally as she had been on the occasion of his previous visit; her head held as high, her attitude as unbending. Only when she had greeted Jenny and—to his surprise—turned to give him her hand, he found it was cold and not quite steady. "When will he be back in town?" she demanded.

Rightly interpreting this as a reference to his uncle, Antony replied guardedly. "To-night, perhaps . . . but more likely to-morrow morning."

The old lady did not seem to find this particularly satisfactory. "Well, so long as you're here," she remarked disagreeably, "you may as well hear what has happened. And what Michael has to say, too." She looked past him at Jenny. "Sit down, child; sit down," she commanded, and turned an unfriendly eye in Antony's direction. Jenny went to join Dorrie on the sofa, and Antony subsided obediently on to the chair he had occupied before.

"Another bottle of Andrew's tonic has been found in Roddy's room," Priscilla said abruptly.

"You mean . . . the vitamin capsules?" He wasn't quite sure whether he found the information more surprising, or the matter-of-fact way in which she introduced it.

"Of course I do." But Antony was momentarily impervious to the impatience in her voice. They might hope to prove then, the substitution theory; but only at the cost of having the prosecution say the poisoned bottle had been introduced by Roddy himself. Premeditation . . . it only made things worse.

"But the police must have searched his room, when they arrested him," he said, looking for the bright side.

"If you think you can prove they were planted," said Edward Blake, obviously following his thought, "I wouldn't count on it, if I were you." Antony looked at him inquiringly. "It's not a large bottle, you know, and was pushed down inside a pair of socks."

"Thick, knee-length ones," said Dorrie. "He had them when we went ski-ing."

"So the police search might well have missed it," said Edward, rubbing it in.

Antony's face was expressionless. Another point of argument, no more than that; though Counsel would doubtless give the unfortunate detective concerned some bad moments in the witness box, the defence stressing the thoroughness of his search, the prosecution trying to persuade him how easily the hiding place could have been overlooked. "I suppose it's no use hoping,'' he said, "that they are still where you found them.''

"June very properly brought them to me,'' said the old lady austerely.

"June?''

"The housemaid,'' Dorrie explained. "We were packing some more things for Roddy. And the socks were in a plastic bag with a sweater he wanted and some moth-balls.''

"I see.'' He turned back to Priscilla. "Was the package just as it came from the shop?''

"So far as I could tell.''

"And you opened it?''

"Naturally. How else could I know?'' She nodded as she spoke towards the mantelpiece, and Antony walked across with his hands in his pockets. White paper, and a blob of sealing wax; a brown-glass bottle about five inches high with a sadly uninformative label . . . the chemist's name, the doctor's name, "The Tablets, Mr. Andrew Gaskell'' . . . no date, no prescription number even. Rather ostentatiously, he made no attempt to touch the package, but turned to look down at the old lady. "These will have to go to the police,'' he said. And saw her mouth close in a thin stubborn line.

"Will it help Roddy?''

He avoided the question. "It's something I've wanted to prove,'' he said. "That another bottle existed, similar to the one Roddy handed to his father on Tuesday evening. This, I think, is the package he collected from the shop last Monday.''

"It has always been obvious, Gran,'' Edward explained, "that if Roddy is innocent someone else changed his bottle for one already prepared.''

"Then this will help him,'' said Mrs. Gaskell, her eyes still on Antony.

"Not . . . not positively.'' Again it was Edward Blake who undertook to explain:

"You see, Gran, they'll say it is just as likely Roddy had made his preparations in advance. Won't they, Maitland?''

"I'm afraid so. But still, this is evidence we must present—''

"I didn't bring you here to tell me my duty, young man.'' Priscilla sat nodding to herself for a moment, and then said briskly, "Gilbert shall do it. But not until you've heard what

Michael has to say, Mr. Maitland. I won't have the police interrupting us.''

Michael Pratten, in spite of the old lady's dislike of people who hovered, had remained standing all this time between the sofa and the door. He now said in a quick, nervous way, apparently addressing the back of Dorrie's neck.

"I don't want to upset everybody, but while you're here, Maitland—" He broke off there and glanced briefly at Antony—apologising perhaps for the fact that he was introducing yet another bone of contention—and then went on in the same hurried way: "It's about what was said when Mr. Gaskell— Mr. Andrew Gaskell—sent for Roddy on Tuesday afternoon. I thought perhaps—"

"Never mind what you thought, Michael," old Mrs. Gaskell interrupted him impatiently. "Go on!"

"A first-hand account is always helpful," said Antony, encouragingly. Left to himself, it seemed unlikely that Pratten would ever reach a climax, and the old lady's intervention seemed to have made him even more incoherent.

"Oh, but this isn't . . . I mean I only know what Jenkinson told me.''

"Jenkinson was the clerk who heard them quarrelling, wasn't he?" Antony spoke abruptly, surprised by his own irritation. Dorrie looked at him reproachfully, and Pratten went on as jerkily as before.

"You see, at the magistrate's court he was only asked if he'd heard their voices, and did it sound as if they were having words? But he heard a little of what they were saying when he was in Miss Somers's office . . . she's—she was—Andrew's typist.''

"What did he hear?"

Michael's manner became more apologetic than ever; he waved his hands wildly, but his eyes were still fixed on Dorrie. "He heard Andrew say, quite distinctly, 'it's not a matter of opinion, there's a right way and a wrong way'; and then, a bit later, 'your grandfather had his own ideas, I don't wish to criticise him; but I will not tolerate your interference in what I feel is right.' And at some point Roddy said, 'I only wanted to keep things as they were'.''

Antony was frowning over this. Nothing to contradict what Roddy had told him; and yet, horribly suggestive. In face of this, Roddy's story could only sound like a feeble explanation, patched up after the event. And—underlining this thought—"I think we must face the fact," said Priscilla clearly into the silence, "that Roddy took the picture from the study."

"He says he didn't."

"He isn't a fool, Mr. Maitland. No doubt he will persist in his denial. But I believe I am right in thinking that you cannot face facts effectively unless you know what they are."

"Perfectly right." He smiled at her, and then turned back to Pratten. "What has Miss Somers to say about this?" he asked. "Was Jenkinson with her all the time Roddy was in his father's office?"

"No, for a few minutes only."

"But she heard nothing while she was alone?"

"She says not. She says she was typing continuously." Something in his tone brought Antony's eyes on him questioningly.

"True?" he asked.

"I don't know." But he added with a sudden burst of candour: "She likes Roddy, I think; so she probably wouldn't say."

"As if things weren't complicated enough already. Do the police know that, do you suppose?"

"I should think so," said Michael cautiously. "There's been an awful lot of talk, you know, one way and another. And Roddy always gets himself talked about, whether there's anything to say or not."

"So I imagine." He caught old Mrs. Gaskell's eye, fixed on him with an anxiety he knew would not be expressed in words, and added with an attempt as reassurance, "It doesn't really mean anything, you know."

"But I don't know," she retorted. "Roderick used to say when you went to law it wasn't just the things you could prove that mattered, it was all the things that could be suggested, until the jury mistook the total for proof. Was he right?" she demanded.

"Well, yes, but—"

"Please don't quibble, Mr. Maitland."

"It isn't quite so simple. I mean, all the suggestion wouldn't be on one side." While she frowned over what was obviously a new thought he turned back to Michael Pratten.

"I imagine it has made a good deal of confusion at the office . . . all this."

"It certainly has. After all, a week ago—" He broke off, apparently realising that the sentence could only end in embarrassment. Edward Blake, who also was still on his feet, came a pace or two nearer and remarked with a casual air which was obviously not intended to be taken as genuine:

"You've got what you wanted, anyway . . . running the whole show."

They made an amusing contrast, Antony thought, eyeing them while this uncomfortable statement hung in the air between them. Here in his grandfather's drawing-room, Blake looked no less elegant than he had on the night of the Watsons' dance. Pratten had not the presence to make an equal showing; neatness and propriety were words which came to mind where he was concerned. And in the same way his worried, half-apologetic air formed a violent contrast to the other man's bright-eyed malice. He said now, huffily: "I'm doing what I can. I really don't know who else knows half as much about the firm."

"I'm sure you're right," said Edward cordially. "But tell me, Michael, whose policies are you following . . . Andrew's, or Roddy's?"

"There has hardly been time . . . the question has not arisen—"

"Hasn't it? Well, when a decision is called for . . . what then?"

"Each case is different . . . each must be treated on its merits."

"Now, where have I heard that before?" said Edward. Pratten flushed angrily.

"How could I know what either of them do in any given circumstances?"

"I should think you could make a pretty good guess."

"Do you think so? Well, let me remind you," said Michael, tight-lipped and angry, "that I'm not the only one who 'got what he wanted' out of Andrew's death."

"Just what do you mean by that?"

"You're down for a nice little legacy in Andrew's will . . . don't tell me you didn't know! So what's to stop you going abroad to live, as you say you've always wanted?"

"Michael . . . Edward!" Priscilla's voice cut sharply into the altercation, stopping Pratten in mid flight, and silencing Blake's retort. "If you must quarrel—" she went on, unsteadily; and broke off with an unexpectedly helpless air.

"If you must quarrel," said Gilbert Gaskell, coming forward for the first time to join the group around the fireplace, "your grandmother's drawing-room, Edward, is hardly the most suitable place."

"But, look here, Uncle Gil—"

"Perhaps it would be helpful," said Michael stiffly, "if I left you." He stood a moment, looking round the group of people, and drew back his lips in a smile that was almost a grimace. "Of course, I sympathise with your dilemma," he said; and it was noticeable that as his anger grew his nervousness had left him.

"I don't understand you," said Gilbert, flatly. And Edward murmured:

"You'd better explain that, Michael, don't you think?"

"You're all of you concerned about Roddy. But if he's innocent . . . well, ask Maitland where that leaves you."

"The answer's obvious, even without Counsel's opinion," said Edward. "I don't believe for a minute Roddy killed his father; therefore, somebody else did."

"Somebody close enough to him to know . . . well, for instance, to know about the capsules," Michael insisted.

"And so?"

"So it would be more convenient, wouldn't it, to think it was me? Not some member of your precious family circle."

"You're being less than fair, Michael." Old Mrs. Gaskell's voice dominated the incoherent protests that greeted this remark. "We have always treated you—haven't we?—as one of ourselves."

"A privilege indeed," snapped Pratten, obviously too angry to accept this statement either as reproach or olive branch. "Since being a member of the family means no more than freedom to participate in its quarrels, it is not an altogether enviable privilege."

"I think you've said enough for the moment, don't you?" said Gilbert Gaskell. There was a look of shocked disbelief about Dorrie and her grandmother; Edward was smiling faintly; but Antony was surprised to note that Gilbert was shaking with anger. Michael turned without another word, and marched out of the room.

Dorrie said, "Oh, but—" and half rose to her feet; then she glanced uncertainly at Jenny, and subsided again. "That was all your fault, Edward," she said. "I think you're beastly!"

"Do you, Dorrie?" His eyes rested on her a moment before he turned away. "I'm sorry, Gran," he said.

"This is a house of mourning, Edward. It is not seemly—"

"No, Gran, of course not. I'm sorry," he said again. His glance flickered for a moment towards Antony before he went on, "You know I couldn't go away," he said. "I've talked about it, I know; but there's Mother to consider."

Priscilla Gaskell looked at him steadily; Antony, watching her, could get no clue to her feelings. At last she said, "Don't forget I want to talk to you later, Edward." And added impatiently: "Where *is* Janet?" and looked at her son as she spoke.

"In her room, I suppose," said Gilbert. "I don't think we need disturb her. She was feeling upset," he added, dividing the information partially between Antony and Jenny.

Priscilla seemed annoyed by the inadequacy of this description. "She was indulging herself in a fit of hysteria," she remarked with asperity.

"Well, you must admit—" began Edward, apologetically.

"Nonsense!" said the old lady. "There is no excuse for such behaviour. As for a reason—" her eyes moved reflectively to Antony's face—"it was something Gilbert said to her."

"Oh, come now, Mother. I was just telling you about my talk with Maitland—" The sentence trailed off as something seemed to strike him. He added, almost to himself: "And then Janet started yelling, and after that Michael told us—"

"He was only trying to help," said Dorrie, defensively.

"Don't be sillier than you must," interrupted Edward with sudden exasperation. "He had it all mighty pat." Dorrie shrugged impatiently, and turned away to look into the fire. Edward eyed her in a helpless way, but before he could add anything the door opened and Janet bustled into the room, closely followed by the parlourmaid who was looking sulky and pushing a laden trolley.

Afternoon tea at number 34 was obviously an institution, and the members of the family reacted to this invasion like well-rehearsed actors. Only old Mrs. Gaskell had no part assigned to her, probably she usually undertook the director's rôle. Now she sat silent, and obviously impatient, while tables were placed, tea poured, and sandwiches and scones distributed. Gilbert took her tea, Edward placed a small plate of sandwiches at her elbow, saying, "There, Gran!" as he did so; but if his intention was to placate her, he had very little success. As soon as the maid had left them she looked across at her daughter, still busy behind the tea-tray.

"Well, Janet?" she said.

"If you mean, is my headache better," said Mrs. Blake, "I must say that it is not. I have been very upset," she stated, looking round her in a challenging way, as though expecting one of them to dispute her claim. "It has brought my neuralgia on again."

"You should have stayed upstairs, Aunt Janet," said Dorrie, "until you felt better."

"How could I? The servants are quite demoralised, and nothing would be done unless I made it my business—"

"Some tea will do you good," said Edward, bracingly, taking the last cup from her and looking round for a place to sit. Finally he took the chair nearest to Jenny, and began to talk to her quietly. Dorrie set her lips tightly together, and picked up her cup; shaking her head in a resolute way at the offer of sandwiches. Priscilla sent one last, inimical look in her daughter's direction, and then devoted herself to her tea. Janet slumped back in her chair with a look of resignation, and Gilbert, after eyeing her thoughtfully for a moment, shrugged his shoulders and seated himself as near Antony as he could.

"I understand from Hargreaves that you saw Roddy yesterday," he said. "Did you find your talk with him helpful?"

"I'm not really in a position at this stage," said Antony shortly, "to tell what is and what is not important." Then he relented and gave Gilbert an apologetic grin. "If only we can stop him giving the impression he's enjoying himself," he confided.

"I see your difficulty." In his quiet way, Gilbert was amused. "I hope you're not regretting your decision to help us," he added.

"No-o." Antony's eyes moved for a moment to Dorrie's face, and he repeated, "No," more positively.

"I agree with you there," said Gilbert. "The only one of us—Roddy included—who's worth worrying about."

"That's rather drastic. Would you really put it so strongly?"

"You'll agree with me," said Gilbert placidly, "when you know us better."

Jenny, taking her cue from Edward, who now seemed determined to behave as though nothing had happened, had embarked on a painstaking description of the first night she had recently attended. Dorrie had turned her head a little as though she were listening, but Antony doubted very much whether she heard a word that was being said. He turned to Uncle Gil beside him and asked abruptly, "You will get in touch with the police, won't you? About those damned capsules."

"That shook you, did it?" said Gilbert, perceptively. "I admit, I hadn't seen its full significance."

"Your nephew had," said Antony.

"Edward? Yes, I wouldn't doubt it. I suppose they'll ask why we were so long reporting the matter, and we shall say we couldn't do anything until we'd had tea." He gave a sidelong glance at his companion and added, "Quite a performance, isn't it?"

"On an occasion less sad than this," said Antony, deliberately trite, "afternoon tea can be a very pleasant function." But he got no rise out of Gilbert Gaskell, who said merely, "Yes, indeed!" and grinned at him.

Jenny's narrative had dried up now; she was listening to something Edward was telling her, and seconding his efforts to draw Dorrie into the conversation. Dorrie was the only one of the family, Antony noticed, who wasn't making a pretty hearty meal, their various preoccupations notwithstanding. Conversation with Gilbert was not altogether easy, because he was assiduous in keeping the ladies supplied; and presently, when the other dishes were nearly empty, he offered Jenny the willow pattern plate that stood on the table at Priscilla Gaskell's elbow.

"You mustn't do that, Uncle Gil," said Edward, interrupting him with a languid protest. "Those are Gran's specials; aren't they, Gran?"

"Indeed they are not." The old lady roused herself to vigorous protest. "That is really too bad of you, Edward . . . most unkind." She turned to Jenny. "My family don't share my taste for anchovy paste, my dear, but my husband liked it and so do I. I hope you'll have one of these.''

Jenny didn't care much for anchovy paste herself; but seeing that Mrs. Gaskell was really upset by her grandson's remark she took a sandwich and bit into it without any show of distaste. The old lady watched her with apparent satisfaction, and then helped herself to the last one on the plate.

''True nobility,'' said Gilbert in Antony's ear.

But they were almost at the end of the tea-party. Priscilla was gracious when they took their leave, but Antony couldn't feel that from her point of view the visit had been a notable success. He was putting various facts in order to retail to Sir Nicholas as they walked back in the chilly dusk across the square. Jenny was silent, too; but when she said as they reached their own pavement, ''I wonder which one of them she'll marry,'' he only grunted at her, and didn't even register the remark sufficiently for his curiosity to be aroused.

This time there were no messages to greet them. Even Gibbs, that martyr to duty, was apparently taking his ease. Antony went up the stairs at his usual speed, and was still too preoccupied to notice that Jenny seemed a little breathless keeping pace with him. As they went into their own hall the telephone was ringing.

Although he had only just left the Gaskells, for a moment Antony did not recognise Dorrie's voice. She said, without any attempt at greeting, ''Gran's ill. Can you come back?''

That brought him out of his abstraction with a jerk. ''Yes, of course. But what—''

''As soon as you'd gone,'' said Dorrie. ''It was . . . horrible. So I range the doctor, and then I thought of you.''

''Of course I'll come,'' said Antony again; and put down the receiver and went out quickly into the hall. ''Jenny—'' he was saying; but that was as far as the sentence got.

Jenny had just come out of the bathroom. Her gloves and scarf were on the table, but she still had her coat on. She said, speaking with difficulty, ''I've been terribly sick, darling, I think you'd better—''

Antony was just in time to catch her as she fell.

CHAPTER XI

IN THE GREY hours of the following morning, Antony was at Waterloo to meet his uncle's train. Sir Nicholas came quickly through the barrier and wasted no time on preliminaries. "How is she?" he demanded.

"Better . . . they say. She's sleeping now." There was a blank look in his eyes, and the older man took his arm without ceremony and began to steer him towards the taxi rank. "It was touch and go," Antony said. "Even quite a small dose . . . she might have died, Uncle Nick."

Sir Nicholas himself was tight-lipped and the more angry because he did not know in which direction this emotion should be channelled. He said briskly: "Are we going back to the hospital?"

"No. No, I don't think we'd better. They more or less chased me out. Said I could come back after breakfast."

Sir Nicholas found this statement more heartening than what had gone before. "You'll be better for some coffee," he said firmly, having by this time had a pretty good look at his nephew, who was grey with fatigue, unshaven, and obviously very cold.

In spite of the early hour the house in Kempenfeldt Square was already awake, and if Gibbs was no more amiable than usual, at least there did not seem to be any particular animosity in his mutterings. As for Mrs. Stokes, she was fussing unashamedly; and though it was her habit to pretend some respect for her employer, she had no such inhibitions where Antony was concerned, and drove him upstairs with quite explicit instructions concerning the taking of a hot bath, putting on a warm dressing-gown, and so on. Later he wondered vaguely whether he had actually obeyed her, but could only suppose he must have done so.

Certainly he was a little warmer when he sat by the study fire some half hour later, sipping a cup of coffee which seemed somehow to have been heated to a degree far beyond boiling point, and apologising for the third time to his uncle. "I'm sorry I got you out of bed, Uncle Nick. I just couldn't think what else to do." The dazed look was still in his eyes, and Sir Nicholas did not comment upon the reiteration, as normally he would have done. Instead, he asked:

"Have the doctors said what made her ill?"

"They haven't said anything. But I know, of course . . . the same stuff that killed Andrew Gaskell." He paused, and looked back without pleasure to the events of the previous evening. "I'd been reading up on the symptoms, you see, so I knew at once. And all I could do was get the doctor; I did try to give her artificial respiration while I was waiting for him, but I can't properly because of this damned shoulder." (Sir Nicholas noted, as a measure of his nephew's perturbation, that for the first time in his recollection Antony had spoken without self-consciousness of his wartime injury). "I did think of the other way, only I didn't know . . . with poison . . . I might just have made things worse." He stopped, and drank some more coffee, and added after a moment: "And I still don't know if that makes sense or not."

"It doesn't matter now," said Sir Nicholas, at his most prosaic. "She's getting better."

"Yes, I know. But I feel it's all my fault, Uncle Nick. I should never have let her come with me." Before his companion had time to condemn this sentiment as useless he added in dismay, "Oh, lord, I forgot all about Dorrie."

"I phoned just now, while you were changing," said Sir Nicholas.

Antony was vaguely surprised to know that his uncle had gathered so much from the disjointed account he had given him in the early hours. He said, "Well, then?" and made the words a question.

"Old Mrs. Gaskell is dead," Sir Nicholas told him. He half expected another outburst of self-recrimination, but Antony took it quietly.

I'm sorry about that," he said, after a while. "But it makes one thing clear . . . it was the sandwiches."

"Something anyone might have eaten?"

"Anchovy paste . . . no one else liked them, apparently." He stopped, and forced his thoughts back to the drawing-room at number 34 the previous afternoon. "Gilbert passed them to Jenny; that looks like an innocent gesture on his part, but it might have been meant to look that way."

"No one could have wanted to harm Jenny," said Sir Nicholas, positively.

"No, but they might not have *minded*. Edward Blake tried to stop her taking one. I wonder—"

"Who else was present?"

"The old lady herself; Dorrie, and Mrs. Blake. Michael Pratten had left in a temper some time before. But the mischief had been done earlier, probably before the sandwiches were made. I must see what Sykes has to say about that."

"Have you been in touch with him?"

Antony shook his head. "The doctor has, I think. At least, I had a message while I was at the hospital that he'd like to see me to-day." He drank the last of his coffee, and passed the cup to Sir Nicholas, who was relieved to see that he looked a little more normal now. "May I have a refill, Uncle Nick? It's so cold this morning," he complained.

Jenny was awake when he got back to the hospital, and clear-headed enough though not really up to talking. He made her laugh with his account of Mrs. Stokes's ministrations, and how Sir Nicholas had suffered under them patiently, without the *sotto voce* comments which would usually have accompanied such an outbreak of solicitude. "Poor Uncle Nick," murmured Jenny.

After that he held her hand until she fell asleep again, but then he was due in court. He went with reluctance, but the discipline of turning his mind from his own affairs to his client's probably did him more good than anything else could have done. But he was physically cold whenever he thought of what had happened; he knew so well now the unpredictable nature of aconitine, and how little might constitute a lethal dose.

He got back to chambers soon after three o'clock, to find

old Mr. Mallory waiting for him with an air of respectful sympathy which he found unnerving. ''Mrs. Watson has been on the telephone several times, Mr. Maitland. I think perhaps you should speak to her.''

''Yes, I suppose so,''Antony agreed wearily.

Aunt Carry was annoyed, and expressed herself freely. ''I should have been told,'' was her main theme; and, of course, she was right. But he had to stop agreeing and assert himself when she proposed that Jenny should go to her when she left the hospital. ''It's very kind of you, but she won't need nursing, you know. The doctor says—''. After that the conversation degenerated into a pretty good dog-fight; and hostilities only ended when he agreed to her suggestion that Liz should come to Kempenfeldt Square for a week of two, until Jenny was really fit. Mrs. Watson had a few more remarks to make about obstinacy and wrong-headedness, but at last she rang off.

Antony sat and looked at the telephone for a while, and thought vaguely that he should telephone Sykes, and for some reason didn't want to. That problem was solved by the inspector ringing him; he agreed to go round to Scotland Yard right away.

The detective greeted him with a worried look, and showed his relief when Antony gave him the most recent bulletin. ''For I don't mind telling you, Mr. Maitland, that's a very worrying business,'' he said. A massive understatement, but no one could have doubted his concern. A constable brought tea. ''You'll feel better for that,'' Sykes said, on a note of self-congratulation, as he passed the visitor his cup; and Antony thought suddenly that the urge to comfort the afflicted with hot drinks seemed to be universal. As well as Uncle Nick, there had been the nurses at the hospital; and now the inspector. But along with this attempt at consolation came the inevitable request: ''And now, Mr Maitland, if you'll tell me—''

He did his best to give a clear and comprehensive account of the events of the afternoon. Sykes took some time to consider what he said, so that Antony at last was driven to interrupt his cogitations with an impatient question. ''I must know, Inspector . . . about the poison.''

''Like you, we assume it to have been in the sandwiches.

The old lady had a lot more than a lethal dose in her, and the anchovy paste is the only thing she ate that would successfully hide the taste of aconitine.''

''Was the jar poisoned, or just the sandwiches?''

''The jar. There was a little left which we took for testing.'' He held out a hand silently for his companion's cup and said, not looking at him, ''The cook thinks it's about a fortnight since she had any, and it's been in the refrigerator since then. It could have been poisoned any time since then.''

Antony understood this pronouncement well enough. ''But Roddy Gaskell could have had no reason to kill his grandmother,'' he protested.

''She was an inquisitive old lady, and a pretty knowing one,'' said Sykes. ''Her death makes very little difference to any of the family financially, and I think we must assume she discovered something.''

''That motive would apply to anyone else, equally with Roddy,'' Antony pointed out.

''But we have no evidence against any other person.'' Sykes was stirring his tea, but stopped with the spoon poised and asked bluntly: ''What are you going to do about this business now, Mr. Maitland?''

Antony met his eyes. ''Full speed ahead, Inspector.''

Sykes was frowning. ''In the circumstances, you wouldn't want to defend the guilty party,'' he said carefully.

''I happen to believe Roddy Gaskell.''

''Do you, Mr. Maitland? Do you, indeed?'' Sykes was stirring again. Antony sipped his tea and wondered what was coming. ''You'll be getting this information from the solicitors in the usual way,'' the inspector said at last. ''I'm speaking unofficially, Mr. Maitland. As a friend.''

''I'm grateful, of course, but I don't quite understand,'' said Antony. But he was annoyed to find that his hand was shaking, and put down his cup in a hurry.

''By now, no doubt, you know something of aconitine,'' said Sykes. ''We have all been taking it for granted it was not too difficult to come by in this country, by someone with a certain amount of botanical knowledge.''

''Or a good book,'' Antony agreed.

''Yes, well . . . the further tests which have been done show that the poison which killed Andrew Gaskell was not derived from the local plant, but from the Indian *aconitum ferox* . . . the most deadly poison known." He held up his hand to forestall an interruption his companion had no intention of making. "Not very easy to trace positively," he said. "Not very easy to obtain either, except for somebody who visited the country. But I understand it is possible to come by such things more easily in India . . . without signing the poison book, you might say," he added with a grim smile.

"Well, Inspector?"

"I must tell you, Mr. Maitland, that Roderick Gaskell was in Nepal about four months ago. He had business in Dacca, and made the journey inland on the pretext of sight-seeing." He seemed to be expecting some comment, but when Antony remained silent he went on: "I realise I am acting improperly in seeming to wish to influence your decision. But as things are I felt that some measure of extraordinary frankness was due to you."

"That's kind of you, Inspector," said Antony. "If I thought Roddy was responsible for what happened to Jenny . . . but, you see, I don't."

"But, Mr. Maitland—"

"I appreciate your concern, of course. You don't want me to do something I'll afterwards regret."

"Such as helping acquit the man who poisoned your wife," said Sykes. "You see, Mr. Maitland, if you come round later to my way of thinking—when the trial is half over, say—you could not then withdraw without serious injury to your client's case."

"You do make it difficult, don't you?" He got up as he spoke, and moved restlessly to the window. "I *think* he's innocent," he said; and was not conscious how he stressed the word. "If he is, I can't let him down."

"We've been at odds before, Mr. Maitland, and I admit there have been times I'd have done better to listen to you; but you can't always be right, you know."

"No," said Antony. He continued for a moment to gaze through the dusty glass; but afterwards he could not have told, from what he saw that day, the view Sykes's office commanded. He could see only Jenny . . . white, exhausted, her face damp with sweat, her hair in a tangle against the pillow, her hand limp in his own. The last time he had seen her in hospital . . . but that was one of the forbidden thoughts, too painful for everyday indulgence. The present was enough, and if he could find the person responsible . . . it might be Roddy . . . Sykes was right, how could he be certain? . . . easy enough to make up your mind to trust someone when your own emotions weren't involved. He turned back to the detective.

"As a friend, I'm grateful, Inspector."

"But you won't act on what I've told you?" As their eyes met, Antony became aware that the other man's attitude had subtly changed, the concerned air seemed to have been overlaid with one almost of calculation. "I might have spared my pains, it seems," said Sykes, heavily. "I didn't realise—"

Antony came back to the desk, and stood looking down at the detective. "You won't believe me, but I've no inside information," he said. "I'd better go," he added, but without making any move to do so.

"Before I start asking you questions which—in the circumstances—you would quite properly refuse to answer," said Sykes, nodding his assent.

"Precisely,"Antony agreed, and this time made for the door without further comment. But his smile as he turned to raise a hand in valediction was only wryly amused.

He spent the remaining time till dinner at the hospital, being ejected at last by a particularly fierce dragon of a sister who told him coldly that "Mrs. Maitland must have *some* rest." He was encouraged to see a glint of amusement in Jenny's eyes as she listened, but when she added her own entreaties he went meekly enough.

Sir Nicholas was sympathetic when he described the encounter. "But I couldn't even get in," he said.

"Well, according to Dr. Prescott, she'll be home by the end of the week. I say, sir, I forgot all about Aunt Carry; she's not very pleased with either of us."

"How did she hear?"

"You told Dorrie, and Dorrie told Liz."

"And Liz told her mother. I dare say we'll survive her displeasure."

All the time they were talking Antony was uneasily conscious that his interview with Inspector Sykes, with the undigested—and possibly indigestible—facts it had revealed, must be laid before his uncle sooner or later. In an effort to delay this, he went upstairs after dinner; but the flat seemed quiet and desolate, and after wandering about disconsolately for a while he picked up a book and went downstairs again. Sir Nicholas was wrestling angrily with yesterday's Ximines. This time, Antony plunged into the matter without preliminaries, saying abruptly:

"I think I ought to tell you sir, that some further evidence has come to light which tends to strengthen the case against Roddy Gaskell."

Sir Nicholas looked up from his puzzle. "What evidence? Have you been in touch with Hargreaves to-day?"

"Sykes told me. Unofficially. He thinks—"

"Answer my question," said Sir Nicholas, softly.

"The poison come from India. Roddy was in Nepal not long ago. Along with the other evidence, it's a big point," he added, as though Sir Nicholas were arguing with him.

"You say Sykes told you." His tone had sharpened now. "What did you say in reply?"

Antony was still on his feet, and had been looking down at his uncle. He turned his eyes now on the book he still held in his hands, and said slowly: "I doubt if you'll like it, sir. I said I should carry on."

Sir Nicholas made no immediate reply. He put down the folded newspaper carefully, and the pencil on top of it; pulled his glasses down towards the tip of his nose and looked at his nephew over the top of them. "You can't have thought I shouldn't be interested," he said mildly.

"No, of course not. I ought to have told you earlier. But I find it rather difficult—"

"There's nothing difficult about it."

"Don't you think so, sir?"

Sir Nicholas said, still in that tone of dangerous quietness, "What exactly is in your mind, Antony?"

"That we ought to return the briefs. But I don't find it an easy decision."

"I should hope not, indeed," said his uncle, primly.

Antony raised his eyes quickly at that; Sir Nicholas met his frowning look with a bland one. "I was sure, sir, you'd think

. . . Sykes told me I couldn't always be right . . . I made sure you'd agree with him about that.''

"I do," said the older man, cordially.

"Well, then! After what happened to Jenny—"

"I think, perhaps, we'd better leave Jenny out of this."

"How c-can I?" Antony, despairing of making an impression, was beginning to lose his temper. "How can you, Uncle N-Nick, for that m-matter?"

"Very simply . . . and that doesn't mean I don't care about what happened," said Sir Nicholas, angry in his turn; and came to his feet with the words. He was as tall as his nephew, fair-haired, a little more heavily built; but as they stood and glared at each other an onlooker might have seen the elusive likeness between them very clearly marked.

Antony was the first to look away. "I'm s-sorry," he said; but the apology was made without conviction.

"Then take your mind back to the problem," Sir Nicholas directed him. "And try to apply a little logic to it . . . if you can. Roddy Gaskell is neither more nor less guilty because of what happened to Jenny."

"N-no, of course. I remember what you s-said the night he was arrested. But, damn it all, Uncle Nick, he might have reason to spare for killing his father, but not the old woman . . . not the old woman."

To his greater annoyance, Sir Nicholas had regained his normal calmness. "You're guessing, Antony," he said.

"B-but this new evidence—"

"Is not conclusive." He paused, and added unfairly, "As I understood it, you made a promise—"

"Yes, I did." He was thinking as he spoke of the night of Roddy's arrest, and of Liz's frantic protests. "If I back out now I may never know, but what if I come to believe he's guilty?"

"Unless he confesses, it will be a belief . . . no more. And you will be just as impartial as you would be with any other client."

"Shall I, sir?" He was turning away as he spoke. Sir Nicholas said, in a flat tone from which all emotion seemed deliberately to have been excluded:

"If I ask it as a favour, Antony, will you go on with this?"

"Why . . . of course!" He whirled round to face his uncle again, but his expression told him nothing.

"And not accuse me again of—er—lack of concern for Jenny?"

"I'm sorry about that, sir." Antony began an apologetic gesture, found the book was still in his hand, and tossed it onto a chair.

"Then let us forget this singularly unprofitable discussion, and turn to other things. May I give you a drink?"

"Thank you, sir."

Sir Nicholas began to cross the room in his leisurely way. "There are one or two things in that confounded crossword puzzle with which you may be able to help me," he said. "At least, if you can't, I shan't be the only one to be kept awake by it."

CHAPTER XII

THE INQUEST on Priscilla Gaskell's death was held and adjourned; and as there seemed no immediate prospect of the police releasing her body for burial, Janet Blake arranged that a Memorial Service should be held on the following Thursday, and prevailed upon her relations to attend by that simple mixture of blackmail and bullying against which only the most strong-minded have any defence.

Gilbert found the idea gruesome, and said so. Edward murmured, "Not in the best of taste, do you think?" and for once Michael Pratten was in agreement with him. Only Dorrie seemed not to care, one way or the other. When they came back from church she escaped from the party as soon as she could; they were assembled in the drawing-room, and there was something indecent about that, with Gran's empty chair, and that awful portrait of the old pirate following you about the room with its eyes. It was not, she told herself carefully, that she had been especially fond of her grandparents; or even of her father. In fact, there could be no denying, her chief emotion was one of gratitude for her freedom. Her father's death had made her financially independent, and now death had also removed the person whose opposition to her scheme to break away from the family would have been most violent. Aunt Janet's protest would turn rapidly to hysteria, and strangely enough she found this much less daunting than her grandmother's overbearing ways had been.

Edward found her in the morning-room about half an hour later, looking out into the square and almost hidden by the long curtains. "Planning some mischief, my sweet?" he enquired.

Dorrie turned her back on the window, and because it was

only Edward she spoke without thinking. "If it weren't for Roddy, I think I'd be almost happy," she said. And added, appalled by her own frankness, "That's a dreadful thing to say, isn't it?"

"Not a bit of it." Edward's tone was cheerful. Her black dress did not suit her, he thought; she looked smaller and paler than ever, with a pinched look about her face that might have been due to the cold. "Come and sit down over here," he invited. "I'm going to light the fire."

She started to protest automatically, before she remembered Gran wasn't there to disapprove of such wicked extravagance. Edward, on his knees on the hearthrug, looked up and grinned at her understandingly. "Mother won't say anything," he promised. And if Dorrie added to herself mutinously, "So long as she knows it's for you," she crossed the room willingly enough and sank into one of the big chairs which flanked the fireplace.

"What were you plotting?" asked Edward again, carefully not looking at her. Instead he kept his eyes on the fire he had lighted, watching as the dry wood kindled and the flames began to leap among the crown of coal.

Dorrie pushed back even further into the depths of her chair; she had always felt at ease with Edward, but suddenly he was a stranger. "Escape," she said, in a small voice; and was not prepared for the force of his reaction.

"Not now," he said, violently. "Not yet!"

"I don't see," said Dorrie, with an assumption of dignity, "what business it is of yours."

Edward scrambled to his feet, perhaps feeling that to look down on her would add authority to what he had to say. "Someone's got to look after you," he said.

"I'm not a child," said Dorrie. "I can take care of myself."

"Yes, of course. But look here, Dorrie . . . what exactly are you thinking of doing?"

"I can't stay here. You know I wanted to go, Edward. Even before—"

"That was different." He saw her shake her head stubbornly, and added with a sort of desperation, "It wouldn't look well, to leave Mother now."

"She doesn't need me, Edward. She's got you."

"That isn't the point."

"If you're going to say, 'what will people think?' " Dorrie interrupted him, "I'm just not interested. I shall go to an hotel," she added.

"All right!" He sounded grim now, and Dorrie moved uneasily in the big chair. "Have you thought what that would be like, my girl, as things are?"

"At least there'll be no one to tell me what I may or may not do."

"They'll nudge each other when they see you," said Edward, ignoring this. " 'That's Roddy Gaskell's sister,' they'll say, 'the one that murdered his father.' And the press will be after you, as soon as they know. 'Why did you leave home, Miss Gaskell? Why—?' "

"At least," said Dorrie, with angry desperation, "you know the answer to that."

"Do I, Dorrie?" Edward was suddenly thin-lipped, withdrawn. She knew she was hurting him, but for the moment she did not care.

"I won't stay with Aunt Janet," she told him, "because of what she's trying to do to Roddy."

"No . . . I see." He stepped back a little as he spoke; no use to try to bridge the gulf while this still lay between them. "She was upset," he said, and heard with surprise that he was echoing one of his mother's more frequent remarks. "She doesn't really think Roddy killed anyone," he added, more positively.

"He's been arrested." Her tone was stubborn still, but he saw that there were tears on her cheeks.

Edward made no move to comfort her. He jammed his hands in his pockets and stood looking down at her sombrely, and after a while he said, "*That* won't help Roddy," in a brittle tone, as though he were losing patience.

"If you mean my leaving home, I don't know why you're so set against it. You've talked often enough about getting away yourself."

"Well, I can't go now," said Edward shortly. "Apart from the trial, I can't leave Mother to face this alone."

Dorrie sniffed, and began to mop her eyes. "If you're calling me a rat—" she said. But there was no conviction in the protest; whatever resolution she had previously achieved seemed to have left her. "All right," she said drearily, "I'll stay here until it's over." But when he tried at last to comfort her she shrugged away his solicitude impatiently. "You've got what you wanted, Edward. Isn't that enough?"

Later still, Michael Pratten found her there alone. It was nearly dark now, and even the light from the fire was dying. "You've had no tea," he said. "Shall I get you some?"

Dorrie shook her head, and tried to speak lightly. "Not exactly 'funeral baked meats,' but I find I don't want anything," she said.

Michael frowned at the flippancy. "You're over-wrought," he told her. "You shouldn't have gone to the service."

"Oh, I think so, Michael. I think I should. Roddy couldn't, so I had to." He missed the hardness in her voice, and thought her protest pathetic.

"You're very brave," he said.

Dorrie thought wearily that she was calm now because all her tears were shed . . . there seemed to be no feeling left, only emptiness. "I was going away," she said, abruptly. "But Edward says I mustn't. I suppose he's right."

"Edward!" said Michael, obviously not liking to be put in a position of having to agree with him. "But this is your home," he added. "Why should you go away?"

"It's Aunt Janet's home, too," Dorrie pointed out. "And she thinks Roddy . . . she's always saying—" She broke off because Michael had come up to her quickly, and bent to take her hands.

"Don't worry," he told her. "She can't really think anything of the kind, I'm sure of that."

Dorrie looked up at him; his hands were warm and comforting, and she was grateful for the sympathy in his eyes. "Then why does she say it?" she asked.

"She's trying to protect Edward . . . of course," he said. And put his arms round her and held her close when he saw the stricken look in her eyes. "As soon as it's over, I'll take you away," he promised.

In the deserted drawing-room, Janet Blake was mechanically straightening chairs and plumping cushions. The last of the funeral guests had gone; she found it easier to think of them like that, less distressing than having to remember that her mother still lay unburied. Mr. Hargreaves had explained to her about the inquest: that the adjournment would most likely be until after the trial was over, in case Roddy was named in the verdict and that very fact prejudiced his chances. "He isn't being tried on *this* charge," the solicitor had said.

It was all very dreadful, and the trial would be an ordeal; in fact, she didn't know how she could go through with it, if she didn't have her sense of duty to sustain her. It was her duty to tell the truth, and not think about the scandal. After all, it was all of a piece with Roddy's behaviour; he'd been nothing but trouble, that boy, ever since she could remember.

Even Gil had gone, though he had lingered long after the rest; she thought he had wanted to tell her something, but then he had left with whatever it was unsaid. But she wasn't thinking of Gil now, just of Dorrie's unsatisfactory conduct; they had deserved better of her, the little group of relatives who had returned to the house, than that she should absent herself almost immediately, and not even return later to make her farewells.

But that is only, thought Janet discontentedly, what I can expect from those two tiresome children. Dorrie had always been the quiet one, and now it seemed she was as ungrateful as her brother. I gave up my own home to look after them, Janet said to herself (not for the first time); and small thanks I've ever had. Not from Mother . . . and what I gave up for her, nobody will ever know. Certainly not from Father (she looked up resentfully at the portrait above the mantel). He had had all the fun that was going and cared for none of his children, not even his daughter. Not even though everybody said he'd be bound to dote on her, she was growing so like her mother. That had been a lie, it wasn't virtue he was looking for in his descendants. Only Roddy, at last, had caught his interest, and after that the old man had spoiled him shamefully.

If Edward had been half so favoured . . . but he'd no idea of ingratiating himself, none at all. It wasn't to be wondered at if his grandfather had tended to overlook him. There had been, of course, that uncomfortable time when old Roderick decided there'd be a place in the firm for his eldest grandson;

with Edward always talking about going abroad that would have been fatal . . . no getting him back once he'd tasted freedom. She'd put a stop to it, naturally, but still it wasn't fair that Edward hadn't been helped in some other way. She'd told him often enough, "You've never had the chances your cousin gets"; but he only laughed at her, or sometimes replied with the sarcasm that was perhaps—now that her parents were dead—the only thing she feared.

She put down the cushion she had been straightening, and looked round her. The room was tidy enough now, except for the ashtrays. The cigarette stubs were the sole reminder of the afternoon's activities. She frowned a little over the ones that were lipstick-stained. Years ago Gilbert had tried to get her to take up smoking . . . good for the nerves, he told her . . . some such rubbish. But if it weren't for her neuralgia, she was always perfectly well; and everyone admitted she had energy to spare. She picked up the first ashtray, and threw its contents on the fire as though she were performing a ritual.

Walking home in an effort to shake off the depression engendered by an afternoon spent in company with his relations, Gilbert Gaskell wondered irritably how on earth Janet had ever got like that. She had bought a new dress for the ceremony, it was true, but it was a shapeless affair, no style about it. She *would* wear lisle stockings, and her flat-heeled shoes could certainly have done with a visit to the repairers, though they'd have been better thrown away altogether. He had to go back a good many years to the time they had been growing up, to remember her as a normal, rather pretty girl; and as he thought about that another memory stabbed him. "Jeannie with the light-brown hair" Ted Blake had called her, laughing and teasing her as he so often did; and Janet had flushed, because his tone made the words a compliment, but then she had seen her father watching her from across the room, and had become instead self-conscious and solemn. She'd always had that streak of sanctimoniousness, but it wasn't till much later when she came back to London after Ted died, that he really noticed the change in her; when she started neglecting her appearance, and going in so determinedly for the helpful activities that must be so trying for the poor souls at the receiving end. Certainly it had annoyed the old pirate; Gilbert disconcerted the passers-by at this point in his reflections by laughing aloud at the thought, his mirth an odd contrast to the funereal clothes he had donned for the occasion. He wasn't very far from home now, but on a sudden impulse took the turning which would bring him to Edward Blake's top-floor flat. As he went up the stairs he hoped he would find his nephew in, all this way for nothing would be tiresome to say the least. But Edward answered his knock with gratifying promptness; and he was alone.

It was a pleasant enough place, though self-contained only in the sense that it was at the top of the house, so no one had occasion to pass through it; Gilbert had seen the gas-stove on the landing, and the bathroom, he knew was shared. The living-room was big enough for it not to matter that you couldn't stand up in some of the corners, but it was too barely furnished for Gilbert's taste.

"Thinking of moving, my boy?" he asked, seating himself cautiously on a modern-looking chair; the thing seemed solid enough, but what was he supposed to do if he wanted to relax? It was no more than a perch, when all was said and done.

Edward had muttered something about sherry, and gone immediately to his bookshelves. He turned as his uncle spoke, and frowned at him. But after a moment he shrugged. "That's fighting talk, Uncle Gil," he said. "I've had so many insinuations from Michael—"

"Never mind him." Gilbert waved aside the information, which he found, indeed, rather uncomfortable. "I came to talk to you about Dorrie," he said.

Edward made a sudden swoop, and produced the sherry from behind the lowest row of books. He looked troubled as he came across the room with it, and he did not answer until he had completed his task and provided his guest with a glass. "I spent some time this afternoon persuading her not to leave home just now," he said.

"Well, you know," said Gilbert apologetically, "it is an awkward situation . . . even if she is your mother."

Edward disentangled this rather obscure remark without too much trouble. "I don't blame Dorrie for being upset," he said. "But it makes it difficult."

"The thing is, she needs someone to look after her, with Roddy away."

"Yes, I know. But it won't help to have her going to an hotel." The glass he was holding went down on the table with a snap; Edward got up again, and began to move restlessly across the room and back. Gilbert eyed the movement with disfavour. "There's nothing I can do," said Edward, "until the trial's over . . . and perhaps not then."

Gilbert thought that over, and then asked: "What do you mean?" with an unfamiliar sharpness in his tone.

Edward was silent for so long that it seemed he was going to ignore the question; but after a while he stopped prowling and said in an abrupt way which was very unlike his usual manner: "If Roddy is found guilty . . . do you think that can happen?"

"I hope not. I hope not, my boy. But everything that's gone on lately has been something that 'couldn't happen to us'," said Gilbert. "And I don't see what the result of the trial really has to do with it."

But Edward didn't seem to be listening. He had come back and picked up his glass, but he didn't sit down, and he didn't look at his uncle. "If Roddy is acquitted I shall ask Dorrie to marry me," he said, in a hard voice. "Otherwise . . . well, Michael seems fond of her."

"I hope you don't mean what you seem to mean," said Gilbert, shocked. "If you do . . . I can only say, I thought better of you."

Edward laughed, and said more naturally (that is, in the rather affected tone that never failed to annoy his uncle): "Didn't you know I was a cad?"

"Well, I don't suppose," said the older man, rising and preparing to leave, "I don't suppose the girl would have you, anyway."

"I don't suppose so, either," said Edward, moving towards the door. He opened it with a flourish. "My apologies, Uncle Gil. I really don't seem to have helped you much with your problem. You'd really do better to refer it to Michael, you know."

CHAPTER XIII

AFTER ALL, it wasn't until Friday that Jenny was allowed to come home from the hospital. Antony, getting in fairly early after a conference with a client he strongly suspected of being several times a bigamist, found her comfortably installed on the sofa, with Liz in attendance. The room was uncomfortably full of flowers, and Liz was obviously taking her responsibilities seriously; managing to convey such an aura of professional severity that he could almost, he complained, hear the rustle of a starched uniform. "And I warn you, Liz, I've had enough of that kind of thing."

Liz gave him a distant smile. "My duty to my patient," she began, and then spoiled the effect by giggling. "It's such heaven to be here," she said; and immediately was serious again. "Mother's so dreadfully cross, just now. I hope you'll let me stay."

"As long as you like," said Jenny. She had a little colour now, but her movements were languid, and her voice still a trifle husky. "I shall need you, Liz," she said, positively.

"Yes, but . . . how long will it be?" asked Liz, going to the heart of the matter. "Until the trial," she explained. Her eyes were fixed on Antony intently; he resisted the impulse to look away, and said as casually as he could:

"Probably about three weeks. Otherwise it would have to be held over to the next session."

"Does . . . does that give you time—?"

Jenny didn't say anything, but she put out a hand and touched his sleeve. He knew well enough what she meant, and curbed his impatience and answered the question gently. "There is always a lot to be done in preparing a case," he said. "But . . . yes . . . time enough." He wished he had

125

been more encouraging when he saw the animation drain out of Liz's face; but he knew at the same time there was no real encouragement he dare give her, even if he weren't so damnably confused himself.

It was Sir Nicholas's simple belief that a patient discharged from hospital was well on the road to recovery. Considering the opinions he had often expressed concerning "expert" witnesses in the field of medicine, Antony found this unreasonable; and unwisely said so when his uncle expressed a desire for his company later that evening.

"You'll do Jenny no good, mooning over her," said Sir Nicholas. "And perhaps you'll be a little bit more capable this evening of calm discussion." This was not altogether fair comment, but Antony took the remark and its implications quietly enough, and accompanied his uncle to the study as soon as dinner was over.

"I've been talking to Mallory," said Sir Nicholas, watching as Antony unplugged the percolator and carried it across to the side-table. Not altogether a startling pronouncement, but he was gratified to see the younger man look uneasily over his shoulder.

"I'm sending Willett to India, sir," he said, rather quickly.

"So I understand." As this brought no immediate comment he went on dryly, "If I am to justify this expenditure to Mallory, I must really have some idea why the trip is to be undertaken. I presume it is not for his health."

"No," said Antony. But his smile was half-hearted. "It's on Roddy Gaskell's account, of course."

"Of course," nodded his uncle.

"Well, I didn't want to send him," said Antony, virtuously. "But Hargreaves . . . well, he isn't exactly helpful."

"You don't need to tell me that; but why India?"

"The poison, sir . . . I've been talking to Doctor Raven."

Sir Nicholas got up and began to feel along the mantelpiece. Antony, putting down his cup, cast a knowing eye at the table which stood by his uncle's chair, deduced it was his cigar-cutter that was missing, and produced the implement from the drawer which also held three spare boxes of Swan Vestas, four Royal Sovereign pencils with broken points, a tangle of rubber bands, and last week's folded *Observer* with Ximines's crossword puzzle now almost completed. Sir Nicholas thanked him absently, sat down again and picked up his box of cigars.

"I have been wondering," he said, "when you proposed to do some work on the Gaskell affair." Antony let this pass, and he added, still placidly, "You're not trying to prove a negative, I imagine; do I gather the doctor has given you—er—some line to follow?"

"In a way. It's all in his report, highly technical, and a good deal more to come, I'm afraid. I don't envy you the medical evidence," he added, not without malice.

"I am sure, my dear boy, it will give me no trouble. After all," his uncle pointed out, "you will have done the spade work."

"Yes, there is that. Well, as a line it's rather tenuous, but what is important in my mind is that the whole family seem to be in the habit of buzzing around the world like snipe—"

"That is a bird with whose habits I am not really familiar," said Sir Nicholas. His cigar was going well now, and he paused to eye it with approval. "But I do remember a very severe-looking stuffed snipe in a museum when I was a boy; and whatever that bird did or did not do in its spare time, I am sure it would have felt 'buzzing' to be both undignified and unnatural."

"Anyway," said Antony, declining to be drawn, "I've got Hargreaves going on that . . . where they've all been, and when, and why. Including Pratten, of course."

"Even so, it is difficult to see why anyone should have brought home so unlikely a souvenir as aconite—"

"That's what makes me think there may be something in what Dr. Raven says. But we've got no choice. We've got to suggest an alternative place of origin."

"And then, at best, we'll have raised a doubt. Not even a reasonable one," said Sir Nicholas sadly.

"No, and there's another thing that's occurred to me, sir, the prosecution . . . who's got it, by the way?"

"Halloran."

"Oh, lord, has he? Well, then, I don't think Halloran is going to let you get away with this substitution theory too easily."

"We've reverted now to the capsules?"

"Yes. Our point is that someone had them ready. Only one was poisoned, you know, but the way they were packed it was bound to be the first one taken."

"What does the chemist say?"

"Well, to begin with, nobody remembers anything."

"That would be altogether too much to expect," commented Sir Nicholas, tartly.

"I mean, usually Mrs. Blake ordered them, but anyone might have done so without their being surprised. And anyone might have called for them . . . Andrew, Roddy, one of the clerks or typists from the firm."

"Are you under the impression that you are being helpful?" asked Sir Nicholas. He spoke coldly, and Antony gave him a questioning look before he went on.

"The next thing's a bit better. When they looked at their records they found that two lots of capsules were supplied within a few days of each other, about three weeks ago."

"Did this cause no comment?"

"They weren't poison, you know, nobody checked up on them. And if they had noticed, they'd just have thought a mistake had been made, and the next order would be a little longer delayed."

"Three weeks," said Sir Nicholas, thoughtfully. "How does that fit in?"

"It means the extra lot was purchased either the Friday before Roddy came to see me, or the Monday after."

"If we argue on those lines," said Sir Nicholas, "we are tying the motive for Andrew's murder directly to the problem of the Velasquez." Antony frowned over this for a moment.

"We have to do it, though, to counter the argument that only Roddy could have inserted the poison. And when we've made our point, the prosecution come back with the fact that the spare bottle was found among Roddy's things," he said, gloomily. "One queer thing, sir, in spite of all their searching, the police haven't been able to find the aconite."

"We're not really proceeding very fast, are we? What was your point about Halloran?"

"Only that he'll say it would be equally to Roddy's advantage to have made his preparations in advance."

"Of course he'll say that. He isn't half-witted."

"He might try to argue that no one would have had them so long prepared."

"He might do, but he won't," asserted Sir Nicholas. "He'll say they were poisoned well ahead of time, and then he'll make the most he can out of the quarrel that afternoon, go on to stress Andrew's cryptic remarks at the dinner table, and say that was what decided Roddy to use what he already had ready. And we'll reply with a flimsy rag of a story about an argument over the firm's policy, and try to make the jury believe the only reason Roddy gave his father the capsules at that precise moment was because Janet reminded him about them." He looked at his nephew accusingly, and asked: "Was there any sealing wax in the house?" in a tone which seemed to expect—perhaps even to hope—that the answer would be unknown.

"There was a half-used stick in Michael Pratten's desk in the study. Red," he added, "the same make the chemists use."

"I thought as much," said Sir Nicholas, with gloomy satisfaction. He deposited an inch of ash carefully. "I can see you're going to make me read the doctor's report myself," he remarked. "But what else did Hargreaves have for us?"

"To begin with, some information regarding Janet Blake's evidence. But you won't like it," he warned.

"Probably not."

"It's damnably circumstantial. The capsules: she ordered them, she asked Roddy to collect them, she didn't see him on Monday evening, but on Tuesday she reminded him about them and saw him hand them to his father; Andrew, who had already been without the wretched things for two days, put the bottle in his pocket; they were together most of the evening—the old lady was with them too—and at eleven o'clock he swallowed one of the capsules, according to custom, with a glass of water the parlourmaid brought."

"Rather a meagre nightcap," said Sir Nicholas, reflectively.

"Yes, sir. The only thing there is any doubt about is the exact time Andrew was taken ill; but it's only a question of whether it was ten minutes, or perhaps fifteen, after he took the capsule."

"To interrupt Janet's story for a moment, what about fingerprints?"

"Only Andrew's on the bottle, sir. He threw the wrapping paper on the fire."

"And the talk at the dinner-table?"

"She's quite clear it was Roddy Andrew meant. Says her mother had told her as much beforehand . . . that Andrew suspected him, I mean. The detail's there for you, but that's what it boils down to."

"You're quite right, said Sir Nicholas. "I don't like it at all."

"The rest is, how Roddy got on with his father; and the things they disagreed about. You know."

"I'm afraid I do."

"As for the rest of the stuff I got from Hargreaves, not much more than gossip, really." Sir Nicholas's exclamation seemed to disparage this offering, and Antony sat up straight and went on with more emphasis. "Not altogether uninteresting, sir. For instance, the policy disagreements were quite genuine."

"I cannot conceive that it was otherwise."

"Old Roderick, of course, was a go-ahead chap . . . yes, I know you know that, Uncle Nick. Andrew was cautious, Roddy just the opposite; you know that, too. What interests me is that Michael Pratten is said to be more progressive than Roddy. You haven't seen him, sir; he doesn't look like that."

"Are you just talking, Antony, or is this leading somewhere?"

"I just thought it was interesting," said Antony, meekly.

Sir Nicholas contemplated the information. "No," he said at length. "Who is Pratten, anyway? What is his background?"

"He's the son of a friend of the Blakes, who was killed—Michael's father, I mean—in an air raid. I don't quite know why the old pirate concerned himself with Michael, but he certainly helped him complete his education . . . he's a year or two younger than Edward Blake, I believe."

"And later he went to Roderick as his secretary. That may explain why he stayed with the Gaskells so long."

"It might explain why he stayed with the old boy, but not why he stayed with Andrew," Antony protested. "Not living at number 34. I don't suppose he liked Andrew, nobody ever did so far as I can make out. And as they were in radical disagreement—"

"From your look of satisfaction I am bound to assume you think you know the answer to that conundrum," said Sir Nicholas, crossly. "Pray do not keep me in suspense."

"Jenny says he's in love with Dorrie," said Antony, his tone suspiciously mild. Sir Nicholas directed at him another of his sharp looks.

"That, I suppose, could provide a reason—"

"Yes, but it also brings him slap into the centre of the stage in the matter of motive," said Antony. "He could have got the idea into his head that she wouldn't like the publicity Andrew intended, and so removed the picture. After that one thing led to another . . . *viola tout!*"

"I don't know which I dislike more," said Sir Nicholas repressively, "your habit of gesticulating like a Frenchman, or the vile colloquialisms which at other times disfigure your conversation."

"I'd say, on the whole, the slang distresses you more," said Antony, unrepentant. "But don't you like my alternative villain, sir?"

"I might get more excited about him if I didn't know you were equally prepared to present hypothetical cases against half a dozen other people."

"Not half a dozen," Antony protested. "Well, there's Gilbert, of course. He might have pinched the painting to keep, but that wouldn't explain how it got into Roddy's safe."

"He could have put it with the charts, intending to get hold of it later—er—when the heat was off," said Sir Nicholas, affably.

"Good lord, Uncle Nick, what have you been reading?"

"Just listening to your conversation, my boy."

"Oh, well . . . I see what you mean."

"I hoped you might," said the older man, blandly.

"And that seems to dispose of Gilbert, doesn't it? The other 'case' is Edward Blake . . . he's a hot favourite, really."

"Why?"

"Financial motive . . . he wanted to live abroad. Now he says he can't anyway, because of his mother. I think he protests too much. And he's in love with Dorrie, too . . . at least, Jenny says so."

"Then I've no doubt she's right. Er—which of these two young men does Dorrie favour?"

"The oracle didn't say."

"In any event, I have never heard that it was a normal part of courtship to murder the father of the lady you admire," said Sir Nicholas.

"No," said Antony; and there might have been a shade of regret in his tone. Sir Nicholas grinned at him in a friendly way.

"If you've no more theories to propound," he suggested, get back to Hargreaves's report."

"You've had it. There's just Jenkinson's evidence (the

clerk at Gaskells', if you remember), and Miss Somers, who was with him when Andrew and Roddy were shouting at each other. I went down to see her myself, because I thought she might be helpful; but we wouldn't dare use her.''

''Why not?''

''She's quite clear and definite about her evidence: she saw nothing and heard nothing out of the way. And succeeds in making it obvious that she's lying; probably—curse her!— with the best of motives.''

''And Jenkinson?''

''Exactly as Michael Pratten reported him. We can shake his interpretation of what he heard, I expect, but not until Halloran has had his fun with it first.''

''Encouraging,'' grunted Sir Nicholas. ''Well, you'd better leave me those reports to look at, and go and make sure Jenny is obeying doctor's orders.''

''I suppose so.'' He got up and stood with his back to the fire, looking down at his uncle. ''I hope it won't drive you mad, having Liz here,'' he said.

''She's a nice enough child,'' said Sir Nicholas, avoiding the question in a cowardly way.

''Yes, but . . . she's so vitally concerned. She's really mad about Roddy. And I don't know about you, sir, but it gives me the jitters,'' Antony admitted.

''If you mean, it brings home the responsibility you have assumed in this matter, I can only say I am glad of it,'' said Sir Nicholas, repressively. A little daunted by this complete reversal of mood, Antony went away to his own quarters. Liz had heated up the bedroom to an impossible degree, in preparation for Jenny retiring; and looked completely scandalised when he suggested diffidently that a little air might not be a bad idea . . . and—perhaps—only *one* bar of the electric fire . . .

The disagreement was only settled when Jenny roused herself to arbitrate. Antony, lying awake later with the cool, damp air blowing on his face, found himself reflecting with something like admiration on the character of his newest client. He was inclined to feel that to commit bigamy—even once—presupposed a fair degree of courage. Though, of course, the chap would keep them apart, he supposed. When he went to sleep he dreamed, confusedly, of Scheherazade.

CHAPTER XIV

"I'M FRIGHTFULLY sorry about Jenny," said Roddy Gaskell, when Antony went to the prison the following week. "You're sure she's all right now?" He was looking as he spoke at a point above his visitor's head, where a dusty shaft of sunlight made a chequered pattern high on the wall.

Antony said, "Quite sure." And then, abruptly: "I shouldn't be here if I thought you responsible, you know."

"No, I suppose not." Roddy was looking unusually subdued this morning, so that Antony added, with sudden irritation:

"It won't help matters if we sit here and commiserate with each other."

"I suppose not." He brought his eyes away at last from the impersonal ray of sunlight, and looked reflectively at his companion. "Do they really think I wanted to kill Gran?" he asked.

"It isn't more unlikely," Antony pointed out, "than that you poisoned your father."

"But the motive! Honestly!" said Roddy. "First I'm supposed to have tried to protect her, and then—"

"That isn't how it will sound. As Uncle Nick tried to point out, they'll build up the motive over the years: lots of little things, until at last it seems a solid structure. Besides, to be honest, it wasn't only concern for her that made you oppose your father's plan; I imagine you were equally anxious about the old pirate's good name."

"That's true enough."

"And granted the first crime . . . well, the rest follows, I'm afraid."

Roddy had a grimace for that. "Hargreaves was here last week," he said. "He made damned depressing company."

"I'd have come myself," said Antony, answering the thought rather than the words, "if I'd been able to. And Uncle Nick has gone to Leeds Assizes."

"Well, now you're here," said Roddy. He sounded resigned, rather than gratified. "I suppose that means more questions."

"A few," Antony admitted. "For one thing—this won't be brought up at the trial, of course, but it might give us a lead—can you help me narrow the list of people with opportunity to poison the anchovy paste?"

"Anybody . . . everybody," said Roddy. He grinned suddenly, savagely, and spread his hands in an extravagant gesture. "Any of my dear family," he repeated. "Take your pick!"

"That," said Antony bluntly, "is just what I'm trying to do. Are the police right when they say the poison could have been added any time within the last fortnight?"

"Cook's the only one could tell you that, I should think. When last Gran had the anchovy paste, I mean. Or Aunt Janet might remember."

"Mrs. Blake is the prosecution's witness."

"Oh, I see," said Roddy, blankly. He waited a moment, and then went on with a show of diffidence: "I think it would be several weeks since she had that kind of sandwich. And none of the rest of the family ever ate them. So I expect it's true I could have put the stuff in before I was arrested . . . if I'd wanted to."

"And who else had the opportunity?"

"Anyone living in the house for a start. Gran liked the servants to go to bed early; that meant we were all of us familiar with the kitchen . . . if anything was wanted in the late evening, you know."

"Would that include your uncle and cousin?"

"Edward certainly. Uncle Gil . . . perhaps."

"I must say," Antony remarked, sourly, "you're being remarkably helpful."

"Well, I can't help that," said Roddy. He gave his companion an uneasy look and added: "I suppose no one has any idea how much of the damned stuff there still is about?"

"No," said Antony.

"Well, of course not! But I can't help thinking . . . have you seen Dorrie?"

"Liz saw her last week." He paused for a question, but as none came he added: "If it comforts you at all, I don't think she's in any danger."

"Why not?" The question came sharply. Antony shrugged, and gestured vaguely, and after a while Roddy went on in a dissatisfied way, "I suppose if she keeps her nose out of things—"

"That wasn't precisely what was in my mind."

"What then?"

"The murderer," Antony reminded him, "has an interest in preserving the theory that you are responsible for what has happened."

"He managed to kill Gran all right, without destroying the illusion."

"Well, at least, there aren't likely to be any further outbreaks . . . not without very good reason."

"I don't want to sound as if I doubt your word," said Roddy, too politely, "but that doesn't comfort me at all."

"Then tell me," said Antony, wrenching the subject round forcibly, "what sort of a job do you think Michael Pratten is making of running the firm?"

If he had wished to distract the prisoner's thoughts, he had obviously chosen the right subject. Roddy said forcefully, "I'm worried to death," and then grinned ruefully. "As far as I can make out," he said, "he's doing all the things I used to tell Dad I wanted to do."

"Well, then."

"It's all very well. I think it's the right policy; the old pirate could have got away with it, all right, and I know Dad was too cautious. But Michael's got the bit between his teeth, and I just don't know where it will end."

"Don't you trust him?"

"Do I?" Roddy stopped to consider this point. "I'd have said it was just his judgment I doubted; but since you ask me . . . how do I know?"

"Has he been abroad lately?"

"To Europe, several times. To Montreal, last spring."

"Not further afield?"

"Not recently. Not since he went to Australia with Grandfather about eighteen months ago. A sort of checking-up process, really."

"The sort of thing your cousin would have enjoyed?"

"Edward? Yes, I expect so." He relaxed as he spoke, and for the first time smiled at his companion with real amusement. "He went to Bombay once, but he took Aunt Janet with him. You know, with the exception of an occasional weekend, the poor chap has never succeeded in getting off on his own."

"A devoted son?" asked Antony, idly.

"Yes, I think so." Roddy seemed to be giving the question more thought than it deserved. "But I think in this case the motive was more financial. He can't afford extended trips, and the old pirate wouldn't finance them unless he took Aunt Janet along."

"Haven't you got that wrong? He *couldn't* afford to travel . . . before your father died."

"Oh, lord, so we're back at that?"

"Isn't it true?"

"True? Yes, it's true enough. But—"

"I wish you'd just answer my questions, Roddy, without trying to draw conclusions from the answers you give me."

"That's all very well. How can I help thinking? There's altogether too much time, and not enough to do with it."

"I suppose so."

"And, anyway," said Roddy, with an air of triumph which he did not seem to realise was illogical, "the same thing applies to Dorrie, and I'm certainly not wondering about her."

"How did that come about?"

"The old pirate left us all some shares in the firm . . . all the grandchildren, that is. But there was a sort of trust during Dad's lifetime; he made the will when we were children, and never realised we'd grown up, I expect. The result was, the capital couldn't be touched, and even the income only with Dad's approval. It didn't matter to me . . . that's true, as it happens. But I don't think Edward's salary amounts to very much; and Dorrie has been itching for a little independence."

"And your uncle and aunt?"

"Uncle Gil? He's always had *some* money; I think he had

a godfather who hadn't any family, something like that. I don't know any details, of course, but it was enough to keep him from having to join the firm . . . he'd have hated that. Anyway, Dad's death wouldn't have made any difference to him . . . any more than it would to Aunt Janet.''

''Has he been abroad?''

''To Italy, quite frequently. To Paris, sometimes. I don't remember anything else.'' He had been talking for some time quite unemotionally, but now he looked up and caught his companion's eye, and banged his hand suddenly down on the table in front of him. ''I'm trying to give you plain answers,'' he said. ''But it's closer than ever now . . . since Gran died. I mean, it must have been one of us.''

There didn't seem to be much to say to that. Antony, passing the questions he wished to ask in quick review, gave the interview another twist. ''When the charts from your safe were at number 34, Roddy—''

''What about them?''

''You took them home on Wednesday, the week before you came to see me?''

''Yes.''

''And took them back on Friday, after he had reminded you about them?''

''That's right.''

''Did he know they had gone back that day?''

''I suppose . . . well, come to think of it, I don't think he did, because he asked me about it again.''

''When was that?'' The question came sharply, but Roddy frowned over his reply, taking his time.

''I don't really remember. Is it important? A good while later . . . no, it couldn't have been so very long, could it? I didn't take much notice.''

''How long before he died?''

''The week-end before . . . perhaps.''

''And then on Tuesday evening he told you all he knew who had taken the picture—''

''Well, you needn't sound so pleased about it,'' protested Roddy. ''As far as I can see, that just sounds as if he thought it was me.''

''Not necessarily. On second thoughts, though, I don't much like the sound of it myself,'' he added, honestly.

"No," agreed Roddy; and rubbed his forehead with the back of his hand.

The bigamous client was intent on giving the authorities a run for their money, and his affairs detained Antony until late that evening. He found his womenfolk having their coffee by the fire, and dined alone on a steak that—thanks to Liz—was just a little too rare, and seasoned by a barrage of questions. He lied his way through the answers sympathetically enough, but was feeling decidedly ruffled by the time he placed his coffee-cup on the mantelpiece and took his favourite position with his back to the fire. "Did you hear from Uncle Nick?" he asked.

"He phoned this morning," Jenny told him. "The case was over, but he didn't know whether he might be detained. So he asked me to remind you to look up any precedents on the Grover business, and to see if you couldn't hurry along Doctor Raven's report."

"He ought to know better," said Antony bitterly. "Whenever I ask him he talks about the difficulties; and when he does tell me anything I only understand one word in five."

"Is that about Roddy's father?" asked Liz.

"It is," said Antony. He glowered at her; and whether this achieved the desired effect of discouraging curiosity, or whether the fact suddenly came to mind, she said with an air of surprised recollection:

"I saw Dorrie to-day."

"Oh," said Antony. He turned to retrieve his coffee-cup, and sipped for a moment before he went on: "What had she to say?"

"Quite a lot," said Liz, and began to retail it, speaking rather quickly, and more loudly than usual. "She said it was awful at home, with Aunt Janet in a state of gloom and penitence; and Michael was hardly ever in, because he was so busy at the office; and when she decided to go to an hotel, Edward persuaded her not to. Uncle Gil took her out to dinner one evening, to cheer her up, and Aunt Janet behaved as if it was an orgy, and practically had hysterics again. She's having a perfectly horrible time," she added, with an air of defiance that seemed to expect contradiction. Jenny murmured sympathetically, Antony concentrated on his coffee, and after a moment Liz added in a quieter tone: "It makes her feel worse, of course, being worried about Roddy." She was making no parade of her own feelings, so that Antony felt suddenly ashamed of his irritation. But a moment later sympathy and contrition were alike forgotten. "I saw Edward too," said Liz.

"To-day? Where did you meet him?"

"I didn't exactly meet him; at least, I was outside his office when he came out, so we went and had a drink." She was speaking with a great air of candour, and Antony grinned at her.

"Out with it, Liz. Why did you ambush him like that?"

"Because of Dorrie. I don't think she ought to stay at number 34."

"Is that Edward's affair? I should have thought her uncle—"

"I talked to Uncle Gil first . . . days ago. But he was being . . . well, I didn't think he was going to tell me what he really thought," said Liz. "And Dorrie said Edward persuaded her not to leave, so I wanted to ask him why."

"I should have thought that was obvious," said Antony, dryly.

"Yes, it would make talk, and Mrs. Blake *is* his mother; but I didn't think of that," said Liz.

Antony passed his empty cup to Jenny, but his eyes were still on his cousin. "He must have found you an embarrassing companion," he remarked.

"I daresay he did," said Liz, with spirit. "And if you think I'm sorry about that . . . I'm not! He wasn't in a nice mood." She paused, and pondered this statement. "He was being enigmatic," she amplified.

Jenny was filling the cup to precisely one-eighth of an inch below the rim: a standard Sir Nicholas insisted on, which had by now become second nature to her. "I expect," she said gently, her eyes on her task, "I expect he didn't like your questions."

"I don't care about that." Liz sounded impatient.

"Obviously not." Antony took back the cup, eyed it blankly for a moment as though he had forgotten its purpose, and then said smoothly: "Are we to be privileged to know his reply?" He was not conscious of the parody of his uncle's manner, but he did expect this to renew Liz's belligerence, which seemed to him desirable. Instead, she gestured helplessly, and said:

"It didn't make sense. He said he was match-making. But I thought he was in love with Dorrie."

Antony found his wife's eyes on his face. "Does it make sense, Jenny?" he asked.

"It might," said Jenny, looking away; and he was horrified to see that her eyes were brimming with tears. He forgot Liz; forgot, for the moment, the Gaskells and their problems. His coffee was spilled as he put the cup down on the tray in a hurry and went on his knees beside her.

"Don't worry, love . . . there's nothing to worry about." She looked at him then, and her hand came up to fumble for the handkerchief in the breast pocket of his jacket; meeting her eyes, his further words of reassurance were never uttered.

It was to this distracted scene that Sir Nicholas, finding his knocking ignored, entered a few moments later. He looked the group over in silence for a while, and finally enquired, in a tone which betrayed only a mild interest: "You must forgive me if I am curious. What is going on?"

Antony said: "Hallo, Uncle Nick," and gave him a look which (the older man said later) contained no evidence of intelligence at all, not even recognition. Jenny blew her nose. Liz said despairingly: "They're talking in riddles, and they won't explain." She seemed near to tears herself, and Sir Nicholas—incorrectly putting this down to distress, not temper—looked alarmed and backed away a little.

Jenny raised her head at last, and said in a voice very unlike her own: "I'm not crying, Uncle Nick."

Encouraged, Sir Nicholas came forward again. "Of course not," he agreed.

"It's just that I was tired," she said; which perhaps was true enough, so far as it went. After waiting a moment in case she wished to amplify this statement Sir Nicholas turned and looked down at Liz.

"Perhaps you will enlighten me, my dear," he suggested.

"I was telling them I'd been talking to Dorrie," said Liz. Antony, still on his knees, twisted his head so that he could look up at his uncle.

"She isn't very happy," he said. "And I don't expect it

helps, that Mrs. Blake is so very sure of Roddy's guilt.'' He looked again at Jenny, seemed satisfied with what he saw, and scrambled to his feet. ''There's nothing we can do, sir.''

''You think not?'' Sir Nicholas's voice was misleadingly gentle. ''About the main cause of her unhappiness I agree we can do nothing immediately, but I see no reason why she should put up with Janet's delusions.''

''There doesn't seem to be anywhere for her to go,'' said Liz. ''I'm angry with Edward, but I do agree . . . she wouldn't like an hotel.''

''Is she a witness?'' demanded Sir Nicholas, ignoring her and continuing to fix his nephew with a commanding eye.

''The prosecution have intimated as much, though I doubt if they'll call her,'' said Antony. ''So she can't come here,'' he added; and didn't altogether keep the satisfaction out of his voice. If he really wanted to set up a harem, there were easier ways of going about it.

''Obviously not.'' Sir Nicholas's tone set the suggestion aside as ridiculous. ''But there's no reason—is there, Liz?— why she shouldn't come and stay with you, if you go home.''

Jenny said, protestingly: ''Uncle Nick!'' And added, when he turned to look at her, ''I promised Liz she could stay. And she's been so good to me.''

''I know that, my dear. We've imposed on her kindness, and now I'm doing so again.'' His tone was formal. Antony, who was becoming unduly sensitive to his cousin's moods, saw Liz tighten her lips as she listened. They all turned and looked at her, and she gave a rather shaky laugh, and said in a small voice:

''It's not just me, you know. I can't think what Mother would say.''

''No,'' said Sir Nicholas, reflectively. He turned his head a little, and his eyes met Antony's; and for the first time since he came in he smiled with real amusement. ''It's an interesting point,'' he said. ''I feel sure, my dear boy, your curiosity will be sufficiently whetted to make you wish to find the answer.''

CHAPTER XV

As WAS TO BE expected, Sir Nicholas got his way. Antony sustaining with comparative fortitude an interview with Aunt Carry, returned with the news that she was prepared—however unwillingly—to co-operate. The invitation was given, and accepted eagerly; and Liz returned home.

"It's really a very good arrangement," said Jenny doubtfully. "But now I'm sorry for Liz." She paused, and seemed to be considering this statement. "Even more sorry," she corrected herself.

"Aunt Carry can't bully her while Dorrie's there," Antony pointed out; though he wouldn't have bet on it himself. He didn't think Jenny seemed particularly convinced about it, either.

He had already discovered that Sir Nicholas had returned from Leeds Assizes in a mood that was far from mellow. When he recounted the gist of his conversation with Roddy he was told roundly that if all he could produce was a series of inferences prejudicial to their client's welfare, he might as well leave the whole thing to Hargreaves and be done with it.

They were talking in chambers, late on Thursday afternoon. It had been a dark day, and with only the desk lamp lighted the big room was shadowy, and Antony had a queer fancy that it was less friendly than usual. He got up restlessly from the chair he had decorously taken in front of the desk, and crossed to the fire and stood looking down at it moodily. Sir Nicholas twisted his chair round to keep him in view. "Well?" he demanded, after a moment.

"I think it's clear what happened about the picture," said Antony. "I think Andrew Gaskell saw somebody in the study during the time the charts were there, and only afterwards put two and two together and started raising hell.''

"Very probably. Are you under the impression you are being helpful?'' asked his uncle, coldly.

''No,'' said Antony, after a moment's consideration; but he didn't stop talking. ''It still leaves Roddy the most likely person to have taken the thing out of the house that way. But I've been looking at Gilbert's proof: he remembered hearing that the charts had been at number 34—he's the only one who seems to have remembered that—and he guessed what had happened. It reads as if he took it for granted Roddy was responsible; but he isn't ill-disposed, so I expect he'll agree anybody could have added the picture to the bundle of charts, if we put it to him the right way.''

''We'll have to have the respective sizes clear. How big is the Velasquez, anyway?''

''Thirty-six inches by twenty-six. Most of the charts were larger, but there were one or two about the same size.'' He was feeling in his pocket as he spoke, for the envelope on which the precise figures were jotted down; but gave the search up as hopeless after a moment and went on: ''Another thing is the dates.''

Sir Nicholas declined to be drawn by the deliberate vagueness of this remark, but waited without comment for it to be amplified. ''The picture was stolen in 1946,'' Antony said eventually. ''But the codicil to old Roderick's will wasn't made until 1950.''

''Is that supposed to prove something?'' enquired his uncle, disagreeably. Antony gestured indecisively. ''Even if he intended to make that 'bequest' to Andrew, right from the day of the theft, it's quite likely he wouldn't do it straight away.''

''Procrastination is the thief of time,'' Antony agreed, and paused to admire the phrase, as though he had himself invented it. ''But the thing is,'' he added, ''the place behind the panel was constructed that same year.''

''1950?''

''Yes. That makes a difference, doesn't it?''

''You're still harping on this idea that Roderick wasn't the thief. His whole family have accepted the fact, I don't see why you should boggle at it.''

''No, but . . . I think I'll go up to Liverpool,'' said Antony, stubbornly. "The curator of the gallery will be giving evidence about the old pirate's offer to buy the Velasquez, but there's no reason why I shouldn't talk to some of the attendants there."

"No reason at all, if you're determined to waste your time," said Sir Nicholas. "Do you really think it will help Roddy Gaskell?"

"I don't know. I just want to find out." As he spoke, he thought about his recent interview with Roddy, and added with an air of inconsequence, "He was worried about Dorrie. He should feel better, now she's with Liz."

Sir Nicholas had picked up a pencil now, and was scribbling on a blotter. He said, without looking up: "And you have been telling yourself, no doubt, that if Roddy is guilty of the other things that have been done, this air of concern would be a good camouflage—"

"Well, wouldn't it?"

"You would have liked the client whose affairs took me north," remarked Sir Nicholas. "I have seldom met a more muleheaded fellow; I am sure you would have found yourself in complete sympathy with him."

"*Merci du compliment,*" remarked Antony, bitterly.

"Once he got an idea into his head—" Sir Nicholas broke off to put on his glasses, the better to admire the sketch that was forming on the fresh green expanse of the blotter. (Later, old Mr. Mallory would mutter to himself about extravagant ways, and tell one of the junior clerks to have it changed.)

"Meaning, sir . . . you're satisfied of Roddy's innocence?"

Sir Nicholas raised his head, and met his nephew's eyes with a challenging look. "Quite satisfied," he said, deliberately; and started industriously to obliterate his sketch with a rapidly-blunting pencil.

The talk with his uncle left Antony uneasy, and his visit to Liverpool did nothing to put him in a more comfortable frame of mind. A case where every conceivable witness was already being called for the prosecution left little scope for what an anxious solicitor had once referred to as his "special talents." He would have liked some further talk with Edward Blake and Michael Pratten, in both of whom he felt more than a passing interest. The Crown must consider Andrew Gaskell's statement at dinner on the night of his death to be of considerable importance; there didn't seem to be any other reason—except, perhaps, sheer perversity—for summoning these witnesses.

He was resigned to the fact that Sir Nicholas would be sarcastic over his failure to turn up something at the Stonehill Gallery, but he would have liked some small, favourable piece of evidence to produce on his return. As it was, there was nothing to be learned, even when he pursued two former attendants into retirement; though he established to his own satisfaction that old Roderick, at least, hadn't been in the habit of hanging around the place. He had called once to see the Curator, and that was well remembered because the offer he had made for the Velasquez had leaked out; and his picture had appeared often enough in the papers since then to keep his memory clear. He had no luck with the other photographs he took with him, and hadn't expected any after so long. Apart from anything else, Edward and Michael—in their late teens at the time of the robbery—must look very different now.

His researches took him three days, and he went south again with an uncomfortable feeling that if—by any coincidence—a new theft should take place within the near future, he would find himself figuring in the rôle of chief suspect.

He got home to find that Jenny had been making new cushions for the living-room; a sort of declaration of independence, he suspected, on her release from the doctor's care. She was pale still, and though she was determinedly energetic he didn't think it came naturally. But there was nothing to be done about that, she wouldn't take kindly to being coddled.

To his dismay, Aunt Carry made one of her more majestic descents on them that evening, and when she had taken a good look at Jenny said in her sharpest tone: "You ought to get away, child; a change would do you a world of good."

"We'll be going into the country for the Easter recess," said Jenny. "It's not long to wait, and the weather may be better by then." She did not add: "and the trial will be over"; she did not need to, the fact was in all their minds.

"Well!" said Aunt Carry. She did not sound satisfied, but there was some measure of resignation in her tone. "I know better than to argue when you've made up your mind," she added inaccurately; with a glance at Antony to show what she really meant.

"Yes, of course," Jenny murmured meaninglessly; and smiled at her. Mrs. Watson did not exactly relax, but her manner was perhaps a little less austere when she went on.

"I have just come from number 34," she announced. "I wanted to talk to Janet Blake."

"I think I should point out," said Antony, "that when you've heard what she has to say, you've only heard one side of the story."

Aunt Carry looked at him unamiably, but did not attempt to deny that he had read her thought correctly. "I find what she told me very disturbing," she remarked. "And she seems very sure of her facts." But when she went on there was a note in her voice that might almost have been thought to be one of appeal. "She knows him better than anyone," she said.

"Do you think so?" He knew she was worried and unhappy, and tried desperately to think of some way to avoid the argument which seemed to loom inevitably ahead of them. But before he could speak again Caroline Watson said quickly:

"Don't dare tell me Liz knows him. I know she's infatuated, but—"

"It's more than that, Aunt Carry," said Jenny. "I think you knew that when you let Antony persuade you—" She broke off there, with a helpless gesture, as though she could find nothing to add. Antony held his breath, expecting an explosion; but Mrs. Watson, after eyeing her niece stonily for a moment said only:

"When he foisted Dorrie Gaskell on to me, you mean. Well, I don't blame the child for finding Janet depressing company. All she can talk about is retribution, which in the circumstances is hardly helpful."

"Did you see Michael Pratten while you were there?"

"Let me tell you, Antony, I did not need to go to number 34 to see Michael . . . or Edward Blake, for that matter. They have both been continually on the doorstep, ever since Liz brought Dorrie home with her."

"Er—simultaneously?"

"Quite often." She frowned at him, as though daring him to find any humour in the situation. "They are not," she added, "exactly on friendly terms. And when Gil arrives it does nothing to mend matters. He watches Dorrie like a hawk; is barely civil to Michael; and ignores Edward altogether.''

It occurred to Antony that for someone who disapproved of the Gaskell family, Aunt Carry was getting unusually involved in their affairs. He found himself feeling sorry for her, adopted a jocular tone to hide what he felt sure would be an unpopular emotion, and got well snubbed for his pains. After that his uncle's comments on the Liverpool trip were almost in the nature of light relief.

The pace grew more hectic after that, with the pile of papers from Mr. Hargreaves's office growing to formidable proportions. Nothing had been heard from Willett, beyond a series of negative reports; in fact, said Sir Nicholas, everything was negative. Counsel's temper was never at its best on these occasions, and this time Antony felt there would have been something to be said for keeping him behind bars. In fact, he took Jenny to the zoo on Sunday morning for the express purpose of pointing out the resemblance between a particularly magnificent specimen in the lion house and Uncle Nick working on a brief. Jenny fell in with his mood with apparent content; but inwardly she shared his uneasiness.

Doctor Raven's contribution was so far delayed that it was the night before the trail opened when Antony joined his uncle in the study at Kempenfeldt Square and handed him the report.

"The mountain laboured and brought forth a mouse,'' he remarked bitterly.

Sir Nicholas was turning the pages, and did not look up immediately. "I can use the mouse, Antony,'' he said at last, mildly.

"Yes, but . . . it's all we've got, Uncle Nick. I know it means we can cast doubt on the exact . . . on where the poison came from—''

"The word you are seeking is 'provenance','' Sir Nicholas suggested helpfully. Antony disregarded the interruption.

"But it doesn't prove anything,'' he protested, as though his uncle was trying to argue the point. "And you know what juries feel about expert witnesses.''

"I know what I feel about them myself, only too often,'' said Sir Nicholas grimly. "There's been nothing from Willett, I suppose?'' he added. The casual air with which he put the question did not deceive Antony for an instant.

"Nothing," he said, "and even if there were—"

"We cannot avoid the decision any longer. We'll have to call Roddy in his own defence, but I wish to heaven it wasn't necessary."

"He'll be the worst of witnesses," Antony agreed. "But we've got to have his story, sir."

"And can you suggest what I am to do with the mangled remains, after Halloran has finished with it?" asked Sir Nicholas.

"It may not be as bad as that. You've taken him through it often enough—"

"I appreciate your concern for my flagging spirits," said Sir Nicholas, awfully. "Even if I find it a trifle impertinent."

He could play it how he liked from there, but he had a feeling that to quarrel with his uncle at this point would be a serious matter. Instead of the quick retort that was his first impulse he said, pacifically, "I'm sorry," and perhaps Sir Nicholas had been thinking along the same lines for he went on, with a complete change of tone, but speaking as though each word were difficult:

"I think I was less than fair to you, Antony, when I asked you to continue with this case."

"Why sir? I was content to do so, or I shouldn't have agreed—" If he was thinking, as he spoke, that he had a pretty fair idea what was in Sir Nicholas's mind, he gave no sign of it. He thought that Counsel so disliked the idea of his client's guilt, that he had persuaded himself it was certain. He also thought this would be better to remain unspoken between them.

"You agreed at my insistence," Sir Nicholas went on.

"Yes, but now I think you were right. I believe Roddy is innocent."

"Because of this?" Sir Nicholas put out a hand to touch the doctor's report.

"That, and other things."

"Do you think it's proof?" his uncle growled back at him. "Try it on the jury and see!"

"No, I don't think we can prove anything. But that doesn't make any difference to what I believe."

"I appreciate your kindness, Antony. But I'd rather you didn't lie to me."

In view of the deception and subterfuge in which his uncle had been indulging, Antony felt this to be grossly unfair, and nearly went back on his good resolutions by saying so. "As a matter of fact, I'm telling you the truth," he said at last. Sir Nicholas leaned forward and raised one hand in the courtroom gesture in which he demanded the attention of his witness.

"Then tell me this: if you're so sure of Roddy's innocence, are you equally sure you were wise to decide not to ask for Liz's evidence."

"As a matter of fact, sir . . . yes, I am sure."

Sir Nicholas sat back again. "I don't understand you," he complained.

"I can give you chapter and verse, if you like." But he made the offer without enthusiasm; he would be guessing, which would serve no purpose, he thought, but further to exasperate his uncle.

"I should be better employed, I expect, in seeing what Doctor Raven has to say." He picked up the report and eyed it with distaste. "Why can't these fellows write plain English, I wonder?"

Antony took the hint and got up to go. He was feeling tired and depressed, and the more so because he was used to plain speech from Sir Nicholas and disliked the verbal fencing they seemed always to be indulging in nowadays. Half-way to the door he paused, and turned back again; the question was uttered without forethought, and as soon as he had put it he was furious with himself for having done so.

"Do you think we've any chance of securing an acquittal, Uncle Nick?"

The query remained unanswered for so long that the silence between them began to assume a stifling quality. Sir Nicholas said at last, unemotionally: "Since you ask me, no chance at all." He looked down again at the closely-typed sheets of the doctor's report, and Antony turned on his heel and went out without another word.

CHAPTER XVI

THE WEEKS that had passed since the murder had not left winter completely behind, but the first blossom had appeared, and the bushes in the centre of the square showed already a glimmer of green. Coming in out of the sunshine, the courtroom seemed both cold and airless. Antony, a little too casual, stopped to greet an acquaintance in the doorway, and found Bruce Halloran at his elbow as he turned away.

Counsel for the Prosecution was a big man, dark and heavily-built, and Antony held him in considerable respect. It wasn't by any means their first encounter as opponents; and he had also acted as his junior in a number of cases where Halloran had been appearing for the defence. Now his greeting was jovial, and Antony—still in the grip of his depression—braced himself to reply in kind.

"Ready for the fray?" said Halloran. When you were used to his voice booming through the courtroom it gave his ordinary utterances an effect of secrecy, as though he had lowered his voice to impart some confidence instead of just to avoid breaking your eardrum.

"Quite ready, thank you," said Antony sedately. Halloran grinned understandingly. He'd a pretty good idea of the strength of his case, and it was difficult to believe that Maitland had anything up his sleeve this time. He looked across the room to where Sir Nicholas, already in his place, was conferring with an agitated-looking solicitor. "Harding's chosen a pleasantly dramatic affair for his last case, hasn't he?" he remarked. "He always had an eye for a sensation."

It was perhaps as well that he started to move across the court as he finished speaking. He missed altogether Antony's look of stupefaction, and heard only the rather reserved note in his voice as he echoed: "His *last* case?" Halloran looked over his shoulder and smiled at him.

"No need to be cagey with me," he asserted. "There've been rumours, you know."

Antony found himself in his own place with an imposing-looking document in his hand and no clear idea how he had got there. An agitated growling from the solicitors' bench told him that Mr. Hargreaves had still something to impart to Counsel; it never even occurred to him that he ought to be listening himself. He turned the document the right way up and assumed a look of eager interest.

His first thought had taken him back to the evening Jenny made punch, and her anxious questions about Uncle Nick. He might be ill, she had said; and if that were so, perhaps he was retiring and Halloran had got wind of it . . . after all, he was a close friend. But he couldn't really believe he wouldn't have been the first to hear of the decision, once there was anything definite. If it came to that, he couldn't really believe Uncle Nick was ill; but in spite of his doubts, the idea remained at the back of his mind as a rather sickening possibility.

But the only other thing he could think of was sheer melodrama. Sir Nicholas had taken this matter to heart, no question about that. It wasn't the first time Antony had seen him angered by man's inhumanity to man; and the fact that he had known and disliked Andrew Gaskell had only engaged his sympathies further on the side of the dead man's son. Perhaps he'd made a vow never to accept another brief if the verdict went against them! He told himself angrily that the idea was absurd; but he couldn't think of anything else, and he couldn't quite get it out of his head.

One thing was certain, he couldn't ask him. Their very intimacy made that impossible. If you were close to someone for twenty-five years, with a bond between you of both affection and gratitude, you couldn't ask for their confidence if they wished to withhold it. But the last phrase stung; whatever it was, Halloran had heard rumours . . . but Uncle Nick hadn't said a word to him.

In his preoccupation he had not noticed the excited buzz of talk that filled the court until the usher called for silence and the judge appeared. Mr. Justice Carruthers was a small man with a sad, intelligent face; caricatures of him showed an unmistakable likeness to a bloodhound. Antony thought well of his impartiality, and felt they were lucky to have got him; at least, he had thought that . . . before his mind got into such a turmoil. He pulled himself together, and tried to force himself to concentrate on what was happening. But the preliminaries were always tedious, and too often he found himself back with this new and unforeseen problem. He told himself it would wait . . . and Roddy Gaskell's affairs wouldn't.

Roddy was looking pale but buoyant, and his voice was firm when he came to plead. Antony, far from reassured, reflected that he was creating exactly the wrong impression. His temperament was particularly unsuited to prison life . . . and that was a stupid thought, for who but a vegetable would be resigned to it? All the same, it was obvious that the trial came as a welcome relief from tedium, and the impression that he was enjoying himself was unavoidable, though perhaps not altogether just.

Halloran was on his feet now. Antony realised, with a start, that he had missed the first part of his speech. Well, after all, he knew the main points to be made, and knew Counsel too well to hope that they would win any tricks through the prosecution's inefficiency. But it was quite inexcusable and selfish, he told himself, and set himself to listen.

"When you have heard the evidence," Halloran was saying, "you will perhaps think the causes of disagreement were not so very great; that the prisoner, who had been brought up in the enjoyment of every luxury, did not really have much to complain about. But the fact remains that these disagreements did exist, and in one notable matter had reached serious proportions on the day Andrew Gaskell died by poison. We shall show you in detail, step by step . . ."

Sir Nicholas was listening with an amused and appreciative smile, as relaxed as if he were at his own fireside. Horton, the junior counsel for the prosecution, was writing steadily . . . some new thought had struck him, perhaps, as he listened to his leader. The judge had a melancholy look, and his eyes were half shut so that you might easily have thought him asleep . . . if you hadn't been quite sure he wasn't. Hargreaves leaned forward again to mutter something; Antony twitched an impatient shoulder, and after a moment the solicitor subsided with a dissatisfied grunt. Roddy was listening to all this quietly enough, but even in repose his personality was a forceful one . . . and what was Carruthers going to make of that? As for the twelve good men and true (two of them were women), they were listening with every variety of expression from alert intelligence to apathy; that dyspeptic-looking chap at the end of the front row had something on his mind, obviously, and it wasn't Halloran's speech.

It wasn't until the medical evidence was reached that Sir Nicholas made a move, and by that time most of the spectators—and the jury, too—were pretty well rigid with boredom. First there was the doctor the Gaskells had called in; then the police doctor and finally a sort of Lord High Pathologist who spoke briskly of ventricular fibrillation, and preliminary tests involving syrupy phosphoric acid and sodium molybdate solution, sparing them nothing of detail. By the time he had roamed from the colourless rhombs of pseudaconitine to the button-shaped masses of bikhaconitine, with passing references to methoxyl groups and the veratroyl radical, even the judge was showing signs of restlessness. And the confirmation he cited from the work of such authorities as Wright and Luff, Freund and Niederhofheim, or even Dunstan and Andrews, did very little to reclaim the court's interest. In the interests of clarity, Halloran had some questions to ask, and then Sir Nicholas rose to cross-examine.

"I want to be quite sure I have this clear, so you will forgive me if I seem to be repeating my friend's questions to you." Antony found the phrase going through his mind, "Will those in favour please signify their assent—"; but Mr. Webber must have done so, for Sir Nicholas was continuing smoothly. "You have reached the conclusion that Andrew Gaskell was poisoned by pseudaconitine: in other words that the poison was derived from *aconitum ferox*. I am using the more familiar term; *deinorrhizum* lends itself less readily to the tongue."

Again the witness nodded. "That is my conclusion," he agreed.

"And I am right in thinking that *aconitum ferox* is known to be obtainable from 'Nepaul Aconite Roots'?" Sir Nicholas went on. "My authority uses the old spelling 'n e p a u l', but I take it that there is no doubt Nepal is meant."

"I should say, no doubt at all." Halloran and his junior exchanged bewildered glances. It did no harm to have the matter stressed, of course, but they couldn't see why the defence should be willing to oblige them in this way.

"But there are other aconite plants," said Sir Nicholas. "Our own monkshood, for instance." He stopped invitingly.

'A less deadly form," the witness admitted.

"Ah, yes. We are dealing, are we not, with 'the most deadly poison known'? There is then no room for mistake with such lesser evils as—for instance—the alpine wolfsbane—?"

"Such a mistake would be impossible," said Webber, positively.

"But there is one possibility I should like to put to you." Sir Nicholas stooped, and picked up a stout book which bristled like a porcupine with paper markers. He seemed to have no difficulty in selecting the one he wanted, but though he opened the book he did not immediately refer to it. "Would you not agree that *aconitum luridum* is equally deadly?"

"So I am informed."

"Its origin is said to be the Himalayas," Sir Nicholas told him. "Not a very precise location." He looked down at the book which was open in his hands. "But is it not true that aconite roots marketed in India are often from mixed species, so that botanical verification is desirable if it is necessary to be accurate about their place of origin."

"I would not question your authority, Sir Nicholas," said the witness with a faint smile.

"Then you will not question, either, that the use of aconite as the basis for a liniment is not unknown."

"It is very little used to-day. I would not myself recommend it."

"But if you were told that such a liniment had been prescribed, what would your diagnosis of the patient's ailment be?"

"Rheumatism, most likely. Rheumatism, or perhaps neuralgia." Suddenly he became voluble. "An ointment or liniment was not infrequently used in the past, but the danger if the skin is broken cannot be overlooked.''

''Still, you would not be altogether surprised to hear it had been prescribed in such a case; perhaps by some practitioner whose ideas were less up-to-date than your own?''

''No,'' said the witness, doubtfully. ''But I must remind you, Sir Nicholas, that my tests established definitely the use of the Indian aconite root.''

''There are doctors in India, are there not? But what I am wondering is whether these tests of yours definitely pointed to the Nepaul root, rather than the equally deadly *aconitum luridum?''*

''I have already given evidence on that point,'' said the witness, a little stiffly.

''I did not hear you mention, for instance, that you had made use of infra-red analysis.''

''No.''

''But where the precise geographical origin is in doubt, surely it would have been desirable to do so?''

''My instructions did not represent to me that this point was of any significance.''

''Did they not? You know the process, of course.''

''By repute.''

''And would consider it reliable?''

''If properly conducted. But it is expensive, elaborate and time-consuming,'' said the witness, with another of his bursts of volubility, ''and in the circumstances it was not felt necessary—''

''I see . . . in the circumstances,'' Sir Nicholas repeated, with some evidence of satisfaction. ''Thank you, Mr. Webber.'' He sat down, and glanced enquiringly at his nephew. But Antony was watching Bruce Halloran, who rose to re-examine.

''A small matter only. If the precise location from which the aconite root was obtained were indeed in doubt, would you say this proved positively that it could *not* have been obtained in Nepal.''

''No, I don't think so,'' said the witness, who seemed—not unnaturally—to be becoming confused.

''My learned friend mentioned to you the likelihood of aconite roots marketed in India being of mixed species. That would work both ways, would it not? I mean that a person in Nepal—"

"M'lud," said Sir Nicholas, sepulchrally.

"Surely," said Halloran, in a plaintive tone, "there can be no objection to my attempting to clarify—"

"If you can clarify the matter, Mr. Halloran, you will have earned my gratitude," said the judge, a little tartly.

"I was asking you, Mr. Webber, whether a person acquiring aconite in Nepal might not possibly be given the 'mixed species' to which reference has been made?"

"Yes, certainly," said the witness, with obvious relief.

Halloran sat down. Sir Nicholas muttered, "I told you so!" for his nephew's ear. Antony thought, "Honours even,"and drew a circle on his pad around the word "circumstances."

But it was late afternoon before they could return to the question: when the lawyers were beginning to wonder whether his lordship meant to sit all night, and the jury (temporarily lost to all sense of duty) were allowing their thoughts to wander to a "nice cup of tea" or a "quick one" according to their nature. Inspector Sykes had had a long spell in the witness box, and Sir Nicholas had been questioning him exhaustively about the discovery of the Velasquez in the office safe. The court had earlier had a good opportunity of seeing the picture, and there was something to be said, Antony thought, for Gilbert Gaskell's opinion of it; now the charts had been brought in, and experiments made in bundling them all together. When you knew it was there, the lighter canvas of the picture was obvious enough; you couldn't say more than that it could have been overlooked, especially by someone in a hurry.

"There is just one more thing, Inspector," said Sir Nicholas. "I should like you to hear a portion of Mr. Webber's evidence. Concerning infra-red analysis," he explained.

Question and answer were read over. "Am I right in thinking, Inspector, that when the witness used the phrase 'in the circumstances' "—Counsel paused impressively—"what he really meant was: 'because the prisoner, Roderick Gaskell, was known to have been in Nepal some months ago, *it was taken for granted* the poison was obtained there'?"

"My friend cannot expect the witness to answer a question of that nature," said Halloran, rightly outraged. But Sir

Nicholas did not want an answer; he was quite content to sit down again and wait for Halloran to talk himself out, and for Mr. Justice Carruthers—at last—to adjourn the court.

"So that's that," said Antony to his uncle later that evening. "Now for the second part of the programme."

"I am not altogether happy," said Sir Nicholas. He seemed to have shed his uncertainty now that the trial had started, and in spite of the doubt he voiced he sounded much more confident than he had been the previous day. "It will need very careful handling, and in the absence of any further news from Willett—"

"We may still hear from him," said Antony. "He'd an awful lot of ground to cover, you know. Pratten's ports of call when he was on his way to Australia with old Roderick; and all the places Mrs. Blake and Edward visited."

"And even if we could prove the poison was prescribed, quite innocently, for Janet Blake's neuralgia, we'd still not be so very much better off," said Sir Nicholas, declining to be cheered.

"I know that, but it's all we can do." Antony was prowling restlessly about the study, and Sir Nicholas eyed him consideringly for a while before he spoke again.

"What's wrong?" he demanded.

"Nothing . . . everything," said Antony. In contrast to his uncle, he had worried himself into a state of uncertainty in which he would have jibbed at giving a positive answer if asked his own name. "Did you know Dorrie and Liz were there to-day?" he asked, changing the subject.

"I might have guessed it, I suppose."

"Aunt Carry must be losing her grip. Well, at least it means Halloran isn't calling Dorrie, and that's something to be thankful for. I mean," he added pessimistically, "if they find Roddy guilty she won't have to wonder if it was partly her evidence—"

Sir Nicholas picked up his *Observer* in a marked manner, and began to look about him for a sharpened pencil.

The next day started with the chemist, and the analyst who had examined the remaining capsules and found them harmless. After that they went on to the office staff, and evidence of the quarrel on Tuesday afternoon; which sounded just as bad as Antony had expected. Gilbert Gaskell told the court unwillingly about being called in by his brother to identify the picture found behind the panel, and Sir Nicholas took the opportunity of asking him about Roddy's reception of the news of his father's illness. "He seemed shocked," said Gilbert. "Shocked and horrified." But who was going to believe he wasn't a biased witness?

The curator of the Stonehill Gallery spoke of old Roderick's offer for the Velasquez, and a member of the Liverpool Police gave some rather negative details about the robbery. Michael Pratten was called at this point; for some reason the defence had been expecting his evidence to be called later than this. His job was to testify to Andrew's remarks at dinner the day of his death, and while this was being done Antony wrote, "Shall I?" on his pad, and received in reply a decided, "No!" So he had only three questions for the witness by way of cross-examination.

"Was anything said by Andrew Gaskell on that occasion to point positively—without any doubt at all—to some particular person?"

"No."

"As a colleague of the accused you can no doubt tell us whether he led a secluded existence during the two days he had the capsules in his possession . . . the Monday and Tuesday immediately preceding Andrew Gaskell's death?"

"Secluded? Well, hardly."

"In fact, you would expect him to have been in contact with a good many people during that period?"

"Yes, I would."

Edward Blake was called next; obviously Aunt Janet was to be reserved for a Grand Finale. Sir Nicholas's expression was as inscrutable as ever, but Antony was under no illusion at all as to his dissatisfaction with the arrangement. But he had barely got past the first formalities when the court adjourned. "Saved by the bell!" said Antony. "Do you think Carruthers has a date?"

It was as well for their plans that matters had fallen out in this way. The newspapers were enjoying themselves, and if any rag of the Pirate King's reputation remained after the first day of the trial, it was destroyed that evening. Any out-of-

the-way cross-examination of a witness would certainly have
been reported . . .

Blake's evidence was pretty well a repetition of what Michael Pratten had told the court. He was looking very much
at ease when Antony got up and said, after the briefest pause:

"Have you ever been to India, Mr. Blake?"

The witness's answer was lost in the vehemence of Halloran's objection. Mr. Justice Carruthers looked interested, and
momentarily wide awake. "Is there any relevance, Mr.
Maitland?"

"Oh, yes, my lord."

Carruthers had a private smile for Counsel's innocent look.
So he didn't want to have to explain himself? Well, that was
natural enough. All the same, "I think you should tell us
something of your purpose," he suggested.

"To attempt to show an alternative source of supply of the
aconite, my lord." The judge looked at him, frowning.
"Perhaps I should say, 'a reasonable and innocent source'."

"A laudable ambition, Mr. Maitland. You may proceed."

"Thank you, my lord." (If it isn't too late. What a time to
ask for explanations). "I asked you, Mr. Blake—"

"I was in India once, four years ago," said Edward,
coolly. If the question at first had taken him aback he now
gave no sign that he was worried by it. If anything, he looked
amused.

"Did you make an extended stay?"

"I was in Bombay for about a week, and travelling in the
vicinity for another ten days."

"A business trip, Mr. Blake?"

Edward smiled. "Perhaps I should say, not entirely without purpose." Antony looked at him without saying anything, and after a moment he added: "My grandfather made
the arrangements; I had a number of commissions to execute
for him."

"Did you go alone?"

"My mother accompanied me."

"And while you were there, were you in good health?"

"Certainly."

"No reason to consult a doctor?"

"None."

"Was Mrs. Blake's health equally good?"

"So far as my memory goes. I am quite sure, at least, that she did not visit a doctor while we were ashore."

"I see." (Press the matter? Leave it there? But he couldn't press it at this stage without Halloran demanding a showdown). "Now, Mr. Blake, did you see your cousin, Roderick Gaskell, on Monday, the 8th March?"

"Yes. He called on me that evening."

"You had spoken to him earlier in the day, I believe."

"I had."

"Will you tell us the reason for the conversation?"

"Primarily, to arrange for the evening visit." For some reason, these questions troubled Edward, as the others had not done.

"Primarily, Mr. Blake?"

"I also reminded him to collect a package from the chemist."

"You knew what the package contained."

"Yes, I did. My mother told me when she telephoned that it was my uncle's—Mr. Andrew Gaskell's—tonic."

"And you knew—of course—that Roderick Gaskell had it in his possession when he called on you that evening?"

"I didn't really think about it." He added, reluctantly: "I suppose I could have known; I mean, he hadn't been home."

"How long did his visit last?"

"About an hour."

"Thank you, Mr. Blake. I appreciate your frankness." He got the impression that this abrupt breaking-off of the interrogation worried the witness even more than what had gone before.

Janet Blake's evidence on direct examination took most of what remained of the morning, and it had to be admitted that Halloran's instinct was right in keeping her to close his case. Antony took what comfort he could from the fact that she was unexpectedly calm; the cooler she was the more they could press her, and—even at the risk of hysteria—what she had to say could not possibly be allowed to go unchallenged. He no longer dared look at Roddy Gaskell, having an altogether too vivid appreciation of what his feelings must be. Mrs. Blake's evidence went on in a dreary monotone . . . the discovery of the picture . . . Andrew's decision . . . Roddy's objection to his father's plan . . . the whole edifying story of the relationship between the two men . . . Andrew's remarks at dinner . . . the events of that evening . . . the capsules. If only she would show some sign of malice there might be a hope of the jury discounting what she said. This saintly more-in-sorrow-than-in-anger attitude was obviously having its effect.

There wasn't much left of the morning by the time Halloran finished. Sir Nicholas had been keeping a close eye on his watch, and drawing a pair of scales—with a stout duck in each—on the back of his brief. Antony wasn't particularly surprised when he plunged, almost without preamble into the matter which most interested them; obviously, it should be put forward before Edward told her . . .

"Have you ever been in India, Mrs. Blake?"

She had none of her son's lightness of touch. She stood silent for a moment, frowning at him, weighing the import of the question. "Yes, I have," she said, at last. "Five or six years ago, I should think."

"Do you remember if you had occasion to consult a doctor during the time you spent there?"

"No. I mean, I was quite well."

"Have you ever had neuralgia, Mrs. Blake?"

"Frequently. All my life."

"Then perhaps one particular attack out of so many might have slipped your mind."

"If you mean, could I have forgotten seeking medical treatment among a lot of foreigners . . . the answer is, I could not." She was speaking in a forthright way that reminded Antony of old Mrs. Gaskell; and just for a moment he had a vivid picture of Priscilla, enthroned beneath her husband's portrait, saying sharply, "Don't be a fool, Nicholas," on the afternoon they first became involved in the problem of the Velasquez. He wondered whether his uncle thought of it, too, but didn't think of asking him.

After lunch the cross-examination went on, but there wasn't really much to be done, even with the more uncomfortable parts of her evidence. If she had been indulging in blatant exaggeration . . . "but the trouble is, you *can't* exaggerate about Roddy," said Antony to his uncle afterwards.

One small, significant point was slipped in towards the end of the cross-examination; again an echo of the questions put to Edward Blake. "You say you ordered the vitamin capsules, and asked Mr. Roderick Gaskell to collect them. Did you do anything else in this connection?"

"I phoned my son."

"Why did you do that, Mrs. Blake?"

"I wanted him to remind Roderick . . . I didn't think *he* would trouble to remember what I'd asked him."

"You did not think of phoning him yourself?"

"I never believe in interfering when they're at the office," said the witness. She sounded self-righteous about it, even if it didn't seem to make sense.

"So you would agree that Mr. Edward Blake knew that the capsules had been ordered; and had a very good idea that they were in his cousin's possession?"

For the first time she seemed to be wondering where these questions were leading. She said more sharply, "I suppose he knew," and Sir Nicholas went on quickly to his remaining questions before Halloran could formulate a protest.

After a brief re-examination of the witness, the case for the prosecution was closed. Sir Nicholas had time to make his opening remarks for the defence before the court adjourned. Antony listened, and admired his uncle's turn of phrase, his easy confidence. But for all that, he admitted to himself . . . the main strength of the prosecution's case lies in the weakness of the defence.

CHAPTER XVII

A THING Antony hadn't foreseen was Roddy's reaction to the questions put to Edward Blake; and to Aunt Janet about Edward. Sir Nicholas wanted to see his client before the court convened; in the hope, he said caustically, of encouraging in him some semblance of intelligence in the witness box. Antony went with him, but they might both of them have stayed away for all the good they did. "It's bad enough," said Roddy with vigour, "having to listen to all the things they're saying about me."

"We had to try it," Antony pointed out. "And if somebody had prescribed an ointment containing aconite for her . . . who would have been the most likely person to know about it?" But he came evasive in the face of Roddy's further questions. Sir Nicholas's remarks were obviously unheeded, and his nephew grinned at him when they left the interview room to make their way up to the court. "Count ten," he advised.

So the prisoner came to give his evidence full of bounce and belligerence. He told his story forcefully; but it was no use in deceiving themselves, it didn't go over well. Sir Nicholas retained his usual calm, but to his nephew's ears there was a note of strain in his voice. He glanced at Halloran, and thought Counsel for the Prosecution had probably noticed it too; there was a look of complacency about him . . .

As well there might be. He was a formidable figure when he rose to cross-examine; Roddy took a moment to eye him speculatively, jutted his chin, and only too obviously prepared to do battle. Antony heard Sir Nicholas, seated again beside him, expel his breath in a sigh of exasperation.

And here was Bruce Halloran, coming straight to the heart

163

of things. "You hated your father, Mr. Gaskell." And Roddy replied, as he had done to the same statement in prison:

"As a matter of fact . . . no."

"But you have heard the evidence . . . you have yourself admitted to my friend that there were serious matters of disagreement."

"Certainly," said the witness, cheerfully. "I didn't say I *liked* him."

"Where then, Mr. Gaskell, would you make the distinction; In your understanding, what is hatred?"

"Well, I suppose . . . disliking someone intensely. So intensely you wish to harm them."

"I am glad we are so far in agreement," said Halloran, cordially. "But the dislike you have admitted you felt for your father fell short of this?"

"You might as well ask me outright if I killed him," Roddy grumbled. "I didn't." (The judge cocked an intelligent eye at the prisoner, and then looked from him to Sir Nicholas; he did not speak, but Counsel had no difficulty in interpreting his meaning).

"Let us turn to the capsules then. Since *you* did not insert poison into one of them, someone else did."

"I suppose so." His tone was grudging.

"And this person kept by them a poison capsule—or perhaps I should say, rather, a bottle with the top-most capsule poisoned, and carefully wrapped in imitation of the package the chemist made; someone, I say, kept this package handy on the chance—the bare chance—that an opportunity would occur for a substitution to be made?"

"Well, they must have done, mustn't they?"

"Some intimate friend, then? Some member of the family?" (Now that was clever of Halloran. He had sensed a tender spot, and was proceeding to probe it).

"I don't know that," said Roddy, stubbornly.

"But in the circumstances . . . the circumstances which have been outlined, and which you have agreed existed . . . what other alternative could there be to your own guilt?"

"I don't know. I don't have to know," said Roddy. Antony looked up at him, and thought with a sudden sympathy that wiped away his former irritation, that he knew now why the prisoner's attitude had changed. For all his swaggering, the past weeks had been almost unendurable; he might or might not have guessed who the guilty party was, but he didn't want anyone to suffer the same loss of freedom. And as the thought formulated Antony knew that his own doubts had disappeared; he had tried to convince Sir Nicholas that he was certain of Roddy's innocence, but he hadn't really been sure. Now he was . . . sure, and angry, and horrified at their own small chance of success. He looked round to catch his uncle's eye, but Counsel was on his feet with a routine protest.

The judge shook his head. Sir Nicholas sat down again. Halloran said, smoothly: "I should like you to make this quite clear, Mr. Gaskell. You are asking us to believe in this somewhat casual plot, directed not only against your father, but against yourself?"

"I'm not asking you to believe anything." He added, incautiously: "I told my Counsel ages ago I couldn't account for any of the things that happened."

"But later you decided it would be better to provide explanations?"

"Well . . . I had time to think, you see."

"About the charts, for instance," Halloran prompted.

Roddy rubbed his hand across his forehead. "They were found in my safe," he said, "and I don't suppose the police put them there."

"So you cast about in your mind for the best explanation to cover that uncomfortable fact?"

"No, I . . . I realised what must have happened." He paused, and added with a spurt of temper: "As a matter of fact, I don't see why I have to provide an explanation of anything."

"Don't you, Mr. Gaskell?"

"No, I don't. It isn't what I mean by being 'presumed innocent'," he complained.

"Sir Nicholas—" said the judge, looking up.

"M'lud?" (But how could you exercise remote control over so erratic a witness as Roddy? thought Antony, still too worried to find any humor in the situation).

And so it went on, with Roddy's attitude varying between incautious candour and a recalcitrance that was, perhaps, even more unwise. It didn't even take very long, as these things go; Halloran was having it all his own way, and had no need to labour the points he made. He thanked his victim suavely before he let him go.

"Have you any further questions, Sir Nicholas?"

It was coming up to time for the luncheon recess. "Thank you, m'lud, I will not detain the court for long." He turned and looked at Roddy. "My learned friend has understandably laid great stress on your visit to Nepal," he said, "so I should like you to make one point quite clear. On that occassion did you, in fact, purchase aconite in any form?"

"No, I did not."

"Or otherwise procure it?"

"No."

"Did you kill your father?"

"No, but—"

"Thank you, Mr. Gaskell," said Sir Nicholas, quickly. Only the faintest frown between his eyes betrayed to his nephew that at that moment he would very much have liked to wring his client's neck.

The court rose, and Antony, stacking his papers, was surprised to see Sir Nicholas's clerk crossing the room towards them. Mr. Mallory arrived quite out of breath, and thrust a cable form into his employer's hands. "From young Willett, I thought you should have it at once," he said. "It has been delayed." He looked at Antony, and added accusingly: "I could have told you what it would be, Mr. Maitland. These young fellows—" It was obvious that Willett was going to have to bear the main responsibility for the cable company's misdeeds.

Sir Nicholas raised his eyes from the paper. "He arrives at London Airport at two o'clock," he told his nephew. "With a witness."

"Does he say—?"

"No more than that."

"What will you do? Ask for an adjournment?"

"I suppose—" He looked down at the cable again, and then his eyes met Antony's. "That would be the sensible thing to do," he said deliberately.

"But so much less effective." He took the point in his stride, without ever pausing to think that his uncle's attitude—like his own—seemed to have undergone a change.

"I'm with you all the way, sir. Rub it well in what we're doing, and produce him . . . sight unseen."

"It's risky," said Sir Nicholas. But it was obvious he had already made up his mind. He turned to his clerk. "Send Hill to meet the plane," he told him. "He's to bring them both straight here." It wasn't until Mr. Mallory had left them that he turned to his nephew, and shook his head at his obvious excitement. "I wonder just what's in store for us," he remarked.

Doctor Raven was rotund and cheerful. He rattled off his qualifications glibly, and though he had not the presence of his colleague who had appeared for the prosecution he had an assured way with him that was in its own way equally impressive. For all a layman could tell, the first part of his evidence was a mere repetition of what had been said before, but after a while Sir Nicholas took matters into his own hands.

"You must forgive me, doctor, if I find all this a little difficult to understand," he said, insincerely. "Perhaps you could put the matter a little more simply. You agree with the prosecution, I believe, in thinking that the poison used originated on the Indian sub-continent—" (The witness nodded vigorously). "—but not in believing that its basis was necessarily the 'Nepaul root,' as they would have us believe?"

"That is quite correct. I must stress that I had the greatest help from Mr. Webber in the preliminary stages." The witness became technical again. Sir Nicholas gave him his head for a few moments, and then said:

"Exactly. You felt there was doubt about the precise place of origin? What steps did you take?"

"I arranged for a spectrochemical analysis," said Dr. Raven, simply; as though that made everything plain.

"Did you perform this—er—experiment yourself?"

"The equipment involved is extremely expensive," said the witness, as though that answered the question adequately. "I was fortunate enough to be able to arrange for the work to be done in the laboratory of a large commercial firm—"

Mr. Justice Carruthers leaned forward. "Perhaps this process would be more familiar to us under some other name," he suggested, hopefully.

"Perhaps so, my lord. Spectrochemical analysis," he repeated, "or—if you prefer it—chemical analysis by utilising spectrophotometry."

"Ah, yes," said the judge. And caught Sir Nicholas's eye.

"You were saying, Dr. Raven, that you were present when the new tests were made." Counsel paused, put on his glasses, and looked at the judge with an effect of severity. "The firm concerned is a most reputable one," he said. The judge inclined his head.

There was no stopping the witness after that. He produced a series of glossy prints, and—whatever one might have felt about the subject of his discourse—his tone was almost lyrical as he spoke of them. "You will see upon these photographs bright and dark lines. The bright lines indicate radiation from the chemical sample of a particular frequency, this radiation having been stimulated by the light source which has been used to irridiate the chemical sample. The dark lines show where the light from the source has been absorbed." He paused, and added earnestly: "Photographs of this kind are produced by the use of a spectrophotometer, and show the distribution of energy as a function of wavelength. If I may be brief, my lord—"

"By all means," said the judge, devoutly.

"Each chemical sample treated in this manner will produce a photograph, and from this photograph may be determined the various elements which are contained in the sample undergoing analysis. The chemical composition of the soil in which a plant is grown will introduce into it minute traces of chemicals present in that soil. By this method it may be determined, for example, that a sample of aconite was grown in a particular geographic location—"

"In this instance, doctor," said Sir Nicholas, obviously feeling that the witness had been given sufficient rope, "in this case the sample under analysis was from the aconite which caused Andrew Gaskell's death. Have you reached a conclusion as to its place of origin?"

"I have formed the opinion," said the witness, for once condescending to comparative clarity, "that the poison was extracted from *aconitum luridum,* and that the place of origin was in the Himalayan mountains—the extreme west, quite near the border with Kashmir."

"Not from Nepal, doctor?"

"Definitely, no." The glance that flickered round the court was that of a lecturer, trying to assess the possible intelligence of his class. "I would like to show you two more photographs. One of these shows the spectra from the sample provided for my use by the prosecution; the second is of the emissions from a sample of *aconitum ferox*, which I obtained from Nepal." The judge was looking at pictures of what appeared to be a firework display. The jury in turn eyed them blankly. "I am sure you will agree," said Dr. Raven persuasively, "that the differences in the line structure are readily apparent." As one man, the jury nodded dumbly.

"And these differences," said Sir Nicholas, underlining the point smoothly, "serve to confirm that the aconite which was the poisoning agent did not originate in Nepal, as has been suggested by the prosecution—"

There really didn't seem to be much more to be said on the subject, and Halloran showed no sign of wishing to cross-examine. (Obviously, thought Antony wearily, he could make the points which would tend to weaken the evidence equally well in his final speech). So it was lucky that a slight disturbance in the doorway proclaimed that Willett had arrived and was trying to gain admission. As soon as Dr. Raven had been thanked, and had taken himself off, Sir Nicholas looked up at the judge.

"If your lordship pleases, I should like permission for my clerk to enter," he said. "I want him to tell me," he added, with an air of deliberation as Willett came across the room, "I want him to tell me the name of the next witness."

"Some unexpected evidence?" said Halloran, lazily. But the look he flashed at Maitland was the reverse of dull.

Sir Nicholas explained, making his points with emphasis. "If you would like time to speak with this witness—" the judge suggested, with his air of gentle courtesy.

"Thank you, m'lud, I do not feel it is necessary." He glanced aside at Halloran, daring him to interrupt. "I have no precise knowledge of what the witness will tell us, but I am confident it will help us to reach the truth. And the truth," he added, "will without doubt benefit my client. But if I may confer for a moment with my clerk—?"

Willett had slid into place on the bench behind them. He

thrust a sheet of paper into Sir Nicholas's hand. "The answers to your questions," he said. "I wrote it all out in the plane. And I'm sorry to be so late, sir, but I couldn't make it before."

"And the name of this—er—mysterious person?" enquired Halloran, as Sir Nicholas looked up from the page of notes.

"Munawar Kunju Ali." For all his ability in concealing his feelings, for a moment Halloran looked puzzled.

Munawar Ali was diminutive person, rather square of build, and not unhandsome. He moved with an odd, prancing walk to the witness box, and bowed to the judge before turning to survey the court. There was some little delay over the oath. "No need to swear. I come here to tell nothing but the truth," he said. But when the necessity was explained he seized the Bible and looked again at Mr. Justice Carruthers, a wide smile flashing nervously in his dark face. "I am Christian, your excellency," he explained.

When it came to his evidence, he gave it readily enough. "My name is Munawar Kunju Ali. I am doctor of medicine. I have my degree fourteen, fifteen years from the University of Nagpur."

"You practise medicine in Gorakhabad, which is near Bombay?"

"Oh, yes, sir. I am doctor with the Mission Hospital."

"Four years ago, were you living and working in the same place?"

"Yes. I was." He looked from Counsel to the judge and added confidentially: "I am not fly-by-night, your grace." (On the bench behind, Willett whispered despairingly to himself, "I told him . . . I tried to explain." Antony couldn't spare the time to sympathise with him, and Sir Nicholas was intent on the witness).

"Are you familiar with aconite root?"

"I am, yes."

"It is a poison, but sometimes it is used—externally—in the treatment of rheumatism, or neuralgia?" There was a hush in the court now. Antony turned his head; he couldn't see Dorrie, but Liz was leaning forward eagerly. Then he looked to where the witnesses sat who had completed their evidence: Janet Blake looked as she had done from the first, apathetic, uncomprehending; beside her, Edward sat stiffly, but his eyes were alert.

The witness was nodding and smiling. "Yes. It is used so."

"In a liniment, or an ointment?"

"A liniment, yes."

"You have made use of it in this way yourself, perhaps?"

"Oh, yes."

"Will you take your mind back four years, Dr. Ali. Had you a patient then who suffered from neuralgia?" (Antony turned his head in expectation of Halloran's protest; Counsel met his look, and grinned at him, but made no move to interrupt).

"I had a patient then."

"What can you tell us about this patient?"

"An Englishwoman. I never saw her," added the witness, unexpectedly.

"You never . . . but you prescribed for her?" said Sir Nicholas, a little wildly.

"I shall explain. I know of this lady, she is staying in Gorakhabad with her son. And when strangers stay in Gorakhabad, all the town knows of it. That is not surprising, sir, I think."

"Not at all surprising."

"Then the son comes to me. They must leave early the next day, he says, but his mother has an agony." He was speaking very quickly now, earnestly explaining and for almost the first time since he came into the court he did not smile as he answered. "I think she has the toothache, but then he tells me . . . always, he says, she has this neuralgia, and now it is so bad, but she must travel."

"What then, Dr. Ali?"

"I do not like to give him drugs, when I do not know the lady, you see. So I give him the liniment. And they leave a message for me next day, that she has been so much better."

"Did you tell them what the liniment contained?"

"Oh, no, sir." For some reason the suggestion seemed to shock him. "But the label says 'Poison,' and I have told the man it must not be applied where the skin is broken."

"That's very clear, doctor." Sir Nicholas's tone was as

even as ever. (Now, how do we get round that one? Antony thought). "This man who called on you—"

"Yes?" asked the witness, as Counsel paused.

"Could you identify him? Would you know him again?"

"No. I am sure not." Again he turned confidingly to the judge. "It is long ago, and there is, besides, a sameness about the . . . the features of the English I have known." His wide smile came again. "So I am sorry, your eminence, but I would not know him."

"Can you describe him at all."

"He had a great height." Compared with the witness, this would apply to almost everyone in the court. Dr. Ali pondered. "He had red hair," he said triumphantly. "A bad colour . . . an unlucky colour." Roddy was sitting very still, and his eyes were fixed on a point above the judge's head; but there was a stir among the witnesses now, and Antony suddenly thought of the night of Aunt Carry's dance, and of Jenny as he had first seen her that evening, in her partner's arms.

"Do you remember his name?"

"But, of course, I have it in my book. I bring it to show you." He held up what looked like a battered exercise book, but obviously it was a source of pride. "Your names are so difficult," he said, "but I have it written down. His name is Edward Blake."

There was a hum of voices, a flutter of movement hastily stilled. But Antony's eyes went past Edward Blake, and rested consideringly on his mother's face.

Halloran was disclaiming any idea of cross-examining. The witness turned his wide smile and nervous bow in the direction of the judge. "I am saying good-bye to you now, your holiness," he said; and backed out of the box. And suddenly Antony was tugging at the sleeve of his uncle's gown.

"For heaven's sake, sir—" Sir Nicholas looked down at him, eyebrows raised. "Tell them you want to recall the Gaskells' doctor," he urged.

"I should like permission to recall one of the prosecution witnesses, Dr. Morton," said Sir Nicholas, obediently. "If my learned friend has no objection, and your lordship will agree." He shot a look at his nephew that Antony had no difficulty interpreting, and added hopefully, "I do not suppose he is still in court?'' He was perfectly well aware that the doctor had left two days ago, as soon as he had given his evidence.

Mr. Justice Carruthers looked at Counsel for the Prosecution. ''Do you object, Mr. Halloran?'' he asked.

Bruce Halloran was himself so dark that his smile had always something of the saturnine. He smiled now, allowed his eyes to rest for a moment on Antony, and then looked back at the judge. ''I am sure my learned friend has good reasons for his request,'' he said. ''I do not think we need trouble him to enumerate them. I am quite willing that the witness should be recalled, though I am afraid it may take some time—''

The judge was speaking to the usher. When he had finished Sir Nicholas went on: ''In the meantime, m'lud, as my friend is in a compliant mood, I shall ask permission to recall Edward Blake.'' He turned, as he spoke, and looked straight across the court to where the witnesses were sitting. ''I think there is something he can explain to us,'' he said gently.

Edward was on his feet. He met Sir Nicholas's eyes across the distance between them, and spoke to him as though they were alone. ''I have nothing at all to say,'' he told him.

Nobody saw Janet Blake get up . . . except Antony, and he had been watching her. Nobody noticed her until she had moved a little away from the others, and was standing in the open space between two rows of seats where everyone could see her plainly. She said: ''What do you want to ask Dr. Morton?'' And the high-pitched note of hysteria was now very marked.

Sir Nicholas looked at the judge, but Antony was in no mood to wait on court procedure. He saw his chance and took it, saying clearly: ''We want to ask him whether you showed him your liniment when you got back from India.'' Janet Blake's eyes wavered, and then focused on his own. ''Aconite can be identified by quite a simple test,'' he added (and wondered afterwards why no one made any attempt to stop him); ''and if he warned you—''

''What then?'' she asked him. ''What then?'' And Antony said deliberately, and hated himself as he did so:

''You might have told your son.''

And then came Halloran's objection, and the judge was saying something that was probably a reprimand, and beside him Antony could hear Sir Nicholas uttering an obscure male-diction. And over all this, and the hubbub of conjecture that had broken out among the spectators, Janet Blake's voice was screaming:

"You can't say he knew! I never told him!" Her head was thrown back, and the shabby, black hat she wore was pushed awry on her straggling hair; and fantastically Antony was re-minded as he looked at her of the attitude Roddy had taken up the night Sykes told him he was under arrest. He went on looking at her, and he wanted to look away. "Of course Dr. Morton told me!" she screamed at him. "How else could I have known what to do?" And the screams continued, but now there were no words.

Someone was appealing, almost frantically, for a doctor. Several court officials had moved in the direction of the dis-turbance, and now had paused ineffectually, uncertain what to do. In the confusion Dorrie got up from her place among the spectators; nobody stopped her as she passed the barrier, and came across the room to Janet Blake's side. She put an arm around the older woman, and said something in a low voice; and gradually the screaming died away into a noisy sobbing, and then that in turn was quietened. The two women turned, and began to walk quietly towards the entrance to the court.

Antony stared after them. Somehow the scene had added the final touch of horror to what had happened. He thought stupidly, "She's trapped now; she wanted to get away from the family . . . and now she never will." He watched until they disappeared through the doorway; and then turned back to face the results of the bombshell he had thrown.

CHAPTER XVIII

TWO DAYS LATER—Saturday evening—Edward Blake arrived unexpectedly at the house in Kempenfeldt Square. Sir Nicholas was out, and Antony took the visitor to the study. He couldn't think why Blake had come . . . perhaps for no better reason than a wish to unburden himself. But it wasn't likely to be an easy interview.

What he saw when he got a good look at Edward confirmed his fears. The word "hag-ridden" came into his mind. He poured whisky without asking the other man's preference, and the mixture he handed over was rather stronger than his own. Blake was sitting forward with his hands between his knees. He accepted the glass and put it down immediately, untasted, on the table at his elbow.

"I suppose I ought to thank you," he said. "You see . . . I didn't know what to do." The admission came oddly from a man usually so self-possessed, and he did not look at his companion.

Antony cleared his throat, and said the first thing that came into his head . . . the last thing he had meant to say. "How long had you known?"

"Almost from the beginning," said Edward. "I asked her about the liniment as soon as we heard what the doctors said; but she said she'd thrown it away years ago. Somehow I couldn't quite believe that, and then, when Gran died—" He looked up fleetingly at Antony, and then down at the rug again. "I thought if you could get Roddy off, I'd see she went to a . . . a home, or something," he said.

"And if Roddy had been convicted—?"

"That was just it . . . I don't think I ever faced the possibility . . . I couldn't think what to do." He paused, but did not seem to find the silence discouraging, for he went on without prompting. "Of course, I could have made a dramatic confession, but I don't think I'm cut out for a hero, the idea always seemed faintly ridiculous. Besides, it wouldn't have solved the real problem." He raised his head again, until his eyes met Antony's. "It's an awful thing to say, but in a way it's a relief."

Antony got up with an abrupt movement. He had lighted the fire when they came in, and it was burning up merrily; no real excuse for disturbing it, but the instinct to avoid the other man's eyes was for the moment dominant. He said, as he picked up the poker and stooped to thrust it unnecessarily between the bars of the old-fashioned grate, "I didn't plan it that way, you know. And I didn't enjoy it."

Edward said, "I don't suppose so," in rather a queer voice. He was looking at Antony for the first time that evening, in the sense that he was really seeing him; he wasn't quite clear why he should suddenly find himself feeling sorry for his companion, but the emotion was quite unmistakable. He added, rather quickly: "You used the weapons that came to hand. I can see it had to be done."

The poker went down with a clatter on the hearth, and Antony straightened up and stood looking at his handiwork. "Clumsy," he said after a while, as if that explained everything. Surprisingly, Edward smiled.

"That wasn't what the judge said," he pointed out. Antony turned his head, and smiled slightly. The scene in court had indeed been a lively one, but Sir Nicholas, reserving his own recriminations, had known exactly how to play the hand that had so unexpectedly been dealt him. Edward must have been following the same line of thought, for he added now, "At least, Roddy's free."

"Yes," said Antony. He went back to his chair, and watched the visitor pick up his glass and sample the contents. He was glad now that Edward had come, because there were things he wanted to know with a quite painful curiosity. But there was no hurry . . . let him take his time.

What Edward said was, "That police inspector—Sykes— seems a decent sort of chap."

"He is."

"He said they don't know yet if the doctors will say she's

fit to plead," said Edward rapidly. "But he said, anyway, they wouldn't put her in prison. I always heard Broadmoor wasn't so bad, do you think that's right? I mean, she'd be . . . safe; and perhaps not unhappy." He took another drink, and added abruptly: "I wanted to ask you . . . how did you know?"

"It wasn't exactly knowing," Antony objected. "Well, not at first. You see, there was the fact that the poison came from India and that Roddy had been in Nepal. We had to get round that somehow, at the very least we had to show the possibility of some alternative source of supply. You all of you travelled extensively, but it seemed such an unlikely thing to have picked up. So I wondered if there couldn't have been some innocent reason."

"Mother was complaining about her neuralgia," said Edward, "the day you came to tea."

"Yes, and you see the first thing Dr. Raven told me—before all that spectrometry business came up—was the possible use of aconite for external application. He mentioned neuralgia; and when I remembered you'd both been to India, there was a perfectly natural source—far more reasonable than thinking that Roddy had been in the market for a good poison when he made the trip to Dacca."

"But that wouldn't prove anything," Edward protested.

"Of course it wouldn't. All we could hope was to be able to say: this is the most likely way for the aconite to have come to England. The snag was, as you've realised, that Roddy could have got hold of it as easily as anyone else; but at least it got away from the idea that he was the only one who could have done so."

"Yes, I see."

"But when I thought about it, of course, I began to realise it wasn't all that likely the family as a whole would have known about the liniment, still less what it was made of. At that stage, you know, I wasn't exactly convinced of Roddy's innocence, I was just thinking in terms of the defence. So I took the hypothesis a step further: who would be the most likely person to possess the necessary information? And the answer to that was . . . you. But things were different when I began to think about opportunity. Someone had to have easy access to the capsules, to know in detail the arrangements of the household, to *know* they could count on an opportunity for making the substitution. The answer to that was someone in the house, someone actively concerned with domestic arrangements. And when I thought about the theft of the picture, and later of the poisoning of the sandwiches, the answer was still the same. I'd be willing to bet the anchovy paste wasn't poisoned before the afternoon it was used; and some was added to the jar just to sustain the illusion it could have been done before. But the police had searched the house, and where she kept the stuff is beyond me.''

''I can tell you that,'' said Edward. ''There were some onions hanging up in the cellar, in those string bag affairs. She put the bottle among the ones in the farthest corner; there'd have been plenty of time to take it out again before Cook needed them.''

Antony did not stop to question the source of his information. ''So I began to think about motive, and I wondered . . . well, if you ask me your mother was never one of the puritanical Gaskells at all. I think she had a lot of old Roderick in her.''

Edward gave him a startled look, and said uneasily: ''She made a . . . a sort of a statement. Not . . . not at all coherent, you know, but it gave them a good idea what had happened.''

''Did she take the Velasquez?'' said Antony. ''From the gallery, I mean . . . the first time.''

''That's what she said, and it's the queerest thing. We all thought it was the old pirate.''

''I can't see . . . never mind, go on.''

''It's all a bit confusing,'' said Edward, frowning over his thoughts. ''But I think perhaps you're right about what she was really like. As far as I can make out she desperately wanted Grandfather's approval when she was a child; and people started to say she was like her mother—like Gran, that is—so she tried to be like her in character, too, only it didn't work. She didn't realise he wouldn't take prudishness from anyone but Gran. And then I suppose she was stuck with the imitation—''

''Or perhaps she came to enjoy the part she was playing.''

''It could have been that. I remember when my father was alive he'd tease her, and she'd say something prim in reply, but then she'd laugh, and I never did know whether she meant it. But after she came to number 34 she got worse all the time.''

"The Velasquez," said Antony. "Had she any other reason for taking it than just to score off old Roderick?"

Edward stared at him. "That's it, I suppose. That's just it. She knew he wanted it, and it would satisfy the part of her that wasn't puritan—like you said—and she could hug herself and think she'd gone one better than him.''

"I suppose he found out."

"Yes. That part of what she said was . . . was fairly clear." He gulped nervously at the whisky again. "She took it down to the study once when he was away, and fixed it up on the wall somehow opposite the desk, and sat there to gloat over it. And then he came back unexpectedly.''

"I wonder what they said to each other," said Antony. "Obviously, he agreed to hush the matter up. I wonder too which moved him more: consideration for his daughter or the possibility of adding to his collection?"

"Well, to do him justice," said Edward, who was speaking now much more easily, "I don't expect he stopped to think about 'receiving stolen goods,' and so on. He'd think 'I can't give her away'; and he'd think 'best keep some hold over her, or goodness knows what she'll do next.' So he had the panel made, and he added that codicil to his will . . . and I bet he laughed when he did that. But I don't think he can have realised that Mother was really ill.''

Antony was silent, contemplating that stormy household. He felt dimly now that he could understand the particular concern his uncle had brought to Roddy Gaskell's defence. Edward sat back in his chair, and returned to his story.

"For some reason it maddened her when Uncle Andrew wanted to send the picture back. She didn't mind the scandal, but she wanted to keep her trophy. So she pinched the thing again, and she tied it up with the charts so that Roddy would take it out of the house without knowing. She could easily have found an excuse for asking him to bring them back later. Uncle Andrew came into the study while she was there, and she said she was just tying the bundle more neatly, and it wasn't until much later that he put two and two together and asked her what the hell? *He* wouldn't be likely to do any hushing up, and for all I know he may have guessed when he talked to her what had happened in the first place.''

''I think it's very likely she'd have told him, don't you?''

''She was in a very nervous state,'' Edward agreed. ''Anyway, that was that.''

Antony hesitated. There was still one question troubling him; but for all his companion's present calm, and probably quite genuine relief, it hardly seemed decent . . .

''You're wondering about Gran,'' Edward stated, abruptly.

''Well—'' said Antony. ''Yes, I was,'' he added, with a touch of defiance.

''The funny thing is, Mother's done a lot of talking but she's never mentioned that,'' said Edward. ''Do you think she could have forgotten about it? I mean, she talks as if killing Uncle Andrew was quite a high-minded thing to have done; and she thinks it was all right to accuse Roddy because she felt he ought to be punished for . . . for all the things he'd done that she disapproved of; but if Gran's death left her feeling guilty, she may have put it out of her mind.''

''But why—?''said Antony. ''I mean—''

''That's the easiest thing of all to understand, I'm afraid. Gran always prided herself on knowing everything that went on, and she was pretty good at it, too.''

''You think she found out what had happened?''

''I'm quite sure of it. Do you remember, the day she died, she said she wanted to talk to me?''

Antony stopped to think this out. Cunning enough to see that poison added to the sandwiches would do nothing towards clearing Roddy; callous enough—mad enough?—not to care when Jenny ate one, too. He jerked back from that thought, and met Edward's eyes, and asked:

''What are your plans?'' He spoke casually, because he badly wanted to know.

Edward seemed to be giving the question serious consideration, but after a moment he smiled. ''We were all of us wrong about Dorrie, you know. We thought she needed someone to take care of her, but that wasn't it at all.'' His thoughts had obviously taken a brighter turn. ''She's at home . . . at number 34. And she made Roddy go back there, and now she's busy organising him.''

Antony grinned at that. "She'll have her work cut out," he prophesied.

"She's full of decision all of a sudden. They're going to sell the house, but until they do she says we've just got to take up where we left off. She says every family has its . . . its scandals, and it doesn't do to brood about them. And she says Mother can't help being ill." He paused, and added with the uncharacteristic uncertainty he had displayed on his first arrival, "We're going to be married."

"Well, that's good news," said Antony. His companion ignored the interruption, and went on:

"If you want to know what happened, I'll tell you. Uncle Gil asked me my intentions." In his turn he sounded defiant, and for the first time Antony felt a real amusement at what was being said. "I said, 'in the circumstances—,' and he said I was being a fool; and I reminded him we were first cousins, and he said it would be different if we were both like the Gaskell side, but I'm more like my father and Dorrie more like her mother . . . and that's true! He said that made it all right." He stopped, and perhaps some of his companion's amusement communicated itself to him. "I think he'd been reading a book," he said.

"Very likely." That wasn't a point on which Antony felt qualified to pronounce any judgment, but he was adding his congratulations when he saw Edward had got up to go.

"You've been very patient," he said. "And all this time I've never told you what I really wanted to say. Do you think Sir Nicholas would look after things . . . if there is another trial, you know?"

Antony gave his assurance on this point the more readily because he was pretty sure the question wouldn't arise.

It was a mild evening, and he stood on the steps after he had let Edward out, and listened to his footsteps dying away across the square. It wasn't difficult to guess their direction. He thought Jenny would be pleased with that bit of news; as for himself, he might even sleep to-night.

He was just about to go into the house again when a taxi drew up and Sir Nicholas got out. Antony couldn't see his face until he came into range of the light from the porch; but his step, his whole bearing, seemed to have a buoyancy that had been notably lacking of late. Antony waited to follow him into the hall. "Been celebrating?" he enquired.

"My dear boy!" said Sir Nicholas, cordially. He put down hat and gloves on the table, and stood back as though admiring the effect; then he started to shrug out of his overcoat. "If I come upstairs with you," he asked as Antony came forward to help him, "do you suppose Jenny would insist on making tea."

"I'll hide the kettle," Antony promised.

In the big living-room at the top of the house Jenny had a good fire going, and as she turned her head to smile as they went in Antony felt for the first time for weeks that things were back to normal. Uncle Nick was obviously in spirits again, and perhaps he was going to tell them . . .

"You may have noticed," said Sir Nicholas, taking his usual chair, "that for the past few weeks I have had something on my mind."

"You surprise me, sir," said Antony, making for the cupboard where the drinks were kept, and hoping—as he made a mental inventory—that his uncle wouldn't be too captious in his choice of tipple. But Jenny said, firmly:

"Of course we noticed. And we wondered what was the matter.

Sir Nicholas smiled. "Did you come to any conclusion?" he enquired. Antony swung round, but couldn't catch his wife's eye.

"What will you have to drink, Uncle Nick?"

There was a flicker of amusement in Sir Nicholas's eye as he replied. "Brandy," he requested. "For the stomach's sake," he told Jenny, solemnly. "But you didn't tell me, my dear, did you come to any conclusion?"

"We wondered if you were ill," said Jenny, cautiously. She folded her hands demurely on her lap, and met Sir Nicholas's suspicious look with one of blank incomprehension. But when her husband rejoined them a moment later he saw that her eyes were dancing, and his spirits rose as he thought again that the worries and uncertainties of the past weeks were—in part, at least—over.

Sir Nicholas was saying, "I thought better of your powers of invention." Antony had no intention whatever of regaling him with the more lurid of his imaginings, so he said casually:

"Edward Blake is going to marry Dorrie. Or Dorrie's going to marry Edward," he added, doubtfully. "I'm not sure which."

"Good God," said Sir Nicholas, blankly.

"Yes, sir. Gilbert Gaskell has been reading a book on genetics, and has more or less ordered them to put up the banns. I haven't the faintest idea what the harvest will be." Jenny began to laugh, and he looked at her enquiringly.

"Dorrie is marrying Edward," she said. "She told Michael weeks ago; he proposed to her the day they had the service for old Mrs. Gaskell."

Sir Nicholas and his nephew exchanged looks, for the moment completely in sympathy. "Liz," said Antony, and added unfairly: "How you women talk."

"You were going to tell us, Uncle Nick," said Jenny, on her dignity, "what was on your mind."

Sir Nicholas took up his glass and sipped appreciatively. "Ah, yes," he said. "I learned recently, by a devious route, that I might expect to hear from the Lord Chancellor the next time a vacancy occurred among the Queen's Bench judges. It has been obvious for some time," he added, "that Masterman was about to retire."

"Congratulations, sir." So that was the explanation of Halloran's remark, all perfectly simple when you were in the know . . . though why it should drive Uncle Nick into doing crossword puzzles was beyond him. He ought to be relieved that none of his gloomier forebodings had any substance, but all he was conscious of was a renewal of depression.

"Don't be in such a hurry," said Sir Nicholas, plaintively. "It's a great honour, of course, and I've been greatly exercised in my mind as to whether I ought to accept it—"

Antony looked up. "Then you haven't done so?" And the older man smiled again at the eagerness in his voice.

"I thought it over very carefully," he said, "and to-day I decided to—er—circumvent the offer. It will save a great deal of trouble all round, but I thought I should tell you in case you had noticed my pre-occupation. I believe Conroy will be chosen when the time comes."

Jenny said: "But don't you *want* to be a judge, Uncle Nick?"

"No doubt I am lacking in proper feeling. Do you mind, my dear?"

"No, of course not. I think you'd have made a very handsome judge, but I don't want anything to change."

"That's just the trouble," said Antony, "neither do I." Sir Nicholas's eyes were speculative and a little amused, and he added defiantly: "If you want to know, Halloran scared me stiff by talking about your 'last case'."

"That was indiscreet of him; I didn't know he'd heard the rumour." Sir Nicholas leaned back in his chair and prepared to bait his nephew. "The real deterrent," he declared, "was the possibility of your appearing in my court. I was quite unnerved by the thought that there might be enacted before me the sort of scene you involved me in the other day. While I remain at the bar I have at least some small hope of exercising a restraining influence—" But before he could elaborate any further, the phone rang.

Antony took the call, and a moment later twisted round to grimace at Jenny. All she could hear was an angry crackling from the other end of the line, but she diagnosed it correctly. "Aunt Carry," she said in a whisper. She smiled at Sir Nicholas contentedly. "If she's as cross as she sounds, I'm glad she isn't here," she added.

"Roddy Gaskell has been here for hours," said the telephone loudly in Antony's ear. "I don't believe he will ever go. Of course, I blame myself: I might have known what would happen if I let Elizabeth go and stay with you . . . she's stubborn enough without any encouragement. And I may tell you, Antony, if she insists on marrying him . . ."

Aunt Carry was fighting in the last ditch.